TOO SWEET
TO BE GOOD

This Large Print Book carries the
Seal of Approval of N.A.V.H.

Too Sweet
to Be Good

K.M. Jackson

THORNDIKE PRESS
A part of Gale, a Cengage Company

Farmington Hills, Mich • San Francisco • New York • Waterville, Maine
Meriden, Conn • Mason, Ohio • Chicago

Copyright © 2019 by Kwana Jackson.
A Sugar Lake Novel.
Thorndike Press, a part of Gale, a Cengage Company.

ALL RIGHTS RESERVED
Thorndike Press® Large Print African-American.
The text of this Large Print edition is unabridged.
Other aspects of the book may vary from the original edition.
Set in 16 pt. Plantin.

LIBRARY OF CONGRESS CIP DATA ON FILE.
CATALOGUING IN PUBLICATION FOR THIS BOOK
IS AVAILABLE FROM THE LIBRARY OF CONGRESS

ISBN-13: 978-1-4328-6938-0 (hardcover alk. paper)

Published in 2019 by arrangement with Dafina Books, an imprint of
Kensington Publishing Corp.

Printed in the United States of America
1 2 3 4 5 6 7 23 22 21 20 19

To Will
Sitting in the dark with you
still gives me a thrill

ACKNOWLEDGMENTS

When it's time to write the acknowledgments, it feels like the hardest part of writing the book because I always fear I'm leaving out some critical person and, in the process, muddling the book before chapter 1. That said, I'll start with a heartfelt and sincere thank you to each and every person who has given me any word, smile, wink, nod, or nudge my way during this process. Each of you has been so very dear to me and I can't begin to explain how much I cherish every bit of encouragement. Writing is so solitary, and at times as a writer you get stuck in your own head, with only your own voice. When that voice turns on you and whispers to you words of self-doubt and fear, those words, winks, nods of "you got this" and "you can do it," no matter how small, can mean the world and make the difference between going forward and giving up.

I'd like to also and as always thank my editor, Selena James, and the wonderful team at Kensington Books for believing in me and supporting me once again to bring something new to the public with the fictional Sugar Lake world. Thank you.

I'd like to thank my ever patient, kind, and amazing agent, Evan Marshall, for his grace and for being in my corner.

A huge, special thank you to my friend Farrah Rochon for bringing me all the way home with this one and never giving up on me with her tireless encouragement and daily words. You are such a blessing to my life.

Another huge thank you to Sasha Devlin. I never knew what a gift I'd get when we became buds on Royal Wedding night, but I'm so grateful for it. Let the fandom always bind us and never break us apart, my friend!

Thank you to the Destin Divas: you ladies are so very amazing and inspire me beyond words. And thank you to the wonderful women of Fiction from the Heart. I'm honored to be a part of your group.

My undying gratitude and thanks also for the grace, kindness, and friendship of: Falguni, Priscilla, Kristan, Sonali, Barbara, Rochelle, Hope, Sally, Donna, Jamie, and Karen, you all are amazing!

As always, this and everything I do is with the love in my heart of my family, especially my dear twins, Kayla and William. You two inspire me every day.

My husband, Will. You are such a blessing and still the hero I'll probably never be able to capture in words.

Thank you, dear readers, new and those returning (Wow! Did some of you come back? *blowing you all the kisses*): The thought of you spending time with me and my words is truly humbling and I'm so very honored.

Finally, and firstly, thank you, God, for all these blessings. I hope I'm doing you well.

Always,
KMJ

CHAPTER 1
ONE SWEET DAY

Alexandrea Gale stifled back a yawn as she carried her sister's latest concoction from the kitchen to the bakery's front display counter. This one was something Olivia was calling "Oh Honey Yes You May Pie," and though Drea's yawn was held back, her eye roll could not be contained.

The pie was an almost sinfully sweet, triple layer makeup of peaches, plums, and apples with thin layers of puff pastry in between, topped with pecans and drizzled with honey. It was a sticky, gooey, all-out-decadent taste sensation, and Drea was certain there were enough calories in the pie to expand a person's hips with just a hard enough look. As a matter of fact, maybe she shouldn't be looking at the darned thing straight on. She should probably just squint and take it in sideways.

Drea had been living in Sugar Lake going on nearly a year now, which was way past her limit. The lifestyle change of not racing through New York sidewalks at breakneck speed while trying to make a downtown train or crosstown bus to her next audition or part-time job was wreaking havoc on her what used to be audition-ready hips. Instead she was driving to and fro while living off both her Aunt Joyce's and her sister's cooking.

Drea gave the pie a hard look and frowned. Who was she fooling? Like squinting mattered when it came to Liv's baking. You could squint, but you couldn't hide. The pie would always find you. If not by sight, then definitely by smell, using that enticement as a sensory precursor of what was to come. She took a long whiff of the air surrounding the pie. Sweet, and somehow smooth. Drea could practically taste how delicious it was without even taking a bite of the luxurious treat.

Thankfully, she knew she'd get a reprieve from this particular new concoction. With the way Liv baked, the folks in town would not give a hoot about the calories and the pie would be snapped up in no time. For one: This was the South and Drea had quickly come to learn that though there may be the few who ordered a diet soda with their chicken fried steak, this was the land of the sweet tea, and butter here was measured in sticks, not pats. And for two: Her sister's pies were out of this world. The tastes were spectacular. Olivia, or Liv as she called her, was quickly gaining a reputation as one of the top bakers in the county, and her pies were seriously starting to rival those of Aunt Joyce, who was a local legend in her own right. It seemed since Liv had won last year's big Founder's Day competition — well, no, since she'd come back and finally, once and for all, faced facts and solidified her relationship with single dad, hot firefighter, honey-maker, and all-around Mr. Perfect, Clayton Morris — everything she baked had turned to edible gold. Goode 'N Sweet, the family's bakeshop, could not seem to keep any of her new confections in stock. They sold out almost as fast as she could bake them.

Drea's lips twisted as something in her heart twitched uncomfortably. She fought to inch away from the feeling as recollections of New York, big dreams, broken promises, and lost hope threatened to take over her thoughts. She forcibly pushed them back. It was all good. Great even, she mentally told herself, and put her mind back on her sister. Since she'd rekindled her love with Clayton Morris, Liv's creations were packed with an undeniably more passionate punch. It was as if she'd found her calling, in more ways than one.

Ugh. Now, with phone calls and passion on her mind, Drea wished her own phone would get to ringing. She shut her eyes again and let out a sigh. Why would her phone ring though? It wasn't as if she'd had a job audition or a date in forever. And Drea knew any potential leads she'd gained over the years, were now long forgotten. She snorted to herself. As if those with influence were ever actively pursuing her.

What was she sighing for though? Her sister worked hard, was talented, and deserved every bit of happiness coming her way. And Lord knew Drea didn't actually need or want anything that looked like any part of a man, influential or not, or the befuddlement that a man would undoubtedly bring to her life. But the passion and finding your calling part? Now that she could get behind.

Sure, thankfully — well, technically — Drea was still happy with her decision to stay on in Sugar Lake, even though Aunt Joyce had long since healed from her hip surgery and the shop was well back to running at full steam. But it was coming up on a year since she'd left New York, and a year was a mighty long time in the life of a twenty-something who had dreams of making it as an actor/entertainer. Her career clock felt like an hourglass that was quickly running out of sand. Maybe, at not even thirty and still a few years from it, she shouldn't be feeling this way, but in the entertainment world, twenty-seven and no significant cred on your sheet usually meant you were toast.

Now that she'd made room for the newest masterpiece, Drea stepped around to the front of the pie case to survey how the rest of the baked goods looked. Returning behind the counter again, she made a few small adjustments, just to be sure that everything was lined up and there were no empty spaces. Though it gave her a sense of satisfaction to make sure all was in its place in the shop and she did take pride in how updated the old place looked, it all felt like busywork since the early morning rush was over and they were in a bit of a lull.

Drea tapped her moto-boot-clad toes and looked around. Really, what else was there for her to do in the shop at this hour? Her sister was happy as a clam, busy baking in the back, and her cousin Rena had run Aunt Joyce for a quick follow-up at her doc's office, though she seemed once again as fit as could be.

Liv heard a surprising and uncustomary humming come from the kitchen as she caught the tune of a popular upbeat love song. She smiled. Well, at least Liv was enjoying what she was doing. She was pretty much Aunt Joyce's right hand in the kitchen. And though Aunt Joyce contended that Drea was quite the help to her — having updated the interior of the shop and a little of the exterior with the new back patio area — Drea knew there was only so much updating one could do with Goode 'N Sweet. Between her and Rena helping out, along with Liv in the kitchen with Aunt Joyce, things were pretty much getting on track with the shop. Though no one out-and-out said anything, Drea couldn't help at times but feel useless. Like a glorified space and time filler.

When she'd first arrived at Sugar Lake, she'd been running from dreams that didn't quite pan out. And for a while, being here was good enough. A safe enough hiding space while she regrouped and thought of how she'd piece together some sort of career once back in New York. But the mask she'd been wearing as the easygoing, flighty sister without a care was starting to wear thin. She'd done her part with helping out Aunt

Joyce. It was clearly time for her to pack up and head back to New York and real life. Drea frowned, then shook her head.

New York and real life. That statement should have filled her with excitement, but instead it gave her a sense of despair.

Betty Kilborn was mad. No, she was angry. She didn't particularly like the word *mad.* It was too coarse a word, so she much preferred the word *angry.* It hit the ear in a much more genteel way; that is, in a manner she felt better suited her position and advanced age. Not to mention her newly widowed status. She let out a sigh.

Who was she fooling? If she was being honest — and she prided herself on being so, at least when it came to squaring things in her own mind — she was more than angry, mad, or any such word. No, she was seething. Better yet, she was furious, enraged, incensed even. And the worst part was that she didn't have a way to properly ease her current state of duress.

So, Betty slammed the door of her pristine 1979 Thunderbird convertible. With something pricking in the back of her mind, she gave a glance at the back tire and made a mental note to run by Ed's place when she had the time. The thought of the tire brought Henry to mind again, which only made her angrier. Betty knew in the moment she was being immature. This was not how a widow of her status was supposed to act. But still that slam, her little fit of immaturity, was rewarded by the momentary release of frustration when she heard the loud wham of the metal on metal, and it satisfied her. Somewhat.

"Ease it back a notch, Betty. The world can't handle you when you fully unleash."

Betty smiled to herself as the sound of her beloved Henry's voice came soft and soothing to her mind. He always knew how to calm her. Bring her back down from a rolling boil to a low simmer, where she could see clearly again. Betty quickly blinked. Forcing threatening tears back behind her eyes. She didn't know what she'd do without his ever-calming presence by her side. She gave her head a small shake, gray curls catching the slight breeze as she let out another sigh. Nope. Temper tantrums and tears in the middle of Sugar Lake's Main Street would definitely not do. That she did know.

Feeling slightly more herself, Betty let out a calming breath as she adjusted her flamingo-pink cardigan and tucked her old Chanel bag under her arm. She took care to wriggle her mouth in an attempt to smooth her normally smooth features. Sure, wrinkles were inevitable at her age, but she would not let her current state, not to mention that stubborn grandson of hers, bring them on any faster than necessary.

With a quick glance up and down Main Street, Betty could see that though the hour was still relatively early, the town was already abuzz with activity. Out of the corner of her eye she saw Lottie Douglas and Liz Holiday coming out of Cartland's Cart-Away grocery. Once again, Betty fought to keep her expression neutral as the two women caught sight of her, then gave each other knowing glances before making their way in her direction.

Betty stifled an audible groan. Of course, she should have expected this; this is what she signed on for when she made the decision to come into town today. But seeing the two women now as they prepared to pounce, Betty was starting to feel like this morning's outing wasn't the best idea. Maybe the solitude of home wasn't all that bad if coming into town meant that she once again had to deal with the usual, "How are you making out without him?" and "Isn't it so lonely up in that big old house all by yourself?" questions.

19

Well, Betty figured she'd better get her answers together and fast with Lottie and Liz making quick tracks her way. Betty's eyes went wide as she watched the two women, their little feet shuffling at an almost cartoonlike pace. It would be comical if she wasn't their intended target. Despite their advanced ages, the two women were coming upon her at a breakneck speed, so Betty knew she couldn't very well turn and get back into her car to make a quick escape.

Of all the pickles! Squaring her shoulders, she decided to encounter them head on and took a step forward onto the sidewalk right in front of their path.

"Lottie, Liz," she said with a smile she knew was probably about as weak as communion wine, "you both are looking well on this beautiful morning. Getting your shopping in early, I see. Smart, before the sun really makes things unbearable. Any time after ten and it's just about too much to take."

Both women gave her kindly smiles, the oldest of the two (though when you were seventy-eight and eighty, respectively, did that hierarchy really matter? This was the South and these were Southern women. Of course, it mattered.), Lottie reached a hand out and gave Betty's a light pat. "Look at you, dear," she said. "Out and about, looking just as fine as you may be. And Henry not being gone, but what, a month of Sundays now? I'm sure he'd be tickled seeing you as pretty as a picture in your pink today." Lottie's light tone made this seem as though it was a compliment. But the slight sting Betty felt as the words zapped her squarely in the heart let her know it was not.

Lottie looked around as if she expected someone else to pop up from behind Betty's back. Betty turned around, then looked back at Lottie.

"But are you out to do grocery shopping alone?" Lottie asked. "Why didn't you just call up Bob and have what you needed delivered? If you didn't want to do that you could have rang up either of us or any of the women of the auxiliary circle. We'd have made sure your shopping was done. This is what we're here for. To pitch in during times like this. I know it's hard not having anyone to rely on with your family being what it is. . . ." She dramatically paused and in that pause Betty prayed for the strength not to go off completely on the woman, or at least for the spiritual hand of her dear Henry to come on down and hold her back.

Still Lottie continued, "Busy as they are, but by now you know to consider everyone in this town your family. A shame more of your people couldn't make it to be with you during this time."

Betty stifled her words of rebuttal as Lottie's last remark stirred old feelings to the surface. Suddenly she felt just as close to the Sugar Lake town limits as she did when she first got into town more than fifty years before. As the new Yankee bride come to town after stealing away one of their own — and the town's most eligible bachelor to boot — she sure had had her fair share of barbs from envious townswomen back in the day.

But using her well-honed years of training, Betty squelched her feelings back down and instead let out a slow breath and gave a cool smile. Lottie seemed to understand the meaning behind that smile, and she turned toward Liz for a bit of shoring up.

Thankfully for Lottie, Liz came through with a nod of agreement, so she continued. "Yes, we would have surely pitched in. I could have had someone over in a hot minute. Why, I could have sent my son or my daughter-in-law or any of my grands on by. All it takes is a word, hon. And there is no need for you to ever feel like a bother.

Any of them would be happy to help. We know how hard it is for you with your grandson always on the go. Why, it's such a pity that he had to run off and leave so soon after the funeral. And just when you could use the extra hand. But I suppose he never was really cut out for Sugar Lake life. Got more of the city in him like you, I suppose. Still, it's a shame." Once again, she turned to her hype woman. "Isn't it a shame, Liz dear?"

And, as expected, Liz came through, nodding her agreement and causing Betty to wonder if they were now rehearsing their own Sugar Lake cover of a Vegas act. No matter, Betty was not amused and frankly getting pretty darned close to losing it. It was time to shut this little morning catch-up session down. "Well, it's understandable," Betty said. "My Kellen had very important business to take care of. He's been a true blessing to Henry and me and now I'm more than grateful that Henry entrusted him with the family business, having the foresight to see his gifts so long ago. Though" — she slowed and paused for dramatic effect — "Goodness knows I had to practically chase him out of town. He wanted so very much to stay by my side."

Betty felt momentarily guilty for the lie.

23

Though it was true that Kellen, she knew, felt a bit of guilt over leaving her to head to Atlanta to take care of Kilborn Properties' ever-expanding (thanks to his shrewd dealings and expert ways) businesses. She knew leaving Sugar Lake wasn't all that much of a sacrifice for him. Though he loved both his grandparents, moving to Sugar Lake from New York to live with her and Henry after his parents passed away was never his idea of childhood bliss. An already quiet, reserved boy, Kellen was infinitely happier exploring a fine museum or even just getting lost in the anonymity of traversing down the street in a large city over a stroll through Sugar Lake's rambling woods. He'd never fully acclimated to the lifestyle of a town like Sugar Lake where everyone knew your name and darn near your shoe size and blood type.

And it wasn't like Betty totally blamed her grandson. Being somewhat an outsider herself when Henry brought her to town so many years ago, she thought she'd never get acclimated. Straight from her traveling road show tour company's bus to his old Chevy and from there to the judge, where they were married, and then onto Sugar Lake. Betty almost smiled. Thinking on it once again, as she often did of late: Gosh, was

Henry ever a smooth talker. For the life of her, she'd spent the first few years of their marriage wondering how he'd convinced her to accept his proposal so darned easily and move to this quirky town that she'd never even heard of.

Of course, Betty wouldn't let Lottie or Liz know any of her thoughts about Kellen or Henry though; so she went on, continuing her familial praise as convincingly as she could. "Yes, Kellen didn't want to leave, but I told him he must. These tragedies of life happen, but his grandfather wouldn't want others to suffer because of him, and Kellen was needed for some important meetings in Atlanta. You all can expect great things from my Kellen and Kilborn Properties very soon." Getting out that last bit took all Betty had, especially with the fine fit of a mood Kellen currently had her in.

"Well, let's hope he's not strictly all work, Betty dear. Though death is truly tragic, it does make one start to think on life and the circle of things. He really should get thinking about starting a family soon," Lottie said.

Betty felt a frown pull at the corner of her mouth and fought to temper it back. These women were good. Completely on their A button-pushing games this fine morning.

Betty continued to smile. "I'm sure a family will happen in due time. But Kellen is young and like I said, he's terribly busy. I'm so proud of him and lucky to have him to take up the reins where Henry left off. He has plenty of time for whatnot and all the rest."

Whew. Was she laying it on too thick or was that just convincing enough to get the women off her back and stop tongues wagging for a while? Betty hoped the latter, *but really what did it matter?* This time she didn't know if it was her voice she was hearing or Henry's, and once again the tears threatened to come. He was right. What did it matter?

There was no use wasting her time or the excess energy on what Lottie or Liz thought. The fact remained that her sweet Henry was gone, and in that she'd concede that the meddling Lottie and Liz were correct — she was alone. Henry was gone, her beloved son, Sidney, gone, her daughter-in-law, Alice, gone. Gone, gone, gone, all way before their times in her opinion, not that anyone was asking. All she had left was her grandson, a voice on the phone from Atlanta in between business meetings or property scouting trips or the gym or whatever else it was he did to keep his life so very full while

26

she was here, just where Henry left her, alone in Sugar Lake.

Betty squelched back a sigh as the loneliness she had been feeling in her old rambling house on the hill threatened to overtake her once again. Without her sweet Henry to fill the long days and the even longer nights, to make her laugh with his god-awful jokes or wipe away her late-night tears still brought on by silly childhood shadows of being an orphan, it all seemed so incredibly lonely.

Betty swallowed down on a lump in her throat that had no right being there. She gave Liz and Lottie what she knew good and darned well was not at all a convincing smile and put on her best stage voice, channeling her old days singing and acting out skits on the traveling tour circuit. "I must be off now, you two. I have been dying for some of Joyce's honey biscuits and I will not be deterred." *Oh fudge! Did her voice actually crack?* "You both have a wonderful day, now, and don't you go and be strangers. Don't think I didn't know the purpose of your past impromptu stopovers while my Henry was out doing his morning gardening. Now that he's gone, though, I can't offer such a view. I will try and keep the garden up as best I can, and I can still put together a fine tea and play a mean hand of spades." Betty gave them both a huge grin and prayed her smile wouldn't falter till she was at least out of viewing range.

Thankfully her fast rambling seemed to put the duo off kilter and neither Lottie nor Liz could seem to find the proper response to Betty's off-color, dead man gardening comment. How could they? What proper Southern woman admits to ogling a newly departed man during his sweaty lawn maintenance? It just wasn't done.

Good, Betty thought. It was just the reaction she was looking for. "I hope to see you both soon. Be sure to stop by. I'd love to have the company," Betty lied as she quickly turned toward Goode 'N Sweet, the town's long-standing bakery, without a backward glance. Betty vowed she would not turn around and she would not leave Goode 'N Sweet to head to Cartland's before she was sure that Lottie and Liz were long gone off Main Street and back to the air-conditioned confines of their own homes.

Nearing the bakeshop, she hoped that Joyce Goode was in her usual good mood, and by that she meant Goode in the familial sense and not in the countenance sense, because Betty didn't think she could take another moment of putting on false airs or having them put upon her. No thank you. She'd already had her fill for the day on that front.

Right now, all she wanted was some of Joyce's honey biscuits and maybe a slice of peach pecan pie as a do-you-right mood chaser. She swore Joyce's peach pie could soothe just about any hurt. Sure, she'd take the condolences that were sure to come, and she suspected, keep coming for some time, but now all she wanted — no, all she needed — was a bit of peace and, Lord please, a small bit of the old normalcy back in her life. If she could get a little of that without any of the side of extra judgment, she might just have found a few seconds of what felt like contentment. Then maybe, just maybe, she could make it through another blasted day without Henry.

Chapter 2
Working Girl

Drea leaned back and stretched, sending her back into a full arch, slightly wincing at a twinge of pain she wasn't used to feeling. Wow. Missing out on the three-times-a-week dance classes she used to take back in Manhattan was really starting to catch up to her. By no means a professional, Drea at least had the basics of tap, jazz, and modern, with a smattering of ballet under her belt. Back when she was in New York, she'd kept her body in shape with fusion hip-hop classes, which also kept her up on the latest audition happenings since the classes were populated by club kids who, for the most part, all had the same stars in their eyes as she did.

She thought of the enthusiastic dreamers and wondered how they were faring and if any of them had made it further in the past year than the role of underpaid body roller in some up-and-comer's music video. Keeping up on a few social media apps, she'd heard news of a few hits from some of her old crew. But if you let "the Gram" tell it, they were all living as large as Bey, Jay, and the K-Dash clan on the regular.

Drea shook her head. Who was she to throw stones? A year ago, she would have given her pinky toe, maybe both, to body roll in a music video or hang in the vicinity of any of the previously mentioned celebs. She looked around quickly, saw that the coast was more than clear, then did a quick four-count step and added in a body roll and a saucy shimmy mimicking one of her favorite latest music videos.

Drea tried her best to be happy for her old frenemy and at times professional rival Cassidy when she saw her dancing in the background of a video on YouTube. She and Cassidy had become friends in the loosest sense when they found themselves together in one too many situations. In the same jazz and hip-hop classes and then only two elliptical machines down from each other at the gym. Then when there were open calls for young African American women, well, there they were together again. I guess at that point they were friends. The enemy part didn't kick in until they both ended up as hostesses at the same SoHo eatery and the same so-called entertainment-connected married boss kept promising them both hookups. Drea sighed as she stopped dancing and picked up her cleaning rag once again. She guessed Cassidy won out there, judging by her prominent presence in the video and the fact that Drea was here, arranging pies.

"Now, I wouldn't take you for the sighing type, Alexandrea."

Drea looked up, surprised she'd been so distracted in her thoughts that she didn't even hear the tinkling of the chime that accompanied the opening of the bakeshop's front door. Upon seeing and hearing the arriving patron, she couldn't help the smile that came unbidden to her lips. Mrs. Kilborn — well, Mrs. Betty, as she insisted on being called by her first name like so many of the Southern women in town did — looked lovely in her black pedal pushers with black Keds-style sneakers and a white blouse topped with a lovely pink cardigan. Drea noticed that over her left breast she was wearing the beautiful heart brooch she'd so often seen her wear. It struck Drea then that the brooch may have had an even deeper meaning to the recently widowed woman than just the piece of costume jewelry she'd thought it to be.

Drea pulled her shoulders back and grinned at Mrs. Betty's insistence on calling her Alexandrea. Whenever she saw her it was "Alexandrea this or dear Alex that," never "Drea" as others called her. She guessed it wasn't grand enough for the over-the-top Mrs. Betty. Drea cleared her throat and forced her expression to brighten even more. "Sorry about that, Mrs. Betty. Looks like you caught me at an off moment. I'm so glad to see you!"

Mrs. Betty waved a hand as she came forward. "No worries, dear Alex. We've all been there. And I suppose you still haven't quite fully gotten used to our sleepy little town, you being a big city girl and all."

Drea gave her head a shake and for a moment let her inner thoughts escape as she looked over at the display counter, this time not quite seeing the pretty, colorful pies, glistening rolls, and other assorted pastries. Her mind was wandering once again to thoughts of dreams deferred and a faraway New York. "If only," she mumbled.

"What do you mean, 'if only'?"

Drea looked back over at Mrs. Betty, a bit of confusion in her eyes and instant worry over Mrs. Betty's frown. "Oh, I'm sorry," Drea said. "I didn't mean to go babbling out loud. Pay me no attention." She smiled

33

again. "Why don't you take a seat while I get you some tea and a nice warm honey biscuit. I'm sorry, my aunt's not here, but she should be back soon. She just went to an appointment and to run a few errands."

It was then that Drea noticed the extra tote in Mrs. Betty's hand. It didn't look too heavy, but it was substantial enough and she could see there were some large rolled files sticking out. How silly of her. She rushed from behind the counter to give her a hand. "Here, let me take that from you. I should have offered earlier. I'm sorry."

"Oh, it's no matter, dear," Mrs. Betty said, swooshing her away. "I'm not so old I can't handle this light work. And no worries about your aunt. It's not like I'm in any type of rush. I'm just happy to be out." Though her comment was seemingly benign, Drea couldn't help but notice the slight clouding over of her gaze. Drea stepped back and watched as the older woman took a seat, not at her usual table by the window, but one further back, out of view of passersby, where she could still see all the comings and goings along Main Street.

Her brows tightened as she noticed Mrs. Betty's gaze go furtively up the block.

"Were you waiting on someone, Mrs. Betty? Should I set another place?" she asked as she brought the woman over her tea setup.

Mrs. Betty glanced at her in confusion, then shook her head. "Oh no. I'm definitely not waiting on anyone, dear." She gave a slight smile. "More like avoiding, if I'm being truthful." She lowered her voice. "I ran into Lottie and Liz out by Cartland's and let's just say . . . they had opinions about me being out today."

Drea raised a brow. She knew about Mrs. Lottie and Mrs. Liz from her aunt's interactions with the pair. "Say no more. I completely understand. And we all know how opinions are. I mean everybody has them but . . ."

Mrs. Betty chuckled, and it made Drea happy to see her brighten. However, just as fast, her smile became slightly wistful as her eyes went to the window again and down Main Street. Drea could somehow tell in that moment her thoughts were no longer here with her, or Mrs. Lottie or her trusty friend Mrs. Liz — heck, they probably weren't even in the shop. Drea had a feeling by the look in Mrs. Betty's eyes that her mind, no, her heart, was somewhere walking hand-in-hand down Main Street with her too recently departed husband, Henry.

Drea quickly blinked back sudden tears,

35

thankful that they didn't overflow before the older woman looked back her way. What was her problem?

She ran back behind the counter and made herself busy getting the tea and biscuits prepared the way she knew Mrs. Betty preferred. She added a couple of cookies to the side and a few fresh berries, then brought everything over to Mrs. Betty's table.

"It really is good to have you in the shop today," Drea said. "I've been missing your sunny face and needed a pick-me-up."

Mrs. Betty gave her a smile back. "Thank you for that. Thank you for not asking me what I am doing out or questioning why I'm here."

Drea frowned. "Why would I? You being out is perfectly normal. It's another beautiful day in the neighborhood, as they say. Why shouldn't you enjoy it? Besides, my aunt would be fit to be tied if you came to town and had breakfast anywhere else. And you know you don't want to go getting on her bad side," Drea stated with a smirk.

Mrs. Betty shook her head. "No, that I surely don't." She chuckled, her voice light, tinkling, the sound for a moment lifting Drea's sullen mood. "And I don't know what you mean about a bad side to Joyce.

She's the best people. Tells it like it is and always from the heart." Drea noticed a hint of something loaded behind Mrs. Betty's kind words. She suspected her Lottie and Liz encounter took quite a bit out of her with the emotional time she'd been having. But still Mrs. Betty gave her a smile as she continued. "Nothing can compare to the company you get here in Goode 'N Sweet. That includes you too, you know."

Drea felt a rush of warmth at the surprising compliment and she suddenly didn't quite know what to do with herself. Feeling inadequate and wishing her aunt was there, Drea fidgeted a bit, but paused as Mrs. Betty lifted her biscuit and took a healthy bite. As she chewed, Drea felt a small hint of pride watching the woman enjoy the pastry that she could only attribute to her aunt rubbing off on her. But with her pride, worry edged in. It didn't escape her notice today, the slight bit of gauntness in Mrs. Betty's normally full, brown cheeks, only highlighted all the more by the coral blush she'd applied to try and hide it. Nor did the bright purple shadow she wore conceal the darkness under her striking deep-set brown eyes. Instead, it only drew attention to the sleepless nights she must be having. Drea could tell that in the past few weeks (or had it now been a month already since her husband's passing?) that the woman had not been getting proper rest. Clearly, grief was taking not just an understandable emotional toll, but a physical toll as well. Drea could see this visit to the shop today was good and well needed.

The fact that she was thinking such thoughts brought Drea up short. She wasn't the type to notice others' worries. Or at least she didn't used to be. Just go and ask her sister. Drea almost snorted with the thought. But she had an excuse. She liked Mrs. Betty. Sure, she didn't know her much past her aunt and the few conversations she'd had with her upon visiting the old theater up the street she ran with her late husband. But she liked the eccentric older woman all the same.

Drea made herself busy then and thought about Mrs. Betty and her husband as she remembered them just a little over a month before. Even at their age, they'd made quite the pair. She a petite, curvy, brown-skinned beauty. Mrs. Betty wore her silver hair in a short and stylish curly bob that flirted around her cheeks and chin. Her husband was tall and slim, though all at once a broad-shouldered and imposing man in a way that could be called, she was sure, dashing in his day. He was fair-skinned with brown eyes with surprising hints of green that never failed to surprise Drea upon seeing him. They were whimsical eyes for a man she thought could easily command so much distinguished power. That was until he was foiled against his wife, and then Mr. Henry was nothing but softness and smiles as he tucked an errant curl behind her ear, or more outlandishly, was dressed in one of the costumes she'd gotten him into for their Redheart movie theme nights.

Drea smiled, then felt a pang tug at her heart. She'd sure miss their theme nights over at the Redheart. So far, the Redheart had been her one constant form of entertainment in town outside of Jolie's Bar and Grill, and goodness knew, too much of Jolie's ribs and Joy Juice didn't do her any good. Better she spent her evenings out with an old movie, a tub of popcorn, and a soda as her indulgence. Not Joy Juice, mechanical bulls, and smooth-talking Southern boys. She'd left her versions of all that back in the clubs in Manhattan.

Besides it wasn't any hardship for her to do a solo movie night instead of a wild club night, though the fact annoyed her cousin Rena to no end since she'd got it stuck in her head that now that her cousins were in town from New York, it would be a girl's night whenever she could secure a sitter and a night away from her children. Poor fun-loving Rena. After just a few nights out with her, both Drea and Olivia decided they could hardly keep up and opted for more sedate, genteel pursuits.

It wasn't any skin off Drea's teeth, though. She'd come to Sugar Lake to recharge her batteries and regroup after so many disappointments. Spending the evenings in the Kilborns' darkened theater had come to mean solace for her. And there was the added fact that Drea loved the surprise of seeing what the Kilborns would decide to screen for the next week. Crazily enough she'd found herself looking forward to it and their wacky costumes on top of it.

But since Mr. Kilborn had passed, the theater had been shuttered. She could hardly imagine Mrs. Betty continuing those theme nights without him. Half the fun of it was the two of them and what movie characters they would dress up as. Mr. Kilborn was always so quiet and reserved in his demeanor; she didn't know what it took for his wife to get him in those wild getups, but the fact that he did it, week after week, showed his obvious love for her.

Once again, Drea had to swallow back a

sigh. Did love like that even exist anymore? Or was it dying off quickly with the likes of men like Henry Kilborn?

Drea gave Mrs. Betty a smile that she hoped revealed none of her inner thoughts. "Well, company reflects the company it keeps is what I say, and you are always outstanding company. It's great to have you here today."

It was then that a small crash sounded from the kitchen area. Both women looked up at each other in mild shock and Drea pulled an embarrassed face as she heard softly muttered curses coming from her normally mild-mannered sister. She gave Mrs. Betty a raised brow. "Well, it seems duties are calling me out back. I better go and check on my sister. If you don't mind excusing me, I'll be back in a moment."

Mrs. Betty nodded. "No worries, dear. I'll be right here."

Though to Drea it didn't seem like anything major, you would've thought that Olivia's eggs not peaking was a total disaster, right up there with missing a Century 21 sale, but to each her own, Drea thought. After quickly talking her sister down and letting her know that there was a customer out front when her little tirade went down, Drea went back out to join Mrs. Betty.

Heck, it wasn't like she could help out back there. Get an egg to peak. What did that even mean? she thought as she headed back out front.

Once again when Drea looked out, Mrs. Betty seemed to be deep in thought. But this time her mind wasn't wandering — at least, it didn't seem that way. No, Mrs. Betty was intently reading some papers that she had spread on the table in front of her. Drea could tell by the furrow of her brow that whatever she was reading had her distressed. Goodness, she hoped the woman wasn't in some sort of financial trouble.

Drea nibbled at her lip in worry. That didn't make any sense. Though her husband had died quite suddenly, through what she'd gathered from all the town's talk, the family seemed to be well-off. The Kilborns didn't just own the theater, but also were pretty big landowners in town and expanding in more areas in the real estate game — but then again, who knew with town gossip. Either way, Drea thought as she openly stared at Mrs. Betty, something had her seriously troubled, and the fact that the woman was here dealing with it all alone at a table in the town's bakeshop didn't sit well with her.

Where was Mrs. Betty's family? Drea

knew she had a grandson, the so-called business whiz and odd boy wonder, as the townsfolk told it. She'd heard he as of late had been running the family business, groomed by Mr. Henry to be his successor. As to other family, she didn't know much further than that. But why was this woman reading all these documents herself? Where was the young business genius when his grandmother obviously needed him?

Drea had stopped by the repast to pay her respects after Mr. Henry's funeral and didn't see any glimpse of the grandson. She would assume he'd been there, but it was a mad crush of people and she'd only gotten to see Mrs. Betty briefly. The crowd vying for Mrs. Betty's attention and the fact that she was indeed needed at the shop during that time made it so that she could only stay long enough to give Mrs. Betty a hug before heading back to work so her Aunt Joyce could stay and help her friend out.

Just then Mrs. Betty looked up from her papers, feeling Drea's gaze, and gave her a weak smile. Drea felt her cheeks warm at being caught staring. She walked over and picked up Mrs. Betty's cup. "Let me freshen this for you."

"Thank you," Mrs. Betty said. Putting the papers in her hand down, she started to look around the shop as if just seeing it for the first time.

Drea cocked her head to the side, then walked away with the cup. Upon returning, she noticed that Mrs. Betty was giving her quizzical eyes.

Drea frowned. "What is it, Mrs. Betty? Would you like another biscuit too? I'm sorry, I should have offered." She started walking toward the back.

Mrs. Betty shook her head and stopped her with a cool, outstretched hand. "No, dear, not now. But I will take a couple to go on my way out and probably some peach pecan pie; you be sure to set that aside for me. Don't you go and sell out once it gets busy in here again."

Drea was about to walk away when Mrs. Betty's voice stopped her again. "I was just thinking. . . ." Mrs. Betty paused. It was so long that Drea wondered if that was the end of the thought. *But,* she reminded herself, *remember she came in for a reason. She's not home because she's lonely and needs someone to talk to.* Drea smiled and patiently waited.

Finally, Mrs. Betty continued. "It looks so lovely in here. I remember your aunt remarking on the fact that the changes were all due to your keen design eye."

"I don't know about that, Mrs. Betty. I can't take full credit for everything. This is a family business and family always pitches in where needed," Drea said.

Mrs. Betty rolled her eyes. "Come now, it's just you and me and there really is no need to be modest. You did a lovely job here. Between you and your sister, you both helped Joyce tremendously and turned the shop around. Your sister's new recipes have been a wonderful boost to the menu, and you updating the shop has really brought in plenty of new customers. Ambience is everything. How one presents oneself and makes first impressions is always key. You know we've talked about that before. I daresay your New York style gives you an edge there. Not to mention your innate showmanship." Mrs. Betty gave Drea a cute conspiratorial wink and it reminded her a bit of the spark and humor she'd shown in her former self before she'd suddenly lost her husband. She continued, "We know all about presentation and how important it is. You have got real talent, Alexandrea. I can see it."

Drea let out a breath. She didn't mean for it to come out slow and long and breathy like it did, tinged with a hint of regret. But it did, and she couldn't very well suck it back in. "For all that has done me. Oh well. It's nice to be acknowledged by you. Thank you. I really appreciate it, Mrs. Betty." Drea perked up a little; giving voice to her inner turmoil and then accepting the compliment for what it was worth felt nice. But then she took in Mrs. Betty again, looking at the older woman seriously. Drea's eyes went from Mrs. Betty down to the papers strewn across the table. She now saw underneath the legal sheets what looked like architectural plans and designs. She remembered Mrs. Betty's earlier furrowed brow. It all seemed like so much that the woman was taking on. "Mrs. Betty, is there anything I can do for you? I don't mean to pry, but I saw you looking at those papers pretty intently. Can I help in any way? Do you want me to call someone for you?"

Mrs. Betty stared at Drea, perhaps a few beats more than was comfortable, and she looked around the shop once again. She looked down at the papers, then back up at Drea and smiled, the rosiness in her cheeks now coming on naturally and not by her overly applied coral blush. "You know what, Alexandrea, I think perhaps you can. That is, if you're up for a bit of a challenge."

Drea didn't know what it was that made her nod in the affirmative. Maybe it was the blush of her cheeks or maybe it was the sparkle in the older woman's eyes. Or who knows, maybe it was that morning and the wistful feeling of longing she had when putting away that darned Oh Honey Yes You May Pie, or maybe it was the idea of just being given another chance to prove herself, because not only did she nod, but she told Mrs. Betty yes.

CHAPTER 3
WHO'S THAT GIRL?

Kellen Kilborn couldn't believe he was currently pulling in to the Sugar Lake town limits. Well, at least he'd made good time, his black Mustang living up to its Bullitt name. Still, Sugar Lake was the last place he was supposed to be or wanted to be right now. Though just thinking the thought had guilt rising up in his throat. He swallowed it back and focused on where he was supposed to be. Where he was supposed to be was finishing his workout, then heading into his office to prepare for his team's early morning planning strategy meeting to hash out the problems with the Ronson Property Group proposal. But where was he? Not in Atlanta but in quiet Sugar Lake for a strategy meeting of another kind entirely.

All wordplay aside, he'd rather face an entire boardroom than his grandmother this morning. And it was still so darned early, the sun barely rising. She probably wasn't even up yet. His grandfather was the early riser in the family. Kellen knew when his grandmother saw him pulling up at this hour of the morning her hackles would rise, and she'd quickly be spoiling for a fight. Sure, there was the off chance that he'd catch her groggy and off balance and use that to persuade her to see things his way, but honestly, with his grandmother's cunning, those chances were slim to none. These negotiations were probably doomed before they were out of the gate.

Still, here he was. But seriously, where else would he be? The cagey old woman would probably laugh when she saw him.

Yesterday, he'd played right into her hand. He'd been so riled up getting her call just when he'd been pacifying Jamina Ronson about the Redheart not yet being signed over to the Ronson Group. He couldn't tell Jamina that the delay was because of his grandmother's stalling. He was thinking up another deflection right when his other line started to buzz. *What in the world?* Kellen thought. Where was Tracy, his assistant? There was no way this line should be buzzing while he was on such an important call. Tracy knew he wasn't to be disturbed with Jamina Ronson unless there was a dire emergency.

Suddenly, Kellen's heart plummeted and a lump grew in his throat. Thoughts of the last emergency call, from just over a month ago, came flooding back to him. Oh God, he hoped there wasn't anything wrong with his grandmother.

The last conversation he'd had with her had been unusually terse for the two of them. His grandma was never terse, at least not with him. He'd never even argued with her before. Not in all of his nearly thirty years. Hell, Kellen rarely argued with anyone, preferring to keep his true feelings under wraps, thus never giving anyone the upper hand on him by revealing emotions. He had certainly never shown his grandparents anything but kindness and respect. They were the only ones in his life besides his parents to have ever shown him love, even taking him in after his parents died and dealing with him despite his stoic ways.

The only thing he could remember ever having a disagreement with his grandmother about was not being more carefree and loosening up. But thankfully, she'd finally gotten used to his, what she called, "staid young old man ways," and now considered it part of his charm (her words, not his).

But their current argument had no charming side. The fact that Kellen could not get his grandmother to see clearly about the Redheart truly perplexed him. He didn't understand her. The fact that they had a buyer for the old theater willing to pay over the market value for the property should make her happy. Yes, he understood that it was pretty soon after his grandfather's death, but even if his grandfather was alive, he'd consider this a good deal and sell. There really was no longer any need to keep it open. It wasn't like she could run it on her own. Letting it go was probably the best thing. Kellen sighed to himself and pushed down on feelings he wasn't in the mood for feeling. Yes, it was for the best. All things considered.

The time for whimsy was over and now was the time for decisive action. Especially if he was going to bring the Kilborn family and Kilborn Properties' name into the future, he had to make the tough decisions.

Suddenly, Tracy's voice broke through over his intercom: "I'm sorry to interrupt, Mr. Kilborn, but it's your grandmother."

Kellen startled and broke in over Jamina speaking, his heart now racing. "You'll have to excuse me, Jamina. I need to cut our conversation short and take this call."

"But, um, what about the points we still need to go over, Kellen? Wait, how about we meet for dinner later in the week to solidify the —" she began, but Kellen was already halfway gone. He didn't have time to hear her go on. He knew what she wanted. The Redheart for its central location and then after that more of Kilborn land for Ronson's expansion into the Sugar Lake area. He got it. But that all depended on his grandmother and, right now, she needed him on the other line.

"I'm sorry, Jamina, I'll have to have my assistant get back to you," he said, and clicked over to the other line. "Grandma?" Kellen asked, hating the thread of urgency running through his voice. "Are you all right? You're not feeling unwell, are you?"

The voice that came back at him was by no means the sickly one that he was anticipating.

"Don't come at me with that 'are you all right' mess right now, young man. You know good and well I am not," came his grandmother's musical, though clearly irate, voice over the speakerphone.

Kellen didn't know who was more intimidating, his grandmother or Jamina Ronson. Wait, he did know; it was definitely his grandmother. Still, he couldn't show fear.

"So, I take it we're still talking about the Redheart today, Grandmother?" Kellen rubbed his hand across his forehead in frustration. Maybe he should have stayed on the line with Jamina. Clearly, he wouldn't be making headway with his grandmother, not in the mood she was in.

"You know I'm talking about the Redheart, so you'd better come down quick off that hoity-toity business school voice of yours that you got going on right now and remember you're talking to not your 'Grandmother,' but your 'Grandma.' I know you only call me that when you're getting your shorts in a twist."

Kellen felt his lips tighten, which was probably for the best. Better to let no sound escape at this point, he thought as his grandmother continued. "I thought I already made it clear that we were not selling the Redheart, so I don't know what I'm doing currently holding papers in my hand, waiting for my signature to sign it over to RPG. You must have lost what was left of your ever-loving mind if you think you can disregard my words so easily."

Kellen nearly winced at the anger in his grandma's voice. Maybe he'd gone too far. But he thought if she just saw the prospectus in black and white, she'd get a better feel for it. "Of course I don't think that, Grandma. I was just hoping that you could see my reasoning in this." Kellen decided to make his voice more placid. He had to get her to see his way in this. There was so much riding on this deal.

"Kellen, this is not up for discussion. Just like I told you when you were heading back to Atlanta after the funeral, which mind you, was just a few weeks ago — we're not selling the Redheart."

He heard her let out a deep sigh, which let him know she was doing her "let me catch my breath and get my nerves together" thing. Kellen stood and rocked back and forth impatiently as he waited.

Finally, she spoke. "Now, baby, I have all faith in you and you know that your grandfather had all faith in you. I do get that there is a lot on your shoulders and you feel like you must take on the world by yourself right now, but truly you don't. And you don't have to go full steam ahead trying to change the world in a hot minute just because your grandfather is no longer here."

Kellen felt like his teeth were on edge and sensed the possible beginnings of a migraine. Why couldn't she see his way of things? "But, Grandma. This deal would be the first step in expanding our business. They have connections in a lot of major cities that we can use to our advantage. All they want is the Redheart."

"And where is it written that everyone should just get what they want?" his grandma calmly responded.

"But this is pivotal to the deal," Kellen said, trying for restraint while still showing the slightest bit of desperation in his voice.

"Not everything in life is a deal!"

Kellen stilled. His grandmother never yelled. Then he heard her sniffle and he swore someone took an ice pick to his heart. *Please don't let her be crying.* He could take a lot, but he could not take her tears.

She spoke again and thankfully sounded more like herself. "Baby, I know we have put a lot on your shoulders, you being in such a position at such a young age."

"I'm not that young, Grandma. I'm closer to thirty than I am to twenty. And I've been pretty much doing this job for five years, even when Grandpa was alive."

His grandmother sighed and once again Kellen knew he'd done it. He regretted bringing up his grandfather and the past. Dammit, he usually wasn't so careless with his words. "I'm sorry, I didn't mean to say that. I guess I am young and dumb in some ways."

"No, baby, it's perfectly fine for you to bring up your grandfather. And it would seem we're both hurting. More than we may be able to say. You doing what you're doing and continuing his legacy makes me happy and proud. And yes, you have been handling a lot for Kilborn for quite a while, quite beautifully. You've made us both very proud over the years. But, dear, you have to know I'm not budging on the Redheart. So, like I said, even though it may not make all the best business sense to you right now, we will not be selling. I don't know if we'll ever be."

Ever be? Her words sounded so final, it was like a steel door closing in his face and Kellen's dreams of expansion and big city skylines seemed to crumble before his eyes.

"Grandma, please listen to reason. The theater is pivotal to the Ronson deal, which means it's pivotal to the future of our company. Do you understand what I'm saying here?"

"Boy, you forget who practically taught you how to wipe your behind. Understand? You'd better watch yourself," she snorted.

Kellen felt more heat rise then, though not quite from anger and more like embarrassment. "Yes, ma'am."

His grandmother started to laugh then, which did nothing more than confuse and infuriate Kellen. What could she possibly have to laugh about? "Grandma, how could you possibly be laughing? This is very serious."

Suddenly, Kellen paused. Wait a minute. It had only been weeks since Grandpa passed. Maybe his grandmother was having some sort of grieving shock to her system. Guilt started to gnaw at Kellen. He knew he shouldn't have left so soon after the funeral, but he had business to take care of. Now he wished he'd done a better job of convincing his grandmother to travel to Atlanta with him. It wasn't like he'd had parents to stay with her.

Just then, Kellen's mind started to wander to his late grandfather and them casting out in that old fishing boat. The boat had seen better days long before Kellen, but his grandfather wouldn't give it up and took pride in taking them both out on the lake in the early morning hours before the sun got too high in the sky and the Georgia heat unbearable. If his grandfather only knew how much he regretted never telling him how special those moments were. But it was too late for that.

His grandmother's voice brought him back to the here and now.

"As a matter of fact, you don't have to worry about the Redheart at all, young man, because I've got it all under control."

Suddenly, every hair on the back of Kellen's neck rose to full attention. "What do you mean you've got it all under control?" he asked, fear making his mouth go a bit dry.

"Just what I said — I've got it under control." A hint of excitement lightened his grandmother's voice and it had Kellen's mind whirling. He never understood how his grandfather was able to put up with his grandmother's wild mood swings. But he held on as she continued to take him on this emotional roller coaster of a phone call.

"Well, I've come in contact with a fabulous designer, Alex. And the two of us have come up with great plans to continue the vision your grandfather and I had for the theater and make it even better. I reckon that by the next time you're back in town, you'll hardly recognize the old place. Why, as a matter of fact, I think I'll hold a grand Hollywood-style party for the big rededication day. Doesn't that sound terrific? And the best part is you don't have to worry about a thing. Just leave it up to me and Alex and we'll have the old girl shining in no time."

Alex? Wait a minute. What charlatan had gone and gotten his claws into his grandmother and messed up his potential deal while he was unawares?

Kellen was momentarily dumbstruck, but he knew it couldn't last; he had to find his voice. "Grandma, what have you gotten yourself into, going and hiring a designer? Please don't do anything further and don't make any more rash decisions. There's too much that can go wrong with this plan and, like I said, I need that theater for what I've got going over here."

"*Like you said?* Like I said, you don't have the theater. The theater is mine. Just like the company is mine. Don't you forget it, young man." She cleared her throat, pausing momentarily before speaking. "Well, I've got lots going on today, sweetheart. I really must go, ta-ta!"

Ta-ta? Was she really dismissing him like that? And who said "ta-ta" nowadays?

"Wait, we've got a lot to talk about. Grandma, don't hang up. This conversation is not over," Kellen yelled.

But his grandmother's laughter filled the air before trailing off, followed by a soft click and then silence.

Kellen closed his mouth, refusing to be made more of a fool if only to himself. He made it through his last few meetings and his evening workout. Though he upped the pace on his run and went in extra hard with his Wednesday night basketball game, sleep still eluded him, and at three a.m., instead of slumbering as he should have to prepare for the next day's meetings, he'd found himself on the road to Sugar Lake to have it out over the Redheart property with his grandmother.

As he pulled his Mustang to the curb on Main Street in the early morning hours, Kellen was once again surprised by the rapid changes in town. There were so many updates. The new coffee shop, the trendy new boutiques, and an art gallery. Taking it all in strengthened his resolve to make the Ronson deal work. He didn't want to think about regrets. He didn't have the time or space for that emotion. Sugar Lake had never been truly home to him. In his heart, he knew he hadn't found that home yet, and maybe he never would. But the closest thing he had to it was his office and the feeling he got when making good on a killer deal.

Kellen's brows drew together as he spied the front of the Goode 'N Sweet bakery. This was not the bakeshop he remembered. It had been a while since he visited Miss Joyce and the bakery, having skipped it on his last few trips to town. At first, he was taken aback by the look of the place — still country classic, but now there was an updated new twist. It still had the signature brown-and-pink stripes on everything with the Goode 'N Sweet name, but Kellen saw that the store had been updated with a new bit of whimsy, giving it a Southern-meets-Parisian twist. Also, gone were the old frilly curtains that had been in the windows darn near since he was a boy. Now in their place, the large pane glass window was adorned with a border of what appeared to be hand-painted pies and cakes that made a person smile upon looking at them and long to come into the shop and have a taste.

Kellen frowned. Nothing about that whimsical border screamed Miss Joyce, the bakeshop's proprietor. Though the woman was genius in the kitchen, and her baked goods had an undoubtedly whimsically delicious taste on the tongue, there was nothing about her that he would consider whimsical. Kellen hoped Goode 'N Sweet hadn't changed ownership, because he really wanted one of Miss Joyce's honey biscuits right now, and taking a few sweet treats to his grandmother wouldn't hurt his negotiations. He'd learned that trick from his grandfather. Food wasn't the way to just a man's heart.

Kellen got a glimpse of the CLOSED sign

on the shop and frowned further still. He flipped his wrist and looked at his watch: 6:47. The shop didn't open until 7:00. He still had thirteen minutes before he could attack the growling in his stomach. Kellen took a whiff of the air and caught the sweet aroma of Miss Joyce's honey biscuits. Well, at least it smelled like Miss Joyce was still baking. He bounced on his toes as he saw a bit of activity in the back kitchen area.

Surely Miss Joyce would let him in a moment early. He cupped his hands around his frames and peered through the window again. This time he saw a figure start to exit the kitchen, her arms laden with a couple of pies that she was bringing to put into the case. Kellen rapped on the door.

The woman seemed startled seeing him and she jumped back a step. Crap, he didn't mean to scare her. Kellen held up a hand, but stilled as her eyes, face — well, everything — connected with him.

Who was this woman and where was Miss Joyce or Rena, Miss Joyce's niece who usually helped out? This cinnamon-skinned beauty, who was currently giving him a look that could easily ignite a campfire, was definitely not the always good-natured Rena. It was now Kellen's turn to step back.

He watched as the young woman's brows

tightened and her full lips did the same in what seemed to be an innate sense of caution as her eyes pierced him with darts of fire. Kellen took another step back, though for what, he wasn't sure. Still, it seemed somehow necessary for his own self-preservation. Then, without thinking, he leaned forward as if longing to get closer to her and see more.

For a moment, Kellen felt as though his tired morning eyes were playing tricks on him. Her skin glowed in the most beautiful, almost ethereal way, and her full lips, tinted the color of eggplant, seemed to cast some type of spell. Was this some pie-wielding fairy? Her hair had the same spell-casting quality in the way it haloed her head and framed her face, then came together in a side sweep of long twist braids that flirted down past her shoulders. For a moment Kellen forgot to breathe as swirls of never felt emotion wrapped around him unbidden.

But he did remember. He remembered when she jutted her chin out at him and gave a sharp yell, breaking the momentary spell she'd cast on him. "Still closed!" she barked before turning abruptly and hurrying back to the kitchen area without so much as a backward glance.

Kellen swallowed. *Closed?* Assuming it was now fast approaching seven o'clock, what kind of customer service was that? What happened to service with a smile and the customer is always right and all that? Frustration started to edge out his hunger and his momentary lapse of reasoning. Kellen wasn't used to being dismissed and was annoyed it was happening more and more as of late. First with his grandmother and now with this bakery . . . being.

Well, Little Miss Pie Witch would have something to explain when he gave Miss Joyce an earful about her. Sure, good help was hard to find, but Miss Joyce couldn't just go around hiring anybody to open the shop in the morning. Hiring somebody of this type, she'd be out of business in no time. Kellen looked down at his watch and felt his anger go that much higher. 7:02. Closed? They were supposed to be open at 7:00.

Kellen rapped on the shop's door again and once again the cinnamon beauty came from the back, her arms once more laden with baked goods. And yet again, she didn't seem to be in any bit of a rush. As she put the pies in the case, for some reason, Kellen felt the overwhelming need to rap on the door some more.

He watched as she raised one of her perfectly arched brows a most satisfying way and her lips curled up on one side. Kellen couldn't help but give her the same lip curl in return. She cocked her head to the side in a challenging way and suddenly that self-preservation need to step back hit him once again. His hand stilled as he stared. "Don't move, man. Be strong," he told himself.

But all bets were off when she came from around the counter, and Kellen sucked in an almost audible rush of air. *Whoa, was she a looker!* Wait. Seriously, did he just think the word *looker*? Who did that? A 1940s sailor on leave? But really, she was, and it wasn't as if she was wearing anything all that spectacular. The pie witch/fairy, or whatever she was, was wearing some sort of tank top and what appeared to be cut-off denim shorts with a pink-and-brown-striped Goode 'N Sweet apron over top, and that was it. All of it. The ensemble was finished. Done. All except what appeared to be well-worn black motorcycle-type boots that Kellen got a glimpse of when his eyes finally made it down the long, expansive trail that was her perfectly sculpted legs. By the time his eyes were done with their descent, his stupid heartbeat was so loud in his ears that as she finally made her way to the door, that he had to make an effort to tell himself to listen carefully or be made a fool.

He heard her flip the lock on the front door and open it. There was the tinkle of a chime. All the while his blood rushed and there was a thump, thump, thump. She looked at him, then past him to his car, then back at him with shrewd eyes that made him suddenly and for inexplicable reasons want to throw some mud on the shiny black sports car and dirty it up. But then she spread her pretty lips in a smile of welcome that didn't quite hold the Southern charm he was used to, and right then and there, Kellen knew he was in serious trouble.

"You gonna let my arm break off or what, Suit?"

"Huh?" He was confused by the question. Her words seemed familiar but somehow not quite right, and were totally unexpected.

"Oh, did I forget? Welcome to Goode 'N Sweet. Now, my arm is getting a bit tired. You gonna let it go numb or what? You were the one who seemed in an almighty rush to get in." Her voice held the slight edge of fast-paced business to it and none of the Southern lilt that he was used to from the townspeople of Sugar Lake. Kellen blinked.

Wow, she was tall. He was tall and she could almost meet him eye to eye with only the stacked heels of her boots on. Then things started to register.

"Wait, did you just call me *Suit*?"

Her brow rose again.

Kellen decided then and there to get his head together and that she might be a little bit too, well, everything, for her and his own good. Though he was wearing a sports jacket, it clearly was not a suit and even if it was a suit, what right did she have to go calling him *Suit* and tagging him with some sort of a nickname? Yes, she may be beautiful, and he could tell she already knew she was, but she also needed to realize her place, which right now was serving the paying customer.

"Your sign says you open at seven and it is now well after seven. I mean, if you're not open for business on time, you could lose potential customers that way."

With that, she turned and looked at the clock on the back wall, then slowly turned to look back at him with a shrug. "Three. It's three minutes after." She sighed. "So, it would seem you're right. I am so sorry to keep a punctual man like you waiting. But, wait you did." She looked at him incredulously, gave him a quizzical up and down and cocked her head to the side. "Well, sir?" she asked, her voice now dripping with honey. The *Suit* dropped, and the *sir* said not with half as much reverence. He honestly didn't know which was worse. "You said you are in a rush, so what are you still doing out there on the sidewalk? Like I asked before, you going to let my arm fall off?"

Suddenly feeling ridiculous through no fault of his own, Kellen walked into the shop, on the way catching some sort of intoxicating scent that had nothing to do with the biscuits. He was suspiciously afraid that it might be emanating from her. Hibiscus? A slight musk? Whatever, it was all the way heavenly. He cleared his throat and walked further into the shop, his hands tightly fisted at his sides.

Kellen could hear the sounds of more people in the kitchen area. He immediately recognized Miss Joyce as she was speaking with someone else in the back and he felt a bit of relief at the familiarity of it. Whew. He didn't know why, but this woman made him nervous. However, he knew he couldn't very well go and ask for Miss Joyce to come out. Kellen decided to just go and take a seat at one of the tables by the window. He still had a little time before it was safe to wake his grandmother. Maybe he'd just have a biscuit or two and a cup of coffee before grabbing a few sweets to take up to her. Flies, honey, and all that. He should at least be properly nourished and armed for that upcoming fight.

Kellen looked up from his seat, then noticed the odd expression on the young woman's face. "So, uh, not in a rush then?" she said slyly. "Can I get you a menu? Though most people prefer to just go to the counter to choose what they'd like to have."

He gave her a tight smile. Though he understood her confusion, having never seen him before, she probably thought he was one of the tourists in town and didn't know he already knew Miss Joyce's menu backward and forward. He shook his head. "I'm not most people. Still, there is no need for a menu. I'll take a coffee with three sugars, no cream, and two honey biscuits."

Though she'd tried her best to keep her expression neutral, Kellen still caught the briefest, slightest frown from the pie witch before her expression went back to a fairy smile. He tried not to smirk at the tiny victory of besting her. "Be right up," she said. "I should have known you were decisive as well as punctual."

Just like that Kellen wanted to sneer at her backhanded compliment, but she turned on her fast-heeled boots and was off to get his coffee before he could respond. Instead he adjusted his glasses. He wouldn't complain, as he was given the amazing view of those long legs.

But she was quick, and before he could get fully comfortable, she was back, coffee in one hand and biscuits in the other. Kellen's hunger grabbed him anew. "Order up, Suit. I hope I didn't keep you waiting long."

Kellen frowned once again, and this time gave her a raised brow. "So, you're looking to keep going with this Suit thing, huh? It really is terrible customer service. How would you like it if someone called you . . ." He looked her up and down, pausing at her hair, but dismissing that when he saw the challenge in her eyes — nope, wasn't going there. Then he went over her body, fighting to not leer and to be as respectful as possible. Finally, his eyes landed on those darned boots. They looked like they fit her perfectly. Sexy and cool but with a polished, edgy finish due to the silver buckles and cool studding that went up across the toe and around the top edge. Kellen looked back into her eyes. "What if someone called you Boots, for example." He was surprised to catch a hint of a smile at the corner of her mouth and a spark in her eyes.

She shrugged. "Boots, huh? I think it's cute. I love these boots." She twisted her feet left and right.

He frowned. "Well, they're completely impractical for the Georgia heat."

She crossed her arms. "And your suit jacket works in this weather?"

Lost for words, Kellen picked up a biscuit and shoved half of it in his mouth, taking a hearty bite. This time he didn't hold back on the groan that overtook him. Goodness, there was nothing like Miss Joyce's baking. Her biscuits were absolute heaven, second to only her pies. The woman was a culinary genius. If she ever wanted to expand and take her business into supermarkets, he'd be the first in line with investment money. Suddenly, Kellen wasn't regretting his impromptu decision to get on the road as much as he'd been a half hour before.

"So, tell me. Are you meeting a potential client here this morning? Let me guess, you're another one of those wannabe gentrifiers who's got their sights on Sugar Lake? How many acres are you looking to buy? And please, don't say you're angling to make an offer on the shop, because if you are, we're definitely not selling."

Kellen's head shot up toward her. *We're?* What did she mean by *we're*? What could she have to do with the ins and outs of this shop? But Kellen didn't have a chance to question the odd query because just then the shop door chimed and in came a couple of local firemen, pulling her attention their way.

"Morning, Ducky, Brax, Dave. Good to see you this morning," the former Miss Pie Witch, now Boots, said, all smiles for the firefighters who came in and were annoyingly all smiles back at her. Wait a minute, where was that brassy attitude that he got when he'd entered the shop?

Kellen quickly took a gulp of his hot coffee and almost choked as he watched the exchange between her and the men, who were oh so obviously fawning over her. His lips went all twitchy. They were all shoulders, teeth, and muscles, and Kellen wondered if there were check marks for those qualifications on the firefighter's application.

Shoulders: check.

Teeth: check.

Muscles: check.

Kellen continued to watch while she served more arriving customers as the shop picked up business. A couple of elderly people came in and then more tourists after them. The whole time Kellen tried not to seethe as Boots seemed light, bubbly, and friendly with each customer, totally engaging, and everyone seeming to love her right back.

So . . . what? It was only guys in sports coats or the first customer of the day who got the hard end of her studded boots? Kellen polished off the second biscuit, letting out a sigh.

"If you don't get more handsome every time I see you, young man?" Kellen's eyes shifted left and right. "Stop looking so modest, Kellen, you know good and well I'm talking to you," Miss Joyce said, coming over to give him a rather rough slap on the arm before softening with a warm hug as he rose to greet her.

Kellen smiled as he felt some of his earlier pent-up tension finally start to leave his body. Thankfully, Joyce Goode never changed, and immediately he felt a pang of remorse over not getting to see her when he was in town for his grandfather's funeral. He'd given her a thank you and hugs at the repast for all her food, but still, he should have stopped by the shop. It wasn't like he was a stranger there.

"It's nice to see you, Miss Joyce. I'm sorry I didn't make the time when I was last in town. I really should have."

"Oh, that's no worry. I know how busy you were. And times being what they were and have been, I know it's tough, baby. I'm glad to see you looking better. You were a bit shell shocked last time I laid eyes on you. Rightly so." He could see the concern as she looked over his face. "I know how hard this has been for you all."

Kellen shook his head. "You don't have to worry about me. I'm fine. Been just working a lot is all."

She peered at him more intently before looking down at his empty plate and frowning. "Did you just get into town?"

"Yes, I just pulled in about a half hour ago. I stopped here first because I didn't want to barge in on my grandma too early. Plus, I thought I'd bring her a few treats."

Miss Joyce raised a brow. "Trying to butter her up, huh? And you want to make me a part of it?" She shook her head and laughed. "Don't get me involved with your troubles, Kellen Kilborn."

Kellen fought not to blush. Of course, his grandmother would confide in Miss Joyce if anyone. Though Miss Joyce was a few years younger, she and his grandmother had struck up quite a friendship and, though she was friendly with lots of the women in town, his grandma didn't call that many close or true friends. Joyce Goode, she did. So Miss Joyce probably knew that Kellen was in his fair share of hot water with his grandmother.

Miss Joyce waved a hand as if his missteps with his grandmother were the slightest of blips and started to speak. "Well, what did you have? It must not have been that much of nothing since this plate is clean as a whistle."

He shrugged. "I'm good. I had a couple of biscuits." He let his gaze go toward the cinnamon beauty again. She was finishing up with a couple of young dudes who looked to be boaters with too much time on their hands. Or maybe it was too much hands for their time. "The new girl set me up fine."

Miss Joyce scoffed. "Is that it? Just a couple of biscuits and you drove all the way from Atlanta this morning? What to do with you young people and why didn't you tell Drea that you were here and have her get me from out back? I would have come up front to set you up myself. What does she know?" She turned and yelled over her shoulder. "Drea? Honey, please get another honey biscuit and a pecan roll. Oh, and go on in the back and grab a couple of them sausages that I brought in with me this morning and bring them out here too for Kellen."

Kellen noticed how Boots, who he now knew as Drea — though Boots fit her so much better — scrunched up her nose a bit as she looked over at the two of them, clearly questioning who he was to Miss Joyce and why was it that he deserved a special sausage from out back. He could tell that a few of her other customers had the same thoughts by the quick but envious once-overs that had him fighting back a smirk, though he did spare Drea a glance and was rewarded with a hot glare in return. But for all her heat, she turned Miss Joyce's way and only nodded briefly as she quickly finished with her customers before heading to the back. Smart. At least she knew there was no messing around when it came to Miss Joyce. It was good to see the older woman still had her reputation. Kellen recalled the summer his grandfather thought getting a little food service under Kellen's belt was a good idea, saying that any job where he served people would help better prepare him for life in the real world. He had to admit his grandfather had been right about that.

Miss Joyce was quite the taskmaster. Which was why the fact that "Boots" had opened the shop three minutes late had Kellen scratching his head in wonder. Miss Joyce was all about schedules and discipline. It was half the reason he'd enjoyed working for her as much as he did. But looking around the shop now, he barely recognized it.

Though he was happy to see the influx of new customers, this updated decor was quite a shock. "The shop is really looking great. I should've seen it sooner. My grandmother told me about the improvements. You did a fine job. And it seems to be a boon to business."

"That it has, but I really can't take the credit," Miss Joyce said. "What my niece lacks in her baking skills she definitely makes up for in her design intuition. And I'm lucky enough to have been blessed with another niece who is amazing in the kitchen. I dare hope she may take over for me in that department when I'm gone."

Kellen frowned. "Don't talk like that, Miss Joyce."

She waved a hand. "Oh, who's talking about dying? I'm just saying I may not bake all my life. I've got a new hip now. Might as well see what other trouble I can scare up with it."

Kellen laughed and patted Miss Joyce on

the arm. "Well, that's one way to make the best of a situation."

"Hey, Auntie, what's the Suit here doing getting all handsy with you? He's not getting fresh, is he?" the young woman said as she put a new plate in front of Kellen; this time it was a much bigger one with a fresh biscuit, a pecan roll, two beautiful sausages, with the addition of a fresh cup of coffee. Though her words came out sharp, when Kellen looked up at her this time there was clear mirth in her eyes.

"Oh, stop it now, Drea. Why are you always so full of sass? Kellen's an old friend and here he was just complimenting you."

The young woman looked around, saw no one at the counter, pulled out a chair, and sat. She crossed her long legs and smiled widely.

Breathing got difficult. Kellen's sports jacket suddenly grew incredibly tight. She gave him an exaggerated pose as she put her head in her hands and flipped her hair. "Complimenting me? About what?" she asked.

Her aunt leaned forward and gave her a swat across her thigh. "Like I said, you are way too much. Don't you have better things to do than preen for the customers?"

She looked around the suddenly empty

shop. "No customers at the moment but him, so, no, I don't. I know you don't want me back in the kitchen with Olivia." She looked back at Kellen. "Right now, I think at this table, taking this compliment is the safest place for me and all involved."

Miss Joyce looked between the two of them and let out a huff. "Well, I don't. Didn't you tell me earlier you had another appointment today? I suggest you go on and get ready for that. You can't go to your new position looking like something out of my back kitchen. Go on and get ready."

"But I don't have to be there till this afternoon."

Miss Joyce shooed her away. "Afternoon will be here soon enough."

Her niece's brows drew together but she held her tongue, then turned to Kellen. "Well, Suit, it seems I must now apologize and take my leave. Looks like you're more than just a handsome man in an off-weather suit. For that, I'm sorry. It was nice to meet you and I thank you for whatever compliment my aunt doesn't think is worthy of sharing with me at this time."

Once again, Kellen watched as she turned on those boots and made her retreat. He tried his best to frown but found it increasingly hard since his frown was at war with the smile that was trying to break out after she'd called him handsome.

Chapter 4
Persuasion

By the time Kellen was close to his grand-parents' place — now, he supposed it was just his grandmother's place — nervousness was licking at the back of his neck again. Driving up the winding hill to the old colonial-style home, he was filled with a sense of dread that he hadn't felt since being a young boy dropped off there for the first time without his parents after the accident.

He swallowed a sudden lump in his throat as a feeling of loneliness he hadn't felt in going on twenty years captured him anew. It was way too easy for that switch to flip and his mind to go off on a memory trip to places he didn't want it to be. Suddenly, he wasn't the man he was now, but the young boy he was all those years ago who would visit with his parents on their summer and holiday trips to Sugar Lake before the accident. Hand in hand, he'd be with his father as both his grands would rush out to meet them with welcoming smiles. Kellen let out a sigh and shook his head. If he didn't want to face the house without his grandfather's presence, how must his grandmother feel being in the house without him? How was she dealing with this big house all alone when even he didn't want to really face it? Kellen gave his head another shake and told himself he was being foolish. He wasn't that young boy anymore. He was a grown man now. A grown man with an adult's responsibilities, and he should be able to face death and loss and all of that head on. He snorted to himself. It was so long ago he should be over it or at the very least past it enough for it to be just a fleeting shadow.

He let out a breath and forced a smile that was more like a grimace, but he hoped relaxed his features as he shook his shoulders. Time to get to business. Today he was back home to talk some sense into his wily grandmother. *Home and sense,* Kellen mentally repeated. He needed to focus on that. His grandma had to see that he was right. It was time for Kilborn Properties to embrace the future and move forward. Forget looking back and reminiscing about the past. It was time to let shadows go and do what they do: stay behind you if you were moving in the right direction, and if the RPG deal went through as he planned, they would definitely be headed that way. If not, Kilborn Properties would stay stagnant and possibly get swept off the map entirely.

As he drove down the winding road, he noted the familiar scent of the air thick with the smell of moss from the oaks. The road soon gave way to the straightaway and the view of the regal old home. Kellen couldn't help but smile as he thought about the old colonial that was his grandfather's pride. A pride that was tinged with a certain amount of pain over owning a piece of land passed down to him from a dark history. Being of mixed heritage, half black, half white, living in the South, his grandfather was a man who knew what it was like to live life with one foot in two worlds. Clearly black, so he was never fully accepted by white Georgia society, but born with enough pedigree, money, and passed down land to not be dismissed straight out. Henry Kilborn was never quite black enough and certainly nowhere near white enough to comfortably traverse life in the sleepy Southern town. So, he did what he could and made his own rules. Henry Kilborn broke convention as soon as he could, and Kellen supposed one of those first acts of rule-breaking was his grandfather romancing his non-Southern, unconventional grandmother, a singer and showgirl, while on leave during his enlistment, and marrying her practically on the spot. Kellen wondered if his grandfather knew that after their one whirlwind weekend together, when he asked her to marry him right then and there and come back with him to Sugar Lake, Georgia, that she was the spitfire she was, that they'd last all the years they did, and that in the end she'd be left here, in the big house all alone.

Kellen made his way around the circular driveway to the front of the house and cut the ignition. He took in the sudden silence as his car went quiet. All he could hear was the sound of trees rustling in the breeze and the occasional bird chirping. There wasn't a neighbor for at least a mile in either direction. That was the beauty of life out on Sugar Lake. Sure, it was getting a bit crowded on the country club side of the lake, but here, all the serenity and charm of country living still remained. Not for the first time he wondered what RPG would mean to that serenity. But that wasn't a place he could go either. It wasn't as if he could stop that progress even if he wanted to. It was counterintuitive to his goals, and if they didn't sell to RPG, then surely some other property owners would.

Grabbing his bag and the treats from Goode 'N Sweet, he made his way up the front stairs debating on using his key or pressing the doorbell when, as if on cue, his grandmother answered his inner thoughts and the door swung open.

"Well, it took you long enough to get here; you left Goode 'N Sweet a full twenty-five minutes ago," his grandmother said.

Kellen looked around above his grandmother's head, pretending he didn't see her. He waved his hands. "I hear a voice and it sounds like my grandma, but it can't be her because I don't feel any hug and I haven't received any kisses." He stepped back and made a big show of looking at the door. "Maybe I'm at the wrong house?"

His grandmother came forward with a swat on his arm. "How's that for a greeting?" she said. "I swear, boy, you must always be a smart alec. I was on pins and needles waiting for you to get here. Then you go and linger at Goode 'N Sweet for Lord knows how long. Why, it took all I had not to get in my car and pull you out of there." She gave him a hard stare. "What made you stay over there so long?"

Kellen suddenly felt slightly guilty over

the question and couldn't put his finger on why. "Grandma, it's early. I stayed to sit and eat and let you sleep in. I didn't expect you to be keeping these types of morning hours. And how is it you knew as soon as I made it into town? What, you have some sort of a town alert system out there at the city limits? Geez, Grandma. I don't know what's quicker, Twitter or the town grapevine."

His grandmother gave her head a shake. "Don't you worry about how I get my information. Just know that I get it. Now, come on in here," she said, her voice lighter as she looked up at him, a smile hinting at the corner of her mouth as her eyes brightened.

Kellen followed his grandmother into the house, dropping his bag in the foyer and only glancing briefly at the formal sitting room on the right and living room on the left that pretty much always stayed in the same pristine condition. He made his way straight through toward the back of the house to the kitchen.

Though the house still had all the original historic land markings, the essentials had thankfully been updated, with the kitchen having been updated the most. The best part of this room was the oversize windows and the skylight added by his grandfather, making it one of the brightest rooms in the house and Kellen's favorite spot to hang out. Kellen placed the box of treats from Goode 'N Sweet on the center island. His grandma looked at the box suspiciously, then gave a shrug. "Well, I see that you didn't come empty handed, but with bribes." She shook her head. "You've got so much of your granddad in you, boy." She laughed. "But you know that just like him, I can tell exactly what your ulterior motives are with one glance, and sweet treats won't get you anywhere? Not that I'm not grateful." She turned then to grab a couple of plates from the cabinet behind her, reaching up on her toes, and Kellen shook his head, marveling over so much spunk in such a little package.

He went over and gave his grandmother a hug from behind. The immediate warmth and release of stress he felt when some of the tension in her rigid spine relaxed and she leaned her head back onto his chest made his heart swell. "You know me too well at this point for me to try to fool you, Grandma. Of course, I'm here with an ulterior motive, but that doesn't mean I didn't miss you too."

She nodded and turned around, giving

him a wobbly smile. "I know, sweetie. An ulterior motive or not, I'm still glad to see your lovely face." But her eyes grew serious as she stared at him more intently. Kellen took a small step back and went around to the other side of the counter.

"Though I don't like to see that tiredness around your eyes, Kellen," his grandmother said. "I can tell that you're putting in way too many hours in the office, and not enough out in the sun getting fresh air and exercise."

"I work out plenty."

She gave a small huff. "Playing at being a hamster on somebody's machine does not take the place of time out in God's good sunshine and breathing in fresh air. You know that, Kellen. I told you about that many times before. Life is all about balancing it out."

Kellen nodded, waving away the pastry his grandmother was offering ironically as she was talking about his health. "No thanks, maybe later. You know how Miss Joyce is. When she saw it was me in the shop this morning, the two biscuits that I had weren't nearly enough for her liking and she had to go on and add more to my plate. That's what took me so long to get here."

His grandmother nodded. "Well, okay, I

guess I forgive you for being so late getting here then, since it was Joyce holding you up. I know there's no fighting her when she's determined to feed a person."

"True and, like I said, I was trying to let you rest. I didn't want to come traipsing in here at the crack of dawn and wake you. I know how you are about your beauty rest, Grandma."

His grandmother gave a laugh, though it was void of her usual mirth, and Kellen instantly felt a pinch twinge at his own heart. "You wouldn't have been disturbing me, baby," she replied. "Seems these past couple weeks I've been getting up earlier and earlier." She let out a small sigh. Then she looked at him and gave a smile once more.

Kellen could tell that there was no truth behind that smile though. "Or maybe not sleeping much at all?" he asked. "Come on now, Grandma, who are you trying to fool here? You go and get on me about needing rest and look at you. I can't go having you get sick too. Please don't do that." He tried to keep his voice light, but knew the thread of worry still came through.

"Oh, don't worry about that, baby. I suppose I just have to get used to sleeping alone." She gave a laugh sounding more like a little girl than her advanced years. "It's been many years that I've had your grandfather beside me, and to suddenly have him gone, well, that's what's expected, I guess. Others say time heals. I suppose time will also have me get used to sleeping in a big old bed without him snoring beside me. Don't you worry; I'll be fine and back to my usual sleeping habits. Besides, your grandfather would get a kick out of it. With me getting up so early, I'm getting so much more done, tending his garden, making sure the trash and recycling are done. By the time eleven a.m. comes around, my little to-do list is just about done. And I can finally admit, maybe a little bit too late, there might be something to his early bird and worms thing he always talked about."

Kellen smiled. He felt they were quickly getting into some uncomfortable territory that would lead into more uncomfortable territory about the Redheart Theater and the Ronson deal. Kellen watched his grandmother make her tea and sit at the counter across from him, taking delicate bites of her pastry, before she cleared her throat, then looked at him straight on. "Okay, you drove all this way in the middle of the night to make a case that you really don't need to make, but you're here, and I know you're not going to leave without making it, so why don't you give it to me?" his grandmother said before taking another dainty bite and giving him an arched brow.

Kellen felt immediately off kilter. If he was in front of a group of CEOs trying to convince them to invest in new space on Mars, he would be more comfortable than he was right now looking at his grandma munching on her pastry with her mind already made up that she was not handing over the Redheart. Why did he even come? He should have saved himself the gas and the annoyance. Besides, he'd already used all his best tactics on her. He'd begged, pleaded, and even tried cajoling, and still she wasn't having it. Oh well, he was here now and he needed to think of a better plan and quick.

"Listen," he said, "how about you tell me what you're thinking for the theater, Grandma. Why is it that you want so badly to hold on to it when you're open to giving up other pieces of property?" He made his voice gentle, not really wanting to approach this, but he knew he had to. "Is it because of your weekly date nights with Grandpa? If that's the case, then I totally can understand it. With Grandpa's death, I know it sounds harsh, but those nights are a thing of the past. Why would you hold on to the theater just for that? You have the memories. Aren't they precious enough? The Redheart itself is nothing more than a drain on expenses at this point. Sentimentality is not a reason to lose out on a potentially huge deal."

Kellen swallowed. Or maybe it was a gulp. Either way, he wished he could take back that last sentence, as he saw the tiniest hint of a tremor at the top of his grandmother's lip. He really was a jerk at times. A cold, heartless jerk, just as he'd been called by so many over the years. But in his gut he felt it was for the best, letting the Redheart go and creating a more stable future for Kilborn Properties and a safer environment for his grandmother.

He watched apprehensively as his grandmother let out a long breath, took another bite of her pastry, chewed it slowly, then swallowed. She followed by taking a sip of her tea. He could tell she was trying her best to hold on to her temper. This was the grandmother he'd seen many times before, when she was dealing with the women of the auxiliary and one of them had gone a bit too far with their sweet Southern charm, the type with a cutting edge to it. If she pulled out a "bless your heart" — which meant anything but — he might as well get back in his car and onto the highway. Kellen braced himself.

"Sentimentality or not, Kellen, the theater is more than just the place your grandfather and I went on date nights. It's also much more than just a passing whimsy for me as you seem to have suggested more times than I've been comfortable with," she said, her voice deadly serious and way more business-like and no nonsense than he was prepared to hear. "Though you're completely gung ho on this Ronson deal and believe that I'm open to selling other properties to them, I'm not as open as you may think. I'm just being, how should I say, amenable to my grandson's ideas because I believe in you and I believe in your business sense." She paused then. And it was filled with enough weight to bring down an elephant before she continued. "The Ronsons, bless their hearts —" Kellen sucked in a breath. *Well, that one wasn't totally shot his way,* he thought as she continued. "— are fine as a family and RPG is a good enough company. At least they see the value in our idyllic little lake area, which is more than I can say for you." She let out a slow breath, and Kellen was tempted to duck out of the way just in case he'd get burned from the fire of it.

"But," she continued, "I'm not all that

thrilled with any company overdeveloping Sugar Lake. I'm not sure they have the same vision as we do. And if their feelings about building and culture don't line up with us, then they're not the people for us to do business with. Now, if we can come up with a way to manage the Ronsons, then I'll entertain it and include my properties. What I'm not entertaining is putting my theater up as a bargaining chip."

Kellen started to feel more than dread then. Oh crap. Clearly even Miss Joyce's sweet magic wasn't working this morning. This trip was more of a disaster than he'd feared it would be. With one chat Kellen now knew he could be destroying not just the Redheart part of the deal, but even the other properties in the process.

"Now, wait a minute, Grandma. Sounds to me like you might even possibly be taking the other properties out of the deal with Ronson. What happened in the span of our conversation yesterday and this morning?"

His grandmother smiled. "I'm not saying that anything happened; I'm just saying that I've had a good think over the evening, and maybe did some digging on my own into Ronson and their business dealings, particularly Jamina Ronson. By the way, you both looked lovely at the dinner you had together the other night."

Kellen's brows flew up and he gave his grandmother a surprised look. So she saw that picture of him and Jamina Ronson together. The one that had made its rounds on the ATL blog scene and on Instagram. Kellen should have known that his grandmother would follow local Atlanta Internet gossip. She was an original fan of *The Real Housewives.* But it would seem that his grandmother did more while she was up last night than a little quick looking into the Ronson Group. She did some downright digging. He let out a sigh. "Grandma, our dinner is not worth mentioning, besides being nothing more than a productive business dinner and a good move."

His grandmother laughed then. "Oh, it looked like moves were being made. On her part at least. I just want to make sure your head stays clear and your priorities are straight."

Kellen frowned. "My priorities are always straight. You know that."

His grandmother shook her head, then sighed. "That I do." She waved her hand in front of her face and like a new person perked instantly. "But that's neither here nor there. Let me show you my plans for the Redheart." She turned and walked over to the small breakfast nook.

Wait. What? Plans?

Kellen's brows were knit tight as his grandmother laid out architectural plans on the island with a flourish. He blinked as he looked over what appeared to be extensive redesign plans for the Redheart. The façade was pretty much unchanged, but the inside was definitely updated, much more than the little his grandparents had done in past years. What? When? How could she have gotten all this done so quickly and without a word from him?

She looked over at him with a sly smile. "They're pretty fantastic, huh? I shocked you, didn't I? Well, *we* shocked you."

"We? What do you mean we?"

She laughed. "I mean your grandfather and I."

Kellen frowned. That did it. This trip wasn't for nothing and he was here just in time. His grandmother was going over the edge.

"Oh, fix your face, Kellen. It's not like I'm losing my faculties, despite the way you're treating me. This is something that your grandfather and I had in the works before his passing. These plans were done up last year by Archer Jove."

"Archer Jove? You mean Prichard Jove's

son? What's he doing drawing up plans and why didn't I know anything about it?"

His grandmother shook her head. "Like you had to know everything or ever took any interest in the Redheart. And yes, Archer Jove. You know your grandfather and I love seeing young folks doing big things and when he set up his shingle for his architecture firm, we were more than happy to have him do a little something for us. We'd always planned to fix up the Redheart properly. We just didn't know there was a time limit on our plans." His grandmother's voice broke ever so slightly then, pitching lower and taking his spirit with it.

Kellen leaned in to give the plans a better look. That was the least he could do, though even from far back he could see this job was way too much for his grandmother to take on by herself. He saw that the concession stand would be updated and there would be a small game room off to the side with what looked to be vintage pinball machines and 80s style video games. There was also what looked to be an area with a couple of small party rooms; his grandmother explained to him that those were for arts and crafts for kids and community gatherings. And then the biggest surprise came when he saw off to the side and around the back of the theater there were plans for a small outside viewing stage. What? Were they now trying Shakespeare in the Park? Not to mention she even pulled out another set of plans that had a remodel of the theater's dilapidated balcony area. Kellen could see the money practically blowing out the window.

"Grandma, what in the world do you have going here? This renovation will cost an astronomical amount of money. We're looking to make money right now on the sale, not send money out the window. This is beautiful, but with everyone going to the multiplex, we couldn't even begin to make the money back to cover the cost of this renovation. We don't have a food court or a big box superstore or any of that."

"And you just made my case right there," she said. "Maybe people don't want to always go to the mall with all that. Maybe there are some folks who want the quaint charm and more laid-back experience. Wouldn't it be nice to have a real night at the theater again?" His grandmother's eyes got slightly dreamy. "Why must everything always be modern and new to be good? The latest is not always the greatest."

Kellen shook his head. She really was holding tight to the past and, though a part of Kellen could see her vision, he couldn't get past the financial concerns he had. "Grandma, what you are talking about here will not just hold us back, it just may sink us."

For an answer, all Kellen got was a pat on his cheek as his grandmother gave him a smile. "Oh my, I don't know if you get your flair for drama from me and if I should be proud or not." She shrugged. "I think these plans are fabulous, and look," she said, pulling out some rough sketches that had more color, showing an old-meets-new Hollywood theme for the theater. "My Alex did a great job with these designs and only from brief visits to the theater and short conversations with me about what I wanted. It's genius!"

Kellen wanted to give a growl. Once again, it was Alex. And once again, he couldn't wait to meet this Alex face to face and give him a piece of his mind. A part of him wanted to even give a piece of his fist, but he knew that was uncalled for. Alex and now Archer were both sprung on him in the past twenty-four hours. Kellen didn't think he could take much more. "Alex, Archer? My, you are just full of surprises. Huh, Grandma?" He looked down at the sketches with the high-priced lighting, large plants, and expensive-looking draperies. "I can't wait to meet this Alex of yours, so free with the designs and plans on someone else's dime. Tell me, did you let Alex know any sort of budgeting when these plans were drawn up?"

She looked slightly confused for a moment, then she waved her hand and shook her head. "It's not how Alex and I work, dear. We work more freely than that. It's quite collaborative, organic and lovely."

Kellen suddenly wanted to scream. Collaborative? Organic? Lovely? All words that didn't belong anywhere near his business dealings.

"You'll see what I mean when you two meet."

"Yeah, I can't wait," Kellen replied dryly.

To that his grandmother gave him a perplexed look. She cocked her head to the side. "I guess you can meet formally over at the theater this afternoon. We are meeting at one. You want to go on ahead and get a quick shower and get cleaned up, then head on over? Alex has a key so should be there by the time you arrive. It's funny, I thought you would've met at Goode 'N Sweet this morning. Alex is there pretty much most mornings right at opening."

Kellen thought of all the patrons who had come in while he was in Goode 'N Sweet.

He hadn't run into anyone who sounded like Mr. Collaborative, Take a Sweet Old Lady for Her Money Charlatan that his grandmother had referred to. And he was glad that he hadn't. If he had run into anyone called Alex and found out it was him on no sleep and no coffee, it would not have been good. "No, I didn't, and it was probably for the best. You know how I am without my morning coffee — like you are when you haven't had your proper sleep."

"Whatever you say, dear," his grandmother said as Kellen headed up the stairs to his old room to shower, change, and head back to town and once and for all meet this Alex. This was it. He'd put a stop to what was going on with the Redheart Theater today.

CHAPTER 5
SERENDIPITY

Drea fiddled with the keys Mrs. Betty had given her and looked down at her cell phone. Where was she? She thought for sure Mrs. Betty would be here by now. Though she'd left the bakery in plenty of time after being surprisingly dismissed early by her aunt, she still ended up getting to the Redheart only just in time, her mind making her body go slower than she liked as it kept wandering back to the Suit with the glasses who took up so much of her morning.

What an odd guy he was. Cool though slightly awkward and reserved. He acted like he belonged in Sugar Lake, and Aunt Joyce knew him and treated him like an old friend, though clearly, he was not *of* Sugar Lake. Who was he? And really, why should she care? He was probably, just like she guessed, another suit. Looking to scam someone. A good-looking one at that, which was the most dangerous kind. But there was something about his all-seeing, pretty, green-flecked, and still-somewhat-devilish eyes that had her mesmerized. She couldn't put her finger on it, but he was nudging at the corner of her mind in the most uncomfortable way, and she hated being uncomfortable.

Drea looked at her phone again and wondered to herself if she really should go on into the theater without the owner like Mrs. Betty had given her permission to. Sure, that was probably her New York thinking kicking in. Mrs. Betty's message said it would be fine to let herself in and start looking around if she wasn't there when she arrived. She had given Drea keys for just that reason. Still she felt uncomfortable. Sure, she'd been in the theater plenty of times, but never alone. Suddenly Drea wondered if it would be a little creepy. All of her times in the theater had been as a patron during the weekly features Mrs. Betty had shown along with her late husband, Henry. And though the theater was never a sellout or even close, still she wasn't alone.

Drea let out a sigh. Now she was just being foolish. Okay. She wasn't a kid. She was here to do a job and Mrs. Betty would arrive soon. If the little old woman could come in and open the theater by herself, what was she doing acting all afraid? Besides, she was excited to get a jump on looking around again and rethinking her plans. The first ones were made up from only what Mrs. Betty sent her previously and her earlier visits to the theater as a patron. Her mind was in a whirl with all she was envisioning for the theater. Mrs. Betty had her so excited after their talk about it. It actually felt good to feel this way again.

Quickly, Drea took the copper keys and started to unlock the two locks on the theater doors. It amazed her that there were only the two and that was it. Just the one for the middle lock and then one for the lower down near the ground. She had a small bit of trouble getting that one to open and it made her think of Mrs. Betty and bending low at her age. Maybe they should discuss that in their plans. Though the woman seemed as spry as they came, either way there wasn't nearly enough when it came to security. Finally getting the brass and glass doors open, Drea let herself inside.

Immediately her senses were hit by the smell of stale, stagnant air, heat, dust, and old buttered popcorn. The first thing the place needed was a good airing out. She turned, leaving the silence in the darkness of the theater lobby behind her, and looked back out onto Main Street in the afternoon light through the glass of the front doors. All seemed relatively quiet. With everything dark in the theater, she wondered if it would be safe to crack open the doors just a little — surely no one would come inside, and it would allow just a little bit of air in, at least until the switches came on and the ventilation got going properly. She needed Mrs. Betty to let her know how to work that.

Making her decision, Drea cracked open the front doors, flipping the bottom latches down in order to have them stay partially ajar. Looking over to her left she was happy to see two brass crowd dividers, fully equipped with the old-style red velvet ropes, and she carried them toward the doors just in case a passerby got the wrong idea and thought they could enter the theater.

Underestimating the weight, it took quite an effort to move them over, but finally Drea was able to tilt them on their sides and roll them into place. She carried the heavy ropes fireman-style, then clipped them into place. Looking down at her now filthy hands, she almost swiped them on her pleated skirt, so used to wearing a work apron at Goode 'N Sweet, but she thankfully stopped herself and found paper towels behind the concession stand.

Goodness, what happened to the meticulously manicured me of a year ago? She shook her head. *Also note to self: Don't wear a skirt to this dust trap. Overalls, a hazmat suit. That sort of thing will do just fine.*

Drea let out a breath and looked around. The place would be quite the undertaking, now that she thought about it. Pretty much just like any New York club. Looks were surely deceiving. And what looked pretty good under the cover of night and with the right mood lighting was a whole different story when it got into the harsh light of day.

For some reason that thought made Drea smile and the Suit came to her mind again. She looked down at the moto boots she still wore, despite her pleated skirt and tank top. Sure, she could have put on a nice pair of sandals for this meeting with Mrs. Betty, but she wasn't a complete fool with the state of the theater, and honestly, when she made the decision to keep on the boots, she had to admit it was with the Suit in mind and a small hint of rebellion. For all his straight-laced appearance and complete annoyance, he was good-looking, suit and all. The man filled out that dumb suit jacket quite nicely and she supposed she made fun of it because she wouldn't mind seeing what he looked like without it.

He was just so tall and broad-shouldered, but not all that muscular, though clearly fit. Like a slim ball player. Suddenly, Drea envisioned him in basketball shorts and a casual T-shirt and she was pleasantly surprised with what her mind came up with. But just as quickly she let the vision fade. Really, first of all, the idea that a man who would wear a sports jacket when the humidity was above 85 percent pushing 90 would ever hang in basketball shorts was just beyond the pale, so she was wasting a fantasy right there.

Besides, she didn't have time for fantasies anyway. She'd honestly spent more than enough time idling and fantasizing on Sugar Lake as it was. She'd do this job for Mrs. Betty and use the time and money from the job to make the tough decisions about the next steps in her life and bring them to fruition. Even her own ever patient, sainted parents were starting to remind her that time was creeping up on her fast and she needed to start making some tough life decisions. Not that they wanted her to completely settle down, but at least she could show a return on their college and after college investments in her.

Drea sighed. The spoiled part of her — and one thing Drea had learned since being in Sugar Lake and availing herself of lake-side self-reflection was that there was a spoiled part — didn't want to admit that maybe her older sister had a point in her years of nagging. Not that she'd tell her that. Still, her parents deserved more from her. Heck, even she deserved more from herself. She thought about it as she turned away from looking out again for Mrs. Betty along the street and then headed further into the theater. The fact that so many believed in her still, believed in her to turn out and do something, if not great, at least worthwhile with her life, was both daunting and slightly exhilarating. And though she was afraid of the feeling, Drea didn't want to let them down. She didn't want to let herself down.

Going through, past the foyer and concession area as if she were a paying customer, Drea stepped into the Redheart's grand theater area. That was, if one could call it grand. Flipping on the overhead light switches off to the right far corner, she smiled when the magical theater was brought to life in all its slightly faded glory before her eyes. According to Mrs. Betty, the main floor held 400 seats and the balcony another 150. However, due to recent leaks in the roof, it had been a while since the balcony had seen any real action, which didn't matter because there hadn't been enough patrons at any given Wednesday night show since the new multiplex opened out by the mall. Drea smiled, thinking of the plans she and Mrs. Betty had discussed. If all went right, that was sure to change. This theater would once again be a social and entertainment event hub. The idea of it gave her a sizzle of excitement that shimmied throughout her body.

Twirling on her heels, Drea turned her attention toward the stage, the screen, and the darkened burgundy curtains. She went back over to the panel and flipped a few switches, bringing more illumination into the auditorium area. She was able to get some light shining on to the boxes; the intricacies of the carvings around them still shone through despite the chipped paint and peeling gold leaf. Drea immediately saw the potential beauty of what the theater could be, once restored. Looking up, she marveled at the celestial skyline fresco painted on the ceiling, once again thinking of how this kind of amazing attention to beauty and detail was lacking in today's mass quickie constructions.

Drea flipped another switch, bringing a spotlight to the center of the stage, and it was as if a little bit of something in her chest made her inexplicably start to step forward down the center aisle.

Feeling silly, outrageous, and maybe a slight bit morbid, she imagined an audience cheering her on either side as she mimicked a scene from one of her all-time favorite movies, *The Rocky Horror Picture Show.* Slowly and dramatically, she sashayed toward the stage, the refrain of "Don't Dream It, Be It" chanting over and over in her mind. Turning toward the right, she made her way up the wooden stairs, did an exaggerated turn, and felt her skirt lift in the breeze. Turning again, she enjoyed the fluttering as she took a bow at center stage for her imagined cheering audience. The heat of the spotlight warming her from the inside out.

Kellen so didn't have time for this.

For his grandmother to be in such a hurry and so excited to get this theater renovation under way, he didn't understand why all of a sudden on the way into town and not minutes from the theater she suddenly remembered something she had to discuss with Miss Joyce over at Goode 'N Sweet. When Kellen suggested they just stop over there briefly and he would wait outside for her so that he could continue and take her along to their meeting with this Alex, she just brushed him off, telling him that she'd be along in a few moments and to continue ahead of her. That did nothing to smooth his mood for the meeting. But shrugging it off, Kellen thought it was perhaps for the best. He didn't need his grandmother coming between him and this Alex person upon their first meeting. He'd much rather size the guy up himself, without his grandmother's interference.

After the earlier conversation, he pretty much had the guy pegged. And if he had his way and given the proper time alone, he was pretty sure he could send him back to whatever hole he had crawled out of by the time his grandmother had made her way from the bakery down to the theater.

Kellen drove his car directly around back, parking in the lot, which would be another thing that, if his grandmother's ideas came to light, would need to be added to her extensive list of re-dos. He pulled into the old manager's spot — the same one that his grandfather had so many times before — as he purposely shook off the feelings of melancholy that came along with parking there.

Kellen cut his ignition, then quickly made

111

his way to the back door, pulling out keys he somehow still had on his ring for so many years. Looking around before letting himself in, he took in the large size of the triple-width lot and the tall structure of the theater. It really was a big old beauty. He remembered as a kid how much he used to admire its distinct architecture. To his young imagination it seemed like the old building held so many secrets and hidden treasures. He used to love to come during his time off from school when his parents were still alive and just explore, never quite finding anything of note, but it didn't matter. It was all a thrill to his eight-year-old self.

Letting out a sigh as his mind switched from the past to the present, Kellen went to open the back door. He frowned as his foot crunched on a bit of broken glass. Looking down, he could see the remnants of a possible teenage hangout party having taken place in the lot recently.

Once again, anger pricked at him as he thought of his grandmother coming back here alone or to the lot with this strange Alex. What was she thinking? How safe could an endeavor like this be for an older woman living alone? Clearly, she wasn't thinking at all. There were no surveillance cameras. And honestly these locks were little more than a joke for any thief worth their salt.

No more games, Kellen thought. He really needed to convince his grandmother to give this up and move in with him or at least closer to him.

Walking into the theater, Kellen was shocked to find the lights already on. The whole downstairs was illuminated — the stage too. He could see the faint outline from behind the screen of someone rocking back and forth, seeming to glide along the stage. Well, somebody was making himself quite comfortable, he thought. What happened to properly waiting out front for a meeting? Did his grandma give this guy the full run of the place?

Heading toward the back of the stage, Kellen prepared himself for his first glimpse of Alex and giving him a piece of his mind. But what he encountered instead stopped him dead in his tracks.

It hit him suddenly as he took in the shadowed figure moving rhythmically on the other side of the screen. The figure was hard to put into focus, but the silhouette surprised him, being that of a woman and not of a man, as he was expecting. She was moving gracefully on the other side of the screen, twirling and bowing, bowing and twirling, her arms swinging free and wide, and though there was no music playing, but rather only silence in the theater, Kellen felt as if he could hear the magical melody that must be playing in her head.

From the silhouette he could see that she was tall and slim, though beautifully curved with long arms that seemed to extend so far, reaching out to forever when she gracefully pointed here and there with a certain amount of freedom that Kellen couldn't quite understand, but for some reason he suddenly wanted to. Her legs, when she gracefully twirled and her pretty skirt floated up, seemed to go on forever too. Long and shapely right down to her pretty delicate . . . Kellen frowned. Wait — were those boots?

Suddenly he coughed, and the woman stopped midspin.

"Is anybody there? Mrs. Betty, is that you?" the female voice asked as Kellen felt everything in him seem to rise to attention.

It couldn't be. He shook his head. What was going on here? Where was the Alex guy he was supposed to meet? A chewing out was supposed to happen. Kellen was ready.

Instead he cleared his throat again. "No, it's not Mrs. Betty. She will be along in just a moment." He started to walk around to the other side of the curtain. "I'm her grandson, Kel—"

"The Suit!"

Kellen's eyes went so wide open seeing the bakeshop girl that he almost forgot to be insulted by the annoying nickname. Almost.

"And you're Boots from the bakery. Miss Joyce's niece. What are you doing here, and I thought we agreed that we had actual names," he said to her, raising a brow.

She crossed her arms across her chest, then gave him a raised brow back. "I don't remember agreeing to that. And I don't remember knowing your name. Did we actually meet?" she asked him teasingly.

Kellen felt all off kilter, which was a totally foreign feeling to him, but seemed to be the way of things in Sugar Lake. He fought to quickly pull himself together and not get caught up in the smile hinting at the corner of her lips or the glimmer of teasing in her eyes. "I know your name, and it's Drea Goode. Like I said, you're Miss Joyce's niece, the one who helped with the shop. Right?"

To that she rolled her eyes. "And you're the grandson that I hear is supposedly smart?" She shook her head. "Presumptuous much? Yes, I'm Miss Joyce's niece, but my last name is not Goode, it's Gale. My mother is Aunt Joyce's sister, Anne."

Kellen nodded, having remembered meeting, he thought, Miss Anne Goode when he was a kid. "Nice to meet you. I'm Kellen Kilborn. But, I still don't get why you're here. My grandmother and I have a meeting today. Did you have business?" he asked, now wondering if Alex was a no-show.

And though she gave a slight blush of being caught in what he supposed she thought was a private, impromptu dance, she shrugged it off, spinning around once again, adding a little two-step to it. She looked up slightly challengingly. "Did you enjoy it?"

Kellen was at first confused. Enjoy what?

Picking up on his lack of understanding, she elaborated. "Your free show. Did you enjoy it?"

Perfect. She was making him sound like some sort of peeper. He shrugged, hoping it came off nonchalant though he was feeling anything but. "It's not like I can say don't quit your day job. Because obviously, you're not entirely untalented and don't lack in stage presence. Let's say, it's better than your customer service skills."

Once again, her eyes went skyward. "You know, I've never had any complaints about my lack of customer service skills before,

Su" — she stopped short, going on to address him by his full name — "Mr. Kilborn. As a matter of fact, I'm quite multitalented. I'm pretty much exemplary in anything I put my mind to."

Uh oh. Right then and there with her seemingly benign words something new started to nudge at him. It was a slightly niggling feeling of excitement, tinged with desire, sprinkled with a hint of longing that he most definitely didn't have time for.

Kellen pushed his feelings down, then he mentally dug a hole and threw them in there to make sure they were good and buried. He was there to deal with this Alex guy, so that he could get back to work and finally get this Ronson deal under way. He gave Miss Joyce's quirky niece a look that he hoped was cool enough to let her know that he was done playing games. "Listen, I'm sure you are, but I don't have time to see any more parts of your show. My grandmother will be here soon and we have a meeting set up with this designer that she's hired to help her renovate the theater. So if you can make your business with her quick, I'd appreciate it." He looked at his watch with frustration, then back up at her. Maybe he'd missed Alex or he was out front waiting for them. How could he have been so stupid? "The guy's name is Alex. You didn't see him when you came in, did you? Was he the one who let you in?"

Once again, she raised a brow, then she gave a little twirl and shuffled her feet a few times and held out her hand to him. Kellen couldn't help but look confused at her outstretched hand. Then he looked up at her and caught the mischievous smile in her that seemed to hold all the answers to questions that he didn't know if he really wanted to ask. So, instead he just stood silently, taking in her full lips and beautiful cinnamon skin as it glistened under the spotlight of the theater, casting a momentarily magical spell on them as if spinning them from the present to the past in the blink of an eye. Finally, she spoke, breaking the spell. "There you go again with your presumptions. I have a feeling it's going to be a real problem for us."

When Kellen didn't move, she shook her head and let out a frustrated huff. "So, you gonna let my arm fall off?" she asked. Kellen felt the thrill race through his body to his heart as he was reminded of the same words that she said to him in the early hours of that morning.

"What are you talking about?"

"Oh, this is wonderful! I'm so happy to

see you two finally meeting. And don't you both look lovely up there on the stage? Just like something out of an old Hollywood movie."

Both he and Boots turned at the same time, Drea dropping her hand and Kellen bringing his up to shield his eyes. They watched as his grandmother walked down the center aisle, her smile wide and her eyes twinkling. "Just perfect, Kellen. You've finally met Alexandrea. And now that the three of us are all together, I'm sure we can come to some consensus on how to restore this theater and bring it to something even better and stronger than its former glory."

Kellen gasped. He didn't know it was out loud, but the woman next to him turned and clasped her hand over her mouth to stifle back the snort of laughter emitting from it. His grandma, on the other hand, did nothing to hold back and she just guffawed out loud. "And they say I'm the dramatic one in the family," his grandmother said. "Boy, you really can go on when you want to."

She was talking, but Kellen was already on his way down the theater steps toward her. "Alexandrea? Drea? Not Alex but Alexandrea?"

"Boots, too, if you want to get technical

about it," the now not-mystery woman said from way too close to his back.

Kellen turned quickly, and she almost banged right into his chest. He put his hands up. "I do not. Getting technical could have happened this morning, or" — he turned to his grandmother — "last night or last week!"

What was he supposed to do now? How could he not only destroy his grandmother's dreams and plans — that was bad enough — but then on top of it he was kicking out Miss Joyce's niece and taking a job from her too? Might as well, when he packed his grandmother up to move to Atlanta, make the decision to never come back to Sugar Lake again. Going against the Goodes was sure to make him and his family hated, to say the very least. Kellen let out a sigh.

Once again his grandmother chuckled. "First a gasp and now a sigh? What? Have you been taking some sort of improv class and not telling me about it? This is getting to be a bit much even for me, Kellen."

She was right; it was much more than a bit much. Boots was Drea who was Miss Goode's niece who was the Alex that was helping to stop the deal he needed to take Kilborn Properties to the next level, and she happened to be — Kellen side-glanced her way and was rewarded by a way-too-smug side glance back — annoying, prickly, and attractive to him as all get out in a way he couldn't quite get his head around.

"Why don't we step out into the concession area, have a seat and we can talk this out? Like we planned." He let out a breath and looked toward this Alex, Boots, Drea, whoever she was. "Miss Goode," he started, but she cut him off.

"Please call me Drea. I'll call you Kellen and we can pass on the Boots and Suit. Is it a deal?"

His grandmother coughed. "Pardon."

"Don't ask, Grandmother. Please."

His grandmother raised a quick hand though she had a smile on her lips. "Fine by me, Kellen, but Boots and Suit sounds awfully cute. And sure, we can go out to the concession and talk. As I said earlier, there really isn't much to discuss; my ideas and my plan still stand firm. I will see this through and you being here to meet Alex is nothing more than a formality. She and I will work lovely together. We're on the same page. Now, if you have any renovation suggestions, I will welcome your input. You are my grandson."

"Thanks for remembering," he said in a low voice.

But his grandmother barely gave credence to that. "Any more than your helpful suggestions will not be tolerated. Any plans to thwart what I'm doing won't be taken lightly."

Kellen didn't miss the seriousness in his grandmother's tone with her last comment. He wanted to practically grind his own teeth to bits, but looking at his grandmother and the take-no-backtalk expression she had on, all he could do was give a tight nod counter to Boots' wide grin of satisfaction. But then his grandmother wiped the smile off her face and stuck it to Kellen even more.

"The more that I think about it, the more I'd like you helping out with the project, Kellen."

"Huh?" Both he and Drea said in unison.

His grandmother chuckled. "See, you two are on the same page already." She waved a hand and went on to explain. "I'm not saying a huge commitment, Kellen. I know how busy you are, but surely during this important time you can make yourself a bit more available for me. You seem to have very distinct feelings about the theater, budgeting, and well, everything. So why don't you make yourself a bit more involved? You and Alexandrea here can both work with me. It can be Grand, Boots, and

Suit! The three amigos!"

He and Drea both looked at her and then at the theater doors. At that moment, Kellen had a feeling Drea was thinking the same thought as he was. Run!

Chapter 6
Breakfast at
Goode 'N Sweet

It was 6:50 a.m. and once again Kellen found himself outside Goode 'N Sweet.

This time he was pacing.

Back and forth he traveled. Five steps forward, five steps the other way in front of the shop as he waited for her to open. *It* to open! The shop to open! Not her. He wasn't waiting for her. "Definitely not," he mumbled to himself by way of assurance. Boots, he meant Drea, or was it Alexandrea, not Alex? Whatever her name was, he was not there, once again before the shop's opening, in order to see her.

Kellen stopped pacing midstep and let out a long, slow breath. Who was he fooling with that lie? In all honesty, he didn't know why he was there, but he couldn't say it wasn't to get another look at the unpredictable Ms. Boots Gale. This is what being blindsided and a night with only two hours of sleep, at best, followed by a night with less than that, would do to a man. He had no reason to be in front of the bakeshop with way more pent-up energy than he knew what to do with.

Kellen flipped his wrist and looked at his watch. 6:55. The heart rate monitor on his watch started to pulse brightly, then flip to the numbers display. What? He was in the official cool down zone of an aerobic workout. It chimed and gave a condescending, in as much as an inanimate object could be, thumbs-up signal, which caused Kellen to grimace. Had he really been pacing that hard? Serves him right for showing up here like this, probably looking a right fool.

Well, at least she'd have nothing to say about today's outfit. Kellen looked down at what he was wearing. He was sans sports jacket — he purposely left that at home, not wanting to hear any of Miss Smartie Boots' wise comments — and was in a casual, button-down cotton shirt and a pair of khaki shorts. But thanks to his power pacing, he was wrinkled and bordering on sweaty. The morning heat came on fast.

"This won't do," Kellen mumbled out loud before thinking to himself, *How would he look giving her the piece of his mind — which he wasn't able to do yesterday with his grandmother on the back of his neck — look-*

ing like something the cat dragged in? He shook his head and turned to go back to his car when the door behind him opened with a familiar light musical chime.

"You going to just walk off after pacing for the last ten minutes? What, are you getting cold feet or something?"

Kellen spun around at the sound of her voice. He looked down at his watch — 6:57 — then back up at her. "Not ten minutes. You opened three minutes early, Boots." Kellen winced as the words he was thinking came flying out of his mouth. "Wait, um, sorry. I meant to say Drea, and I wasn't going anywhere. I was just uh, checking my car," he said.

She gave him a raised brow. "And there it still is."

Kellen fought against the heat he felt licking up the back of his neck. *Starting out smooth as silk, Kilborn,* he thought to himself as he waved his hand exaggeratedly and pressed the button on his key fob. The locking and relocking of his car doors was loud and obnoxious in the early morning quiet. Kellen cleared his throat in embarrassment. Great. Now he just seemed like a rich guy showing off his expensive model car. Beep freaking beep. He looked back at Drea. "Well, good for you opening early."

She smirked at him, and he realized there was no fighting the embarrassing heat as she gave him a slow up and down. "Too late, Suit. You realize you're not making it any better the more you ramble on. You threw the name out first this morning and now the die is cast. I guess the names are sticking. With that little slip of the tongue it seems you're setting a precedent. Boots and Suit." She pretended to mull it over in her head and smiled.

Kellen tried his best to look annoyed while his heart felt anything but.

She continued. "Besides, I think your grandmother said something about it sounding cute. Since she's embracing it, why shouldn't we?"

He frowned. She was pretty free and easy with her use of words like *we.* Kellen decided to give her no comment either way.

"Come on in since you are definitely not running back to your car. What can I get you this morning?"

Fine, so he wasn't running back to his car. Not since he was caught anyhow.

Kellen let out a breath and sidled past her into the coolness of the bakery, letting the sweet, warm smell of butter, sugar, and her own special scent take over as he made his way to the front counter.

This time he wasn't left alone with Boots — darn it, he was doing the name thing again — because Miss Joyce came out from the kitchen quickly and gave him a bright smile. "Two times in one week, lucky us. Why, aren't we lucky, Drea?"

"Are we? Should I head over to the deli and pick us up some lottery tickets?" she countered dryly. He really wanted to laugh, but fought to stay stoic.

Miss Joyce chose to pretend she didn't hear and continued on. "I would say that this is due to you and not the taste of my biscuits yesterday." She raised a brow at Kellen, who opened his mouth to protest, but was stopped by her continuing to go on. "It's not like my biscuits hardly ever brought you in two days in a row before. I can only think it has something to do with my niece here and her working with your grandmother now, or something like that."

Miss Joyce was a shrewd one. There was so much behind her "or something like that" at the end of her little speech. Kellen was grateful for the out. "Now, Miss Joyce, you know your biscuits are excellent — why else would I be here? However, I can say I was a little surprised to find out that your talented niece was the one behind my grandmother's grand new plans for the Redheart. Why didn't you tell me yesterday when we met?" He gave her a challenging stare that was filled with just enough teasing to make it not disrespectful.

Miss Joyce stared at him hard before she smiled. "Now, Kellen, you know that was for your grandmother to tell and not for me to go blabbing about. What goes on with her business is her business. And besides, why would I ruin the surprise before she was able to share? That wouldn't have been sportsmanlike, now would it?"

"I suppose not, ma'am."

"Well, you could have given your own niece a heads-up as to who he was yesterday when I was running around getting biscuits and sausages and all that." It was Boots now who was chiming in, giving Miss Joyce a little bit of pushback.

But Miss Joyce, being Miss Joyce, came back just as quickly. "Now, where would the fun have been in that? From what I heard you two had a right good first introduction." She gave her niece a gotcha grin, then turned back to Kellen. "Aren't your grandmother's plans for the Redheart exciting?" Miss Joyce smiled as she looked into Kellen's eyes. "I think this is going to be so good for her, Kellen. She needs this, that I will share with you. Your grandma, she's a strong one and I know she'll survive. And who knows? Maybe even thrive in her own way, without your grandfather. I don't know, but I do know this here. This reno is the first bit of her old spark that I've seen in way too long. I'm happy to see her doing this; it will be good for her spirit and, if I do say, good for the community."

Just great, so Miss Joyce was totally on board too. That meant she would be just as angry as he'd feared she would be if he went with his real morning mission and took her niece's job at the Redheart away. Well, doubly so; he couldn't forget about the breaking-his-grandmother's-heart-in-the-process part. Wait, triply so since he'd also be letting the community down.

Kellen let out a groan that he didn't know was audible until Miss Joyce chimed in. "What's troubling you, boy?"

Kellen almost laughed at her easy use of the term *boy,* something he'd never heard from mouths in New York or Atlanta. It wasn't something he'd take from the wrong mouth, but in Sugar Lake where a respected older woman like Miss Joyce was like a mother, you took what you took and you did it with respect. Kellen didn't mind.

He welcomed it even. Especially the way she said it. Soft and honestly heartfelt, as if she wanted to truly know what was on his mind.

Kellen spoke. "Truthfully, Miss Joyce, I came to Sugar Lake to convince my grandmother that taking this theater renovation on was not good business sense for us as a family. What she wants to do is directly the opposite of what I want to do with the Redheart. I also worry that she's taking on more than she can handle, both physically and emotionally."

Miss Joyce nodded and something about the way she did it let him know that she already knew most of the story, probably from his grandmother. Kellen gave her a knowing look. "But you already knew that, didn't you?" he said.

"I can't say I didn't guess at your reason for being in town," the older woman responded. "And I can't say that I agree with you or fault you since I won't go minding your business, just as I won't mind your grandma's. Besides, I don't know a thing about your numbers. What I do know is that emotionally your grandmother is strong. Stronger than you think or give her credit for, so in that you don't have to worry. I know you may not understand, but this thing with the Redheart will probably help her to fulfill something that will bring a type of closure that she very much needs right now."

"But," Kellen started, "it's not just emotional. There are other things to consider. There's her age . . . and well . . ." He felt his voice begin to falter as fears he didn't really want to mention strained to make their way out. Thankfully, Miss Joyce threw him a lifeline and he wasn't further pushed into the abyss of embarrassment.

She shook her head and gave him a soft smile. "There you go, doing as you always had as a boy. Your mind going ten steps into a future you and nobody but God has any control over. As for physically, Betty has got a strong support system here. There's me and Drea, who will help her every step of the way. You don't have to worry, she'll hire the right people, get the help she needs, and we will all watch out for her. It's not like she'll be up on ladders and doing the reno herself."

With that Boots cleared her throat loudly and Miss Joyce shot her a look. "No chiming in from you. I learned my lesson last year. No more roof climbing for me. Just you hush it, missy."

Boots laughed. "I didn't say a thing, Auntie. Besides, if it weren't for your fearless ways, Liv and I wouldn't be here enjoying your lovely company."

Kellen didn't know if that was a good thing or not. He remembered the incident when Miss Joyce broke her hip last year taking it upon herself to clean her own gutters instead of hiring help. So that was what had brought Boots and her sister to their sleepy little town. He looked at Miss Joyce. Though she was clearly admonishing her niece, he could now see the pride and joy having her in town and in the bakery was bringing her. He had to admit that though he and Boots may not have hit it off, she was a bright spark to Goode 'N Sweet and it would seem her aunt's demeanor and newly refurbished shop.

Miss Joyce's voice pulled him back in. "You go on and do what you need to do with the business and don't you worry about your grand. She will be just fine. We'll be sure of it."

Kellen took a deep breath, his heart warring with his mind. Just then the shop's door opened and in came a couple of patrons. Miss Joyce reached over the counter and patted his hand. Her cool touch comforted him, reminding him that he never got that type of comfort anyplace but in Sugar Lake. She gave him a smile before bringing her focus to the patrons that had come in.

"Morning, y'all, good to see you. Can I get you the usuals?" *Usuals?* The easygoing word put a chill on all the warmth Kellen had been feeling in the past moments. He'd never seen these town newbies before in his life and they had usuals? What was Sugar Lake becoming? Could just anybody become regulars now? At their affirmative nod, Miss Joyce turned back to Kellen, giving him a quick wink. In her own way she seemed to be letting him know he was special.

"You go on and take a seat. Drea will bring you over a couple of biscuits and coffee. I'll pack up a little something for your grand while you eat."

She started to move away but doubled back and reached out, lightly brushing her surprisingly soft hands across Kellen's temples. "What did I tell you? Stop worrying so much. You'll end up getting crinkles on the corners of those pretty eyes of yours. What good would come of that?"

Kellen looked over, surprised to see Boots off to the side. She was uncharacteristically quiet, and he could tell she was making herself busy arranging things on the counter. He knew that she had taken in the exchange between him and her aunt, adding to his morning embarrassment. But he leaned back and squared his shoulders as she looked over at him, her dark eyes meeting his, and in that look there seemed to be an inaudible click of understanding that took him totally off guard.

She smiled. It was half quirky, half challenging and just what he needed to bring them back to his usual place of resilience. He almost would thank her if she didn't prick under his skin so.

"So what, Suit?" she started, her snappy tone in place. "Can I get you the usual too? Have a seat and I'll bring it to your table."

He decided to give her a little taste of her own medicine. "Fine, Boots. The usual." He shrugged. He didn't know he had a "usual" too or a table for that matter, but he'd sit and let her figure out both.

"Coming right up," she said, moving with a self-assured, knowing efficiency to get his order together.

It was that self-assurance that made Kellen want to rattle her just a bit, the same way she'd rattled him. "Oh," he said, "if you can spare the time I'd like you to meet me this afternoon at the theater at one. I think we need to talk in depth about these plans you've cooked up with my grandmother and what us working in collaboration on them really will look like."

The slight hesitation before she went back into her smooth character was enough satisfaction to put him back at ease and more in line with his true self.

Drea didn't like being caught off guard, but it would seem the Suit aka Kellen Kilborn aka Mrs. Betty's grandson had a particular talent for it. She didn't know what it was, but the man definitely had a knack. It was not easy keeping her expression normal and her emotions in check when he seemed to stir up so much in her.

The man was infuriating. Or at least he infuriated her! Why did she go and open her mouth talking about "the usual"? It implied that she remembered what he'd had yesterday, as if he'd made that much of an impact on her. And that she wanted him to make this some sort of usual thing. Ugh!

She took a breath. It was fine. She was in the service business. Service with a smile. Saying little phrases like that was surely her job. Right? *Right!*

With her mental admonishment, Drea let out a breath as she went to pour Kellen's coffee and add biscuits onto his plate. She wanted to kick herself as she reached for an extra biscuit, and even considered adding one of the sausages her aunt brought from home as a side extra. *What in the world is my problem?* She gave a quick glance to where he went to sit.

Once again, he'd chosen the furthest back table that was still by the front window. It was her favorite table too. It gave a full view of the shop as well as Main Street. It was also the table that spoke to her the most as a New Yorker, fitting her rule of "always keep your eye on the door, know your surroundings and exits." "Humph, how very *Godfather*-like of him," she mumbled to herself.

"What's that?"

Drea looked up quickly, sloshing a bit of coffee over the edge of the cup and onto the saucer. *Crap!*

"What's got you in a tizzy this morning?" It was her cousin Rena. Never one to slip in quietly, as quiet nor understated were not part of Rena's brand. Drea wondered where her mind had run off to in order to have missed Rena's entrance.

"Nothing." Drea knew as soon as she said it that it came out unconvincing.

Her cousin raised one of her perfectly groomed brows, her large round eyes squinting a bit to show every bit of Goode woman sharpness in a look that said, "Yeah sure, and I'll find you out soon enough." But just as quickly, she blinked and smiled. Her purple glossed lips spreading wide and her eyes turning back to their normal disarming, warm, and open brown softness. "Well, good morning to you too, dear cousin. Woke up on the wrong side of dawn, I see?" Rena half yawned and said, "Not that I don't blame you. I'm tired myself. These kids are trying to run my butt into the ground and Troy is being, well, Troy, so you know how much help he is. I swear if he doesn't get them children out and to school on time like he's supposed to, then it's curtains for him. I'm tired of doing it all."

Drea just nodded. According to her calculations Rena and Troy had been more on the out than they were on the in since she'd been in Sugar Lake. He was her cousin's kryptonite, and for the life of her she didn't understand why a woman who was together in all other aspects of her life let a man like Troy keep her in the position he did. A part of her could understand sticking it out for the kids, but when your baby's daddy was no more help than one of your kids and worse, more of a strain, well, Drea just couldn't understand that. But she wasn't about to ride on the Rena-over-Troy runaway train this morning. "I hear you," Drea said with a quick nod. "Let me get this order over."

Drea made to righting the spilled coffee and finishing up Suit's order, but her cousin's voice pulled her up short again. "Ahh, so Kellen *is* back. I'd heard he was back in town. So, the word on the street is true, huh? You two are gonna be working together? Girl! You lucked out! Could it be that's what's got you so distracted this morning?"

Drea turned to her again. And once again the coffee sloshed. "Luck? Maybe you need to rethink your idea of luck, and of course it's not what has me distracted this morning," Drea hissed.

Rena looked down at the messy saucer as Drea followed suit, then looked back up at her. Once again, up went Rena's eyebrow. "If you say so then, but luck or not, that messy coffee cup and the fact that your normally poised behind can't keep your hands straight tells me that something has you riled." Rena shrugged and looked Kellen's way. Against her better judgment Drea followed suit. He sure looked good this morning as he intently scrolled through his cell phone. His intense expression highlighted his strong profile made even more striking by the accent of his dark eyeglass frames against his tan skin. His broad shoulders filled out his button-front shirt in the most perfect way. He'd rolled up his sleeves to reveal deliciously sinewy forearms, one of her hidden weaknesses. She heard Rena sigh from behind her and say, "Yeah, you're probably right. Why would a country boy turn the head of a city girl like you anyway?"

Drea narrowed her eyes and looked around quickly over Rena's barely whispered tone. "Could you not?" she hissed as she went to get another cup and started to fill it. "We're just working together," she whispered. "Not even working together if he has anything to do with it. There is no head turning. Just work."

Just then her sister, Olivia, came out from the kitchen, fresh pie in hand, and peered over her shoulder. "Oh, he looks like a lot of work all right. Hopefully for you there will be overtime involved too."

Rena reached up to give Liv a high five, and Drea hissed, "If you two don't cut it out . . . ! Like I said, it's just work."

"Sure, Drea," Rena replied with a chuckle from behind Drea's back. "If you say so, but you're washing all these extra cups. I just got a new mani yesterday."

Liv giggled from behind her back.

Drea stopped midstep again and took a breath. It took all she had to keep the biscuits balanced in one hand and the full cup and saucer in the other without spilling as she headed toward Kellen in that back corner table.

CHAPTER 7
THE WAY WE WERE

He was definitely not sneaking up on her this time, Drea said to herself as she paced outside the front of the theater at 12:50 waiting for Kellen 'the Suit' Kilborn to arrive.

She purposely left the bakeshop early, changed, and had gotten to the theater in plenty of time to keep her eyes peeled for the not only punctual but perpetually early Mr. Kilborn.

She knew changing was probably going a bit far, but after a busy morning in the shop where an influx of tourists and some sticky-fingered children had her ending up with whipped cream all over her shorts, she'd decided it was worth it to change after all. It was probably for the best, as she didn't think her ultra-casual shorts/tee combo would quite make it for the afternoon meeting.

Drea had rushed back home to Aunt

Joyce's where she was staying out on the lake and changed into a casually styled shirtwaist dress that was loose and nonconstricting and she paired it with bike shorts underneath in case things got a little physical that afternoon. She suddenly stopped pacing and blushed at her mental wording. Not that she would get physical with the Suit, mind you. It was just that she knew the job would take some amount of manual labor on her part. Wait. Who was she trying to convince here? Drea felt her cheeks grow hot and forced her mind on the theater and what she knew needed to be tackled. There would be plenty, that was for sure, but she guessed it all depended on how things worked out this afternoon with the Suit.

It was a shame, but it seemed like he and his grandmother were on totally different tracks when it came to the renovation of the theater. He was staunchly against the top to bottom renovation all together and Mrs. Betty was going completely in the other way. Not that Drea was all that confident in it or at least in her abilities to tackle the job. Sure, she'd done well with Aunt Joyce's shop and yes, she had plenty of confidence in her decorator's eye coupled with the architect's plans, but this was a lot that Mrs. Betty was expecting of her. Drea had a certain amount of experience with set design from college and stage help from her years working off-off, well, so far off Broadway it was beyond outer borough in Westchester, New York. Still she hoped she didn't disappoint the older woman. It felt like so much of her heart was invested in the completion of this project, and then there was the Suit, who wanted her to give it up. Drea bit at her lip and worried for a moment about being caught in the middle of the family feud.

She knew about family squabbles; heck, the Goode family had their fair share of them. She and Liv were pretty much just getting on nice steady ground after years living on their own sisterly San Andreas Fault. Did she really need to be caught smack dab in the middle of someone else's family struggles? Most definitely not. But, she had to admit, she was excited about this job. She stepped back a few feet and looked up at the beautiful old marquee of the Redheart Theater, right now stuck on the last showing from before Mr. Kilborn passed away: WEDNESDAY NIGHT 7 PM: *THE WAY WE WERE*. Boy did she love that movie. She'd gone to the screening that night and the Kilborns looked so happy. Mr. Henry was dashing in his white naval uniform and

Mrs. Betty was adorable in a lovely, black-and-white, wide collar, A-line dress. The pair went full out as they always did, sticking to the theme of the night.

"Just lovely," Drea mumbled to herself, thinking of Barbra Streisand's beautifully whispered line from the story of an improbable love and loss of two clear opposites. It never failed to make even her jaded New York heart flutter.

Just then there was a tap on her shoulder and Drea jumped, turning around quickly, meeting the incredulous gaze of Kellen Kilborn. "Seems I'm always catching you daydreaming, Boots."

Drea frowned. "Seems to me it's more like you're always sneaking up on me. Don't you know how to call out or something and make your presence known? Something a little more polite than a hard shoulder tap?" She rubbed at her shoulder.

He pulled a face. "Bit much, don't you think? Besides, I did give you more than a shoulder tap. I waved and walked right in front of you, but you didn't even see me you were so lost in your own thoughts. What else was I supposed to do? Sorry I didn't have a blow horn. Maybe next time I'll call you. Speaking of, I don't have your cell number, so I couldn't do that."

He paused. "Do you mind sharing?"

Drea felt a blush start to creep up. There he went, catching her off guard again. She tried to play it off as best she could. She pulled her phone out of her cross-body bag. "Sure. What's your number? I'll call you, then you'll have mine."

He slid her a brief look, then rambled off his number quickly. She put it in and dialed him up, quickly clicking off when his cell started to ring.

"Wow, that was fast. You didn't give me time to save it."

Drea shrugged. "It will be in your log."

"What were you so deep in thought about when I got here?"

She looked up and his eyes followed where hers went. "I was just checking out the marquee. It looks pretty good other than some light restoration. There are clearly some bulbs out and it'll need new lettering. The red heart sign that goes on the side of the building, that'll probably be the thing that needs the most work, but it truly is magnificent. I'm sure we'll have to find a company to take care of that, and properly get all the lights back in working order. But it shouldn't be too complicated." Drea felt more comfortable. Good they were finally off their she-didn't-know-what banter for a moment and talking about the job at hand.

"Is anything ever uncomplicated?"

His words, coupled with the sudden straight on earnest look, gave her all sorts of Robert Redford vibes. Drea almost swooned right there on the sidewalk. Darn him! What in the ever-loving crap mongers was he doing hinting at quotes from *The Way We Were*?

She let out an audible breath, wanting to kick herself for making her surprise so obvious but she couldn't help but wonder if he did it on purpose or if there was a romantic hidden underneath the protective armor of his sport coats.

The romantic she'd glimpsed disappeared as Kellen looked at her with a hint of annoyance. Would he ever flash that smile her way, the one he bestowed so freely on his grandmother and her Aunt Joyce? Not that she needed it or any extra bits of his charms, swooning over a movie quote as she was. He shrugged. "It's my grandmother's favorite movie. She made me and my granddad watch it more times than I can count."

He looked up at the marquee again and she saw his expression change. In an instant, his previous smugness was gone, replaced by a distinct sense of what she could only describe as regret.

He really was lovely, completely not her type in his button-down and khakis, but there was something about his disarming gaze and strong jaw, broad shoulders and restrained muscles that seemed to defy his conventional attire. All of that bottled together made Drea feel instinctively drawn to Kellen.

"Are you okay?" she asked.

"What? I'm fine." He turned her way. The steel back in his eyes.

There was her Suit. Drea frowned as she looked at him, confused by the juxtaposition, but on firmer ground when he said, "I guess I'd better get the sign changed to say *closed for renovations.* It wouldn't do to have passing tourists thinking we've got a showing Wednesday night."

"Good idea, but with plenty to do I'm sure there's no rush. We need to prioritize our list."

He looked up at the sign again, his jaw tightening while his eyes grew soft. He cleared his throat, then turned to her, and for a moment she wondered if he had wandered off somewhere in his thoughts. "Nope, better to get on that right away. I'm sure seeing the sign there from the last showing must be hard for my grandmother."

Drea felt an unexpected chill then, while

her heart seemed to turn in on itself. "You're right. It probably is." She sighed. "I'll take care of it."

"It's fine. I can take care of it myself. It's not that big a deal."

Drea shook her head and took in the old movie title and thought of the last time she'd been to the theater and saw Mr. and Mrs. Kilborn there, together and happy. She blinked away threatening tears as she looked at Kellen. "It's just I'm now wondering what feelings the *closed for reno* sign will bring to Mrs. Betty too."

Kellen let out a groan, then rubbed his hand over his jaw in frustration. He sighed. "I don't know. That's what I'm afraid of. Just all of this. That's why it would be better if she didn't take on the project at all."

Drea frowned. "Wait. How did we get from the sign to no project at all? Look, I'm sorry I even brought it up, but you're making quite a leap. This means the world to Mrs. Betty."

He gave Drea a most annoyed look before turning toward the door, pulling keys out of his pocket. "Believe me, Boots, I've heard. I'm up to my ears in how much this means to my grandmother, the community. Heck, you'd think civilization as we know it was resting on the reno of this little theater."

Drea crossed her arms and looked at him. He really was an ignitable one. She looked around as she thought. "Wait, isn't your grandmother joining us for this prioritizing meeting? I wouldn't feel comfortable making any major decisions without her."

He looked up from where he had knelt to unlock the door. Shaking his head, he looked down toward the locks again, flipped them, stood, then opened the door, moving out of the way to let her in. "Trust me, the fact that I'm even giving the time of day to this project will have my grandmother thrilled. I'm sure she'll have no problems with any decisions I make."

Drea stopped short. "Wait a minute, decisions *you* make?" she challenged. "You seem to have shifted from *we* to *you* pretty quickly, Suit. When I took this job, I was hired for my expertise, not to be anybody's yes girl, cosigner, or any such thing. That's not how I roll. And it's not what your grandmother expects from me and ultimately, she's my boss, not you."

It was then that, as if on cue, Drea's cell rang. She pulled it out of her bag and smiled when she saw the caller ID. "Speaking of your grandmother, now look who it is," she said with a smile as she clicked her phone over. "Mrs. Betty, it's so good to hear from

150

you," Drea said, putting the phone on speaker because she knew it would annoy the mess out of Kellen Kilborn and she wanted to show him that she had nothing to hide when it came to his grandmother. Time to wipe the suspicion right off his face.

"Alex sweetheart, I'm sorry I'm not with you right now. I just had a little something to attend to this afternoon, but I know you will get Kellen straight today on all we've discussed so far. I know we talked about a lot yesterday, but he seems to need just a little bit more clarification."

Clarification, Drea thought, *is that what they're calling it*? Though she found it best to keep those words behind her tongue as she raised a brow toward Kellen. Instead, she smiled at him and spoke to Mrs. Betty. "Don't you worry, he's here with me now, listening to you on speakerphone. I'm sure we'll get along just fine. I'll explain everything you and I discussed and we can do a thorough walk-through of the theater this afternoon. I'll be sure to report back to you on how it goes," Drea added, and was rewarded with a grimace from the Suit on the "report back" line. Served him right.

"That sounds wonderful, dear," Mrs. Betty said, sounding quite chipper. But then her voice took a stern turn. "Kellen?"

151

"Grandma." Kellen's tone was both frosty and reverent at the same time, and once again, Drea was reminded of being smack in the middle of a family standoff.

"Remember what we talked about. You two work together well now. I need you to look at things with open eyes and an open heart. Trust Alex, she knows my vision here as I'm sure you know my heart."

Drea could see the slight anguish as it glazed across his features for a moment. This was a man who didn't do well against words like *heart* and things like emotions; she could tell that right away. And she could also tell that his grandmother knew exactly which buttons to press with him. It was then that Mrs. Betty's voice came louder and more chipper over the speaker. "Okay, I must run now. Speak with you dears later. Kellen, I'll see you at home. And, Drea, I'll give you a ring later to see how things went. Thank you so much for taking this on. I hope it's not interfering too much with the schedule."

"No, ma'am," Drea said. "I'm happy to do it. It's a pleasure."

Drea let Mrs. Betty cut the line first and then the two of them were left in silence. One beat and then another and then one more until the feeling was way too weird to be anywhere near comfortable. Kellen finally broke the tension. "Well then, I guess we better get on with it. Since you're the eyes." He waved a hand in front of her to indicate she lead the way. "Please start the tour of my family's theater and show me exactly how my grandmother plans to put us in the red."

Drea raised a brow, but forced a smile. He was a tough one. "Of course. Please follow me."

CHAPTER 8
BEAUTY AND THE SUIT

"As you wish."

Kellen saw the slight falter in Drea's step as she preceded him on her way up the stairs toward the storage area of the theater. Though she didn't quite get his joke, she was indeed surprised by his quick acquiescence and reply of "as you wish" to each of her ideas for the theater.

She'd been leading him for the past hour and a half, going on and on about her and his grandmother's plans for the theater. So far they had gone over rough ideas for the theater's lobby, the expansion of the gaming area, the possibility of adding a couple of craft and party rooms, not to mention how she proposed the concession area needed a practically complete overhaul while still keeping the original fixtures, but restored of course. When he pointed out the fact that restoration in a lot of ways could be just as costly if not more than buying new, she showed an expert propensity for scoffing at that triviality.

Rather than arguing, Kellen was proud of himself for not getting into a tit-for-tat with her. He'd decided it wouldn't do any good anyway and made a mental note to schedule a meeting with Archer Jove. Maybe he could talk to Archer and find a way around this problem. If not in scrapping it entirely at least in finding a way of cutting costs and making the reno less daunting in case his grandmother wouldn't budge. Though in the best-case scenario he could get Archer on his side to convince his grandmother of the hardship of it. Kellen gave himself a mental shake. Who was he kidding? Archer had come up with these plans and he'd surely want this theater as a feather under his cap. Why would he not want to see it through? It would help his reputation and his bottom line too. That was unless Kellen could come up with another enticement to get Archer to see things his way.

He brought his attention back to Boots as she quickly — but he could tell carefully — went up and down each and every aisle, inspecting the seats and the decorative end columns, making notes as well as sketches in her little notebook, taking pictures and every once in a while shooting a quick video clip.

She stopped at the end of row P, took a pic of the old stone column, then proceeded to video it top to bottom, taking in the majestic-looking carved-out lion heads. Then she turned her camera toward herself, looked up at the lion, and belted out a quick refrain from "If I Were King of the Forest," complete with huffs, puffs, and growls.

She really was an odd one, this Booted wonder. Nothing like any of the women he was used to, but he refused to be swayed. Not by her boots, or her antics. Or by her wide smile, bright eyes, and glowing skin.

Though Boots was clearly her own woman, Kellen could feel his grandmother's meddling fingers all over this situation. Nope. No and not gonna happen. He may be in a sticky situation when it came to this theater, but he'd not compound it by getting mixed up with the likes of her. Besides, these were the early stages of the game. It was only day one and he had to get a full lay of the land right now and this preliminary tour was just a means to his most important end.

Once he got a full picture, he planned on getting real and complete quotes and going to his grandmother again with the cold, hard facts.

But for now, he'd endure the designer thrust upon him and go with the flow. And reluctantly, in another circumstance, he'd admit she did have a good eye, great instincts, and knew what she was talking about. Her vision seemed spot on with what he'd heard his grandparents talk about wanting to do with the theater for years. But life and timing just ran out before they were able to make it happen. Like a swift wind, thoughts of his own parents and the dreams he used to hear them giggle and whisper over when he was a young boy blew through his mind. Kellen let them drift out just as fast as they flew in. That's how life was. It was all about timing. Now was not the time for the new Redheart. Sadly, the dream that his grandmother and grandfather shared had passed away along with his grandfather, and no amount of paint, plaster, or new lighting would change that fact.

Drea changed her tone, bringing his thoughts back to the task at hand. "Come on, Suit. Show's over and we still have plenty of ground to cover."

As they made their way up the wide stairs from the first to the second floor, then turned to the right past the balcony in the middle of the employee-only area, Kellen flipped the switch to light the stairs that led to the projector room and archives room. It had been so long since he'd been up there that he was surprised he still remembered where all the switches were.

But Kellen frowned when nothing happened after flipping the lights to illuminate the staircase they needed to take to the archives room. He flipped the switch back and forth, trying again, which he knew was ridiculous, since if they didn't work the first time, why would they the second? Then he flipped the switch a third time for good measure and heard Boots let out a low snort. With a huff, he turned to the left side of the stairwell to try there — also nothing. *How long were those overhead lights out?* Annoyance grabbed at Kellen. There was no excuse for this. He'd hoped they had not been out long because really, his grandfather should have just gotten them repaired. He paused then, guilt twisting his gut. Was he really admonishing a dead old man for not having lights repaired? He was sure his grandfather had done the best he could with him diverting so much of the family funds to new business ventures, the Atlanta investments, and the new staffing that entailed. As their grandson, perhaps he should have been more hands on.

Still, Kellen wondered for a moment if his grandfather or grandmother had been navigating the stairs on their own without proper lighting during their date night screenings. It wasn't safe, and the thought of it made Kellen's blood heat. What if his grandmother, in all her remodel fervor, tripped in here and took a tumble down the stairs? He pulled out his cell and quickly jotted down a note highlighting this as a top priority. Note 1B, right under changing the marquee sign to *closed.*

He looked up the shadowed stairway, then over at Drea. "Listen, I don't think we should head up there today without proper lighting. I wouldn't want you to get into an accident."

She gave him an incredulous look. "You really are quite the company man, aren't you?" she said, a challenge in her eyes and a quirk in her lips. Those lips. They seemed to spark at him. Tempt and tease him while they mocked him. And more than anything, in that moment and quite uncharacteristically, Kellen wanted to kiss the smirk right off her face. Of course, he wouldn't do it. One: because it just wasn't done. At least not without permission. And he suspected that once he'd asked, she'd smirk again.

And two: Though she didn't work for him, she was essentially working for his grandmother, which once, twice, or however many times removed made her now one of his employees, and that meant completely off limits. So she could smirk away. He would not be moved.

Before he could properly get his rebuttal out, Boots and her way-too-quick self had pulled her cell phone out and flipped on the flashlight to high, illuminating the full staircase. With that, she was on her way up, leaving him with no other choice but to follow. Company man or not, Boots was quickly teaching him who was in charge; he had to, even more quickly, find a way to put a stop to it.

She turned back his way, her smile not challenging, but quirky and as bright as the light she was waving. "Come on, Suit, get a move on. We've only got so much daylight left and still plenty to get done." She frowned. "Funny, you didn't strike me as the lollygagging type when you were banging on the shop's door at the crack of dawn. Let's go."

Kellen let out a sigh as he grumbled to himself and headed up the stairs after her. "As you wish."

■ ■ ■ ■

When would Drea learn to look before she leapt?

Looking at the dusty, overcrowded, and unorganized archives storeroom and knowing that there was another one probably identical to this, if not worse, made her think that running up the stairs instead of down was probably not the best idea. Wow. This job was going to be more than she'd anticipated. With her experiences with many a whacky audition in New York she should have known to expect the unexpected, but this chaotic mess was beyond her imagination, she thought as she attempted to climb over boxes that reached her midthigh. They were full of what appeared to be piles and piles of old film reels in various stages of distress. Though most were intact, there were quite a few with nicks and dings that showed their long, hard service in the industry.

"How in the world?" Drea breathed out, looking around.

The Suit let out a long sound that came out like a sigh mixed with a growl, with a bit of a moan for good measure. She turned to look at him and noticed he was staring at the room with an expression that could only be described as bewilderment. "That's what I want to know." He picked up his phone and Drea watched as he swiped before holding his phone up and appeared to be filming the room. Occasionally, he tapped the screen, she assumed capturing stills of the chaos all around them.

Drea let out another long breath, then relaxed her shoulders as she took in the room again. Trying her best to see it in a new light. Finally, she spoke, purposefully brightened, thinking about what Mrs. Betty would want her to do next. "Really, this is not so bad — well, not horrendous, let me just say," she said, looking over the shelves on the back wall and the far left. "Look, there appears to be some sort of filing system already started over here." She pointed out the few orderly stacks of film canisters that were labeled on the shelves. And then on the other side of the room she pointed to the rows of boxes labeled by year, though clearly not in any chronological order. "See right here, it looks like there's already a bit of a system started. The 1930s, 40s, 70s, 50s," Then she turned over to the back wall, her voice fighting to stay convincing. "And here you can see that the canisters are all neatly labeled."

Oh boy, she hoped she was selling this.

As Drea started forward toward the canisters, she found it hard to control her burgeoning glee. She sucked in a breath and let it out. "Oh my goodness! *Casablanca, Breakfast at Tiffany's, My Fair Lady, West Side Story,* it just goes on and on." She turned back to Kellen. "This room is like a treasure chest. I feel like one of those kids in *The Goonies* who just found the pirate ship. This could be the best job ever!"

Wait a minute. Why wasn't he as excited as she was? Just standing there and continuing to film? "What is wrong with you, Suit? How can you not get excited by all of this? Put the phone down and get over here and give all this a look."

But he just answered her with an infuriating head shake as he put the phone back in his pocket. "Okay, I think we've seen enough for today. Neither of us are dressed or equipped to begin to tackle this room right now. It will take cleaning supplies and boxes, an organizing system carefully planned out." He ran a hand over his closely shaved head. "I don't know, maybe a Dumpster or two out back."

Drea felt her hackles start to rise. Was he ever going to get behind this project, even if this room was already organized and meticulous? And maybe if the lighting wasn't busted or if half the other things on Mrs. Betty's wish list were magically eliminated. As Drea watched his retreating back heading toward the door, she doubted it. "Wait," she called, stopping him. "You are going to come up with a plan of attack, right? Or at least hear mine out. This isn't just some sort of ruse on your part to throw your grandmother off the scent. Maybe toy with her while you come up with a way to get her to see things your way."

He turned back toward her, his eyes tinged with annoyance or, she didn't know, maybe it was guilt. Drea tilted her head to the side and gave him a hard stare.

Suit tried to throw her then and gave her what she was sure he thought would pass for a smile, but she knew it wasn't. She'd seen his real smile and this sure as heck wasn't it. "You're quite suspicious, aren't you, city girl?"

"I'd rather think of it as cautious, and I thought we'd agreed on the name Boots. If we're coming up with new names on the fly, please run them through approvals first. I answer to nothing with *girl* attached; *city woman* is fine though I still prefer *Boots.* Now, are we going to get to work in here or not?"

"Not," he countered back.

Drea blinked. Surprised by his quick and unexpected response.

"The workday is over. It's close to after six. I'm not going to have my grandmother chew me out for keeping you here past proper hours. Besides, haven't you put in a long enough day yet? You must be starving. I know I am."

Drea was both embarrassed and shocked. Did the afternoon really get away from them that quickly? She had expected it to be much earlier. Honestly, despite some hiccups of awkwardness and discomfort, in reality it all went by much faster and much more pleasantly than she thought it would. But it was late. She needed to get a move on and, now that he'd pointed out the time, she was hungry too. And in answer to her thinking it, her stomach suddenly cosigned. Loudly.

She looked up at him, refusing to let herself blush. "Well, I guess it is late. Sorry to keep us both from dinner."

"Let's fix it then. Join me at the diner. That way at least we won't both go home hungry."

Drea tripped; she didn't know if it was the wayward box in her path or his words that put her completely off her step. She told herself it was the box, but either way the result was still the same. Right at the end of the sentence she was left suddenly pressed chest to chest, Boots to Suit, in the arms of her reluctant boss.

CHAPTER 9
SOMEWHERE IN TIME

"It's only to come up with a game plan on what we're going to tell my grandmother."

Drea let Kellen's words flip over in her mind one more time before she turned the lock on the front door and let herself in. The fact that he felt they needed a game plan didn't sit quite right with her.

"There you are, Drea. We were starting to think you'd gotten lost over there in that big old theater. Or maybe it was that you were lost in your own thoughts?" her Aunt Joyce yelled by way of greeting from where she was in the kitchen.

Little did she know how close she was to correct on both fronts. Drea was starting to feel lost all right. Lost, tangled, muddled, and a whole host of things that she needed to get under control. But she wouldn't tell her aunt any of that, she vowed as she squared her shoulders and followed the delicious smell of fried chicken and baked yams, making her way to the kitchen in the back of the house.

"Of course I didn't get lost, Aunt Joyce, though it is easy enough to do so in that big old theater. Not to mention it looks like it's going to be quite the job now that I've really gotten a close look at things."

"Now, you're not going to let that scare you away, are you?" Aunt Joyce looked at her with slight shock and horror from where she sat at the old Formica table that had been in the family for as long as Drea remembered. Though the house had had a few updates over the years, namely Aunt Joyce's pride and joy of a den with a big-screen TV, many touches remained from their grandparents' and great grandparents' days in the old rambling lake house.

Suddenly Kellen's face appeared in Drea's mind's eye. Brooding, challenging, and gorgeous. She took a moment to wonder over why his eyes seemed so piercing behind those glasses he wore. Darn it, weren't glasses supposed to make a person more inconspicuous? Not him. With him it was like a reverse Superman thing going on. Drea sighed, then looked at her aunt again, catching her now staring, her eyes full of concern over her cat-eye glasses. She cleared her throat. "No way. I'd never," she said.

"But it does concern me a bit. The fact that it seems like it's going to be a big job that may take me away from the bakeshop for more hours than I anticipated."

Her aunt smiled. "You don't have to worry about that, sweetheart. I knew what a state that old Redheart was in when you talked about the position with me after speaking with Betty. Though Betty and Henry had done some improvements in the past, I knew once you got behind the surface cover-ups, it was probably a right old mess. If what Betty really wants done is going to get done right, it's gonna take quite a bit of your attention and that's perfectly fine with me."

Drea pulled a face and put her hand to her throat pretending to clutch imaginary pearls. She gasped. "Wow, don't act like you'll miss me much, Aunt Joyce. Now, I know I'm not the best in the kitchen, but you don't have to go and boot me out, pawning me off on your friend. I'm not that sad a case. I can always just grab a Greyhound and make my way back to New York."

Aunt Joyce rolled her eyes skyward. "Cut it with the dramatics, gal. You know it's nothing like that. Betty wouldn't have offered you the job if she didn't think you were extremely talented. And I wouldn't have vouched for you if I didn't think the same. Besides, for the record, I'm not letting you completely out of your shop duties that easily. I'm gonna still need you a few mornings a week for the rush, just like normal until Rena can get in after dealing with them chaps of hers. After that, you are all Betty's. Is that good enough for you? Looks like it's going to be more of a haul for you when it comes to long days. You don't need to worry over us though. We will adjust if you can."

Once again Kellen's face came to Drea's mind: those Jedi mind trick eyes and his own impromptu dinner invitation, not to mention the fact that she ended up declining with her quick excuse of getting home and other responsibilities. She couldn't leave it at that. No way could she leave him with the impression that she wasn't up for his challenge. She was never one to run away when there was a Goliath in her path.

Well, not usually.

Sure, she'd run out of New York last year when the going got tough and it felt like her career was never going to amount to more than close-but-not-quite auditions and broken promises. Here she was at a crossroads again. It was time to start looking at situations squarely. She was feeling antsy for a comeback of sorts, although where she was coming back from, she didn't quite know.

Drea grinned, feeling more herself, as her hunger from earlier rose again and she turned to lift the lid off one of the pots, happy to see fresh creamed corn as a side accompaniment with tonight's chicken dinner. She turned back to her aunt. "Yep, that's fine by me. Thanks, Aunt Joyce. Now I'm going to make a plate. Did you and Liv eat yet? Sorry I was so late, but I'm starving now. I've worked up quite an appetite and looks like I'm going to need my strength for tomorrow."

Kellen didn't know what surprised him more when he stepped into his grandparents' home that evening, the silence or the lack of anything being prepared for dinner. His first thought was maybe his grandmother wasn't home when she didn't greet him with her usual loving outburst of energy, but then Kellen noticed her keys in the bowl on the entryway table. He called out. "Grandma! Grandma!" Physically pushing down the immediate thread of fear that threatened to invade his body, Kellen turned to the right and went up the staircase toward his grandparents' bedroom searching for her. "Grandma!" The bed was still perfectly made although he could see just the tiniest imprint from where she had sat on his grandfather's side.

The rest, his pillow, the turndown, appeared perfect, as if no one had slept there for a long while or it was freshly done up like a hotel change out. Kellen looked to the nightstand and could see his grandfather's reading glasses placed as they always were along with a hardback novel he must have been reading before he passed away. Kellen took slow steps into the bedroom; he didn't know why.

This room had been one he'd always felt comfortable entering freely, but not today. Kellen looked at the novel. As per usual with his grandfather being always curious, it was a mystery novel with a historical bent, big and thick. Next to it, well-worn and thumbed through, was his grandfather's Bible. Kellen picked it up. It was small. So small for a man his grandfather's size. It just filled the width of Kellen's hand. He opened it, marveling as he always did at the various underlines, highlights, and markings. The almost threadbare bookmarking had him opening to a page, his eyes going to a familiar refrain. He could easily hear his grandfather then as he told him of letting go and leaning onto God and not his own understanding for direction.

Kellen let out a slow breath. It seemed so much easier to do when he still had his grandfather as a sounding board. Kellen closed the Bible. Right now what he needed was direction toward where his grandmother was. Who would help him with that? He was about ready to call the police. He placed the Bible back on the nightstand and put his hand to his hip, standing and turning toward the window in frustration. He glanced out the window, taking in his grandfather's daily view of the back garden. The sky was quickly darkening, indicating a storm coming in. Kellen's eyes shifted to the gazebo in the middle of the green and that's when he saw her.

She was sitting stock still, looking out over the rolling hills, his grandpa's gardens, and the town below. She didn't move an inch and Kellen's breath hitched for a moment, taking in his grandmother's cocoa brown skin, determined but delicate features, ramrod straight back that showed her inner strength, and he knew immediately what his grandfather saw in her all those years ago. But then the breeze kicked up and he watched as the wind fluttered around her. Her hair moved with the breeze, her shirt fluttered, and even Kellen from the open window caught a bit of a chill, but still his grandma didn't move, not one bit. Kellen once again felt the threat of fear mixed with frustration this time as he shook his head and headed down the stairs toward the back door.

Kellen jogged out to the gazebo, making quick work of the grass that was under his feet. The wind kicked up again as he looked at the quickly darkening sky. "Grandma!" he yelled, though still she didn't turn around. What was going on with her?

Didn't she hear him? The wind was getting stronger, but it wasn't so strong that she couldn't hear his call. Kellen finally made it to the gazebo, his feet hitting the wood hard, and with the clatter of rubber against wood his grandmother finally turned around with a start, her expression one of shock mixed with bewilderment. She quickly masked it by giving Kellen a warm smile. "Sweetheart, you're home already? I didn't expect you back for another hour or so."

Kellen knelt at his grandmother's feet, taking both of her hands in his, immediately noticing how cool they were despite it being early May, with the day's chill just coming on. He reached up and touched her cheek, which was just as cool. "Grandma, it's now after seven. I'm actually home later than I thought I would be. What are you doing out here? How long have you been sitting here? And don't tell me you haven't had any dinner yet."

In response to Kellen's rapid-fire line of questioning, he saw his grandmother's eyes cloud over a bit and turn just a little uncharacteristically hard. She gently slid her hands from his and started to rise. "Don't go looking at me like that, Mr. Kellen. I just came out to get a little bit of air and lost track of time, the day is so beautiful. And as for dinner, I don't have much of an appetite." She looked at him more closely. "But it's after seven like you said and you must be starving. What is wrong with me? I should at least put something on for you. Come on, let's go inside and let me get you something cooked up."

At that Kellen made a face. His grandmother, for all her wonderful talent, had never been one to be quick as a whiz in the kitchen. Her specialties were usually things like bacon sandwiches and pigs in a blanket. Though she could grill a mean steak and her spaghetti Bolognese was top notch, when he thought of meals in this house, it was less about the food and more about the folks.

It turned out that Kellen's grandfather was the genius cook of the family. His grandmother always used to go around bragging about how she'd found quite the catch in Henry Kilborn, his talents being useful in multiple rooms about the house. The fact that she stated this all over town, from Jolie's bar to the ladies' auxiliary, made her enviable far and wide, and he supposed she didn't mind the fact that she kept tongues wagging about her. "Better you control the word on the street instead of it controlling you, Kel," he could hear her say. She'd had a point there.

They made it inside just before the sky opened up after a crack of thunder and Kellen tried not to think about his grandmother getting caught out in the rain if he hadn't gotten home at the time he had. He knew it would do him no good arguing with her about being out, getting caught in the rain and falling sick. No good at all.

His grandmother was always fiercely independent, no matter if she and his grandfather relied terribly on each other for all the years together. Hearing from Kellen that she may need a bit of help would only cause animosity between the two of them, and right now, he didn't need any more than what they had going.

He watched as his grandmother went from the refrigerator to the pantry and back again, making faces and frustrated noises.

"What's the matter?" he asked.

"Nothing. It's just that the day got away from me more than I anticipated, and I should've ordered some groceries from Cartland's to prepare for your dinner tonight. I'm not really seeing anything here that you'd like to have, sweetheart."

Kellen went over to the fridge, opened it, and gave it a longer look than he had that morning. There was some juice, a couple of eggs, cream for coffee, and not much else. He wanted to kick himself for not noticing earlier how sparse things were. This was by no means the stocked fridge he was used to seeing at home in Sugar Lake. Looking toward the back, Kellen spied a few tinfoil dishes and plastic ware containers. Pulling them out, it was clear they were the remains of condolence cake and deepest regrets casseroles from his grandfather's memorial the month before. Kellen quickly went to dump the dishes in the trash only to have his grandmother gasp and still his hand.

"What in the world are you doing?"

Kellen looked at her wide eyed. "What do

you think I'm doing — throwing these away as they're over a month old. It's not like we can eat them. One bite of this and we'll both end up in the ER."

His grandmother skirted around him, pushing him out of the way and reverently emptying the containers out into plastic bags, then putting the plastic containers into the sink.

Kellen covered his nose from the smell of the old food.

Still his grandmother gave him a harsh glare. "Goodness, one would think I raised you in a barn or something. How do you think I can go and throw away perfectly good Tupperware? You know I have to return these to Mrs. Reese and Mrs. Barnett. If I don't, my name will be mud from here down to Claxton and back." She shook her head at him, giving a *tsk*.

Kellen shook his head. "Grandma, those are not Tupperware. They are barely from the ninety-nine-cent store if that. To save us the smell we could have thrown them away and returned them new and better ones."

His grandmother balked. "What? And come off as uppity? Now please. I know I've been out of the city for plenty of years, but even you know that's just not how it's done. Don't go getting ahead of yourself now,

Kellen."

Kellen felt his eyes go skyward as his stomach grumbled. This was clearly another one he wasn't going to win. "Yes, ma'am."

Finally his grandmother smiled.

"Oh well, what are we going to do about dinner tonight? I'm sorry, honey, I should've been prepared."

Kellen reached out and ruffled the top of his grandmother's curls, leaning down to give her a kiss on the cheek. She really was so darned cute to him at times. "What are you sorry about, Grandma? I know you, and I should've called when I was on the way into town and asked what you wanted." He was this close to saying it was what his grandfather would have done, but luckily, he stopped himself before the words came out. Still though, by the slight stiffening of his grandmother's back and ever so subtle change that came over her, he could tell she was thinking the same thing. Kellen soldiered on. He looked out the window at the hard-driving rain. "How about I give the pizzeria a call and we can do a little takeout tonight. By the time I call it in and it's done, I'm sure the rain will have let up. This is Sugar Lake. These storms pass through quickly."

His grandmother shook her head. "I can

do you one better. Since we've gotten so many tourists into town, things have fancied up." She waved her phone. "Have a thing here and I press it and old Cletus will deliver from any of the restaurants in town. He's turned his pickup into a Buber and a food delivery truck."

Kellen frowned, then shook his head with a smile. "A Buber, Grandma? You mean an Uber?"

His grandmother rolled her eyes. "Same difference, Kellen. You know exactly what I mean and don't go making fun of me. Either way, I just press this little button and I have all the menus I want with only a few swipes." She tapped away, then waved her phone triumphantly. It was as if the moon landing had just taken place and instead of Buzz Aldrin, it was old Cletus taking one giant step for mankind.

CHAPTER 10
WAITRESS

"Third time's the charm?"

"I don't know about that, but it's nice to see that you're counting, Boots," Kellen said as he sauntered into Goode 'N Sweet.

Drea snorted to herself as she stepped back, giving him free passage into the shop that morning. She looked down at her moto boots, today paired with a tank and just above the ankle jeans. Sure, maybe she should invest in some new sneakers or a pair or two of sandals, but she liked her boots. They reminded her of her days hitting the audition pavement back in New York. When she was wearing them she felt grounded, and goodness knew she could use all the grounding she could get, especially when the Suit came a-calling.

She looked up at him as he passed, fighting against the smile that threatened to escape her lips. She decided he didn't need unnecessary smiles. He probably got plenty of them anyway. So many smiles from so many women that they were probably commonplace, which was why he was so stingy with them. At least to her. Not that it mattered.

"So, can I get you your usual today?" Drea asked. Kellen was seemingly already deep in thought and not quite listening to her as he started off toward his usual spot at the back table with the good view. Speaking of, her current view of him wasn't so bad. The Suit wasn't in a suit at all. He was completely out of his previously exposed character and wearing a tank that showed off well-defined muscles and a pair of loose gym shorts that highlighted his strong calves in just the right way. It was her basketball dreams come true and made her want to scream at him to get the heck out of her head and wake her from this walking provocation.

Before sitting, Suit turned back her way, embarrassing her for being caught staring and startling her by turning too quickly. "What, are you in a rush or something? Maybe I wanted something different this morning."

Her brows drew together and she looked at him hard.

Just then his phone buzzed and Drea

continued to stare. Kellen looked down at the phone and then back up at her. "Yes?" he said.

"Well?" she replied.

"Well, what?"

"Well, what different thing do you want, Suit?"

He frowned, then seemed to ponder with the phone buzzing again as if asking it the question too. He let out a huff. "The usual," he ground out in frustration, and Drea would have been offended by his dismissive tone if not for the distraction of the other customers entering after him.

She smiled and welcomed Clayton Morris and his daughter, Hope. Like the loyal sister she was, Drea wouldn't comment on the normally spry Clayton's obvious dark circles. A perfect match to the set of luggage under her sister Liv's eyes. Nope, no comment there. She'd just take a guess that the view of the moon must have been lovely over the lake last night from out by Clayton's old fishing shack.

Drea instead turned her attention to twelve-year-old Hope, who was growing lovelier by the day. "Good morning, Hope. What are you doing in so early this morning?"

Hope gave Drea a smile, though her pretty

brown eyes still showed the edges of tired-ness too. "I'm going in with my dad to work today," she said with a yawn. "We're doing reports on careers in school."

"Wow, that's so nice that you chose your dad to study. Very cool. And it's also cool that you can get the day off from school in order to study him."

"I don't know how cool it is," her father, Clayton Morris, said from over her shoulder. "Well, the report part is pretty cool, but it's not like she's studying her dear old dad today. But I guess I won't be too jealous that she didn't choose me."

Drea raised a brow and gave Hope a conspiratorial grin. "So who did you choose?"

Hope looked at her sheepishly, then looked over at her dad, then back at her. "I chose Avery Brooks. I figure she's got a pretty rocking job being the only female on a crew full of fire-fighting men. And she's a paramedic too, so that's kind of interesting to me. Imagine putting out fires and getting to stick tubes down people's throats."

Drea pulled a face. "Yeah, I guess I can imagine it. But I agree, Avery is totally bad-ass. I'll definitely give her that."

Just then Aunt Joyce came out while a couple of the usual patrons came in. Aunt

Joyce came from behind the counter and hugged Hope before greeting Clayton, the rest of the patrons, and then Kellen.

"Hey, looks like you're staying around with us for a bit, huh?" Aunt Joyce asked Kellen matter-of-factly.

"I don't know about that, Miss Joyce. I'm just here for as long as it takes to get things straight with my grandmother. Though it seems she's wasting no time in passing the word around."

Drea stilled. *What did Aunt Joyce mean by* staying *and when did she know about this? I swear, did blood over friendship mean anything to her and Mrs. Betty? What did she know and how long was the Suit staying in town?*

She perked her ears hard while trying to look mildly uninterested as Kellen continued. "But if that means for a bit, I guess it's for a bit. Looks like I'll be doing a little telecommuting," he said as his gaze slipped over to Drea.

Drea shrugged. "Hey, that's your business. From what I've seen so far, looks like we'll be fine without you — no need telecommuting. Don't let us and the theater project hold you up."

By way of an answer, he just gave her a hard stare.

"Well, if you're going to be around for a while, why don't you join us for dinner at Jolie's one night? It will be good to catch up with you. It's been too long since we got in a game of pool," Clayton Morris said, reaching past Drea to shake Kellen's hand.

Drea tried to hide both the shock and annoyance. So Clayton knew the Suit too? Darn these small towns. Even people who looked like they'd never know each other knew each other.

"So how do you two know each other?" Drea asked, not able to hold her concerns behind her tongue.

Clayton shrugged. "It's Sugar Lake; just about everybody knows everybody. But if you want to get specific, this one here and I used to play rec league ball together." He turned back to Kellen. "Hey, if you still play, me and the guys still get in a game twice a week at the school gym around seven — feel free to stop by."

Kellen looked slightly uncomfortable for a moment as he glanced over at Hope, then back to Clayton. "That will be great. And yeah, I still hit the court every once in a while. So I may take you up on that game."

Clayton grinned. "Cool. Just remember we're not kids anymore. No need to come out trying to be all LeBron on us."

The Suit laughed. "As if. Look at you, Mr. Fire Chief. I should call you LeBron." Drea watched as Clayton did the whole "aww man" humble thing and the Suit did likewise. She was grateful for the lovefest breakup when Liv came out of the kitchen, pulling her man's attention away as Aunt Joyce went to help out with customers behind the counter.

Liv put her arm comfortably around Clayton's waist as he bent down to give her a warm kiss. Drea had to admit she was happy that her sister was so open and loving with Clayton Morris, and that they felt so secure in their relationship that they were able to express their love in this way. Even though she rolled her eyes as if she was slightly embarrassed, Hope walked over, accepting the one-armed embrace from Liv as she bent down to kiss her on the top of her head.

"Your family is beautiful," Kellen said. The sight of her sister so free and easy and the Suit's assumed words caught Drea off guard. She didn't know what to do with the unexpected feeling of longing that suddenly grabbed her.

"Yes, they are, and I am a very lucky man," Clayton responded as if it was the most natural thing. Drea swallowed, suddenly so happy for her sister, who a year before almost seemed like a different person. Looking at her now with Clayton and Hope, they did seem like family and it all looked right. Drea suspected that if things continued the way they were a proposal might not be too far off. Though she'd envisioned happiness for her sister, she'd never imagined it quite as right as this, though she was embarrassed to say it.

"What about the four of us getting together over at Jolie's? How's about tonight? You and Drea can come by after you finish working over at the theater and I'll bring Liv."

At Kellen's expression Liv smiled and reached out a hand to him. Drea would have laughed if he hadn't looked so confused and a tad bit horrified. "Trust me, don't look so afraid; it's not like it's a double date or anything. He just teamed us up because I'm this one's older sister. Those are my biscuits you're eating. Well, mine and Aunt Joyce's — I'm not going to overstep and have my aunt happen to slip and throw something at me."

"Good save, girly! Because I was about to throw this dish towel from clear across the room!" Aunt Joyce yelled, once again proving that nothing got past her eagle ears.

"Well, um, thank you. Your biscuits are delicious." The Suit raised his voice. "Almost as good as the originals."

Aunt Joyce laughed.

But then Kellen looked over at Drea and added, "Believe me, I didn't think it would be a date."

"As if. And I don't know. This is my braid-washing night, you know," Drea said as she walked away not even wanting to give this conversation any more brain space than it was currently taking up. Suddenly her heart was beating way too fast and she didn't like the direction any of this was going.

She started in on Kellen's order, resisting the sudden urge to go back and slip in one of Aunt Joyce's sausages. Nope, she wouldn't do it. That was just a little added specialty for his first day back. Now that this was turning into what looked like a regular thing, she should just give the man what he asked for and move on from there. As her sister came back, she gave her a nudge in the shoulder. Drea hissed, "I'm gonna kill your boyfriend, you know that, right?"

Liv chuckled. "With shoulders and eyes like that? You are not. Just be sure to put a couple extra biscuits in his to-go bag and I'll give Clayton a thank-you kiss and tell him it's from you later." She reached in the pie case and added one of her new breakfast meat pies to the Suit's order.

Drea held back the urge to sneer as her sister made her way back to the kitchen, her own little sanctuary, an extra pep in her step and a hum on her lips.

Coming back to Kellen's table with his order, she noted he barely gave her a second glance as he was deep in low tones on a phone conversation. Still, Drea caught the thread of frustration and urgency in his voice as he said something about rescheduling and sending over documents to a person named Tracy. She was about to walk away when his hand reached out and touched her on the wrist, the surprising action sending a sizzle up her arm as it had her turning around abruptly.

He quickly removed his hand and put both up in a defensive posture, letting her know that he wasn't trying to be offensive by touching her. Then, pressing a button on his phone, he looked her in the eye and said, "Thank you." His tone was all business as his gaze met hers squarely. "And I appreciate the little extra. How did you know I was extra hungry this morning?" A slight grin hinted at the corner of his mouth and a bit of sparkle came to his light-colored eyes.

Great. So the food got a smile.

Drea shrugged her shoulders. "Lucky guess," she mumbled.

Just then the door to the shop chimed and more patrons came in, saving her from coming up with any extra conversation. She'd never been happier to see hungry tourists.

Kellen knew he shouldn't stare, but stare he did. He couldn't help it, just like he couldn't help finding himself biking to Goode 'N Sweet at the first hint of dawn that morning. Sure, he told himself, taking his bike out was a replacement for his usual morning gym run, and heck, the excuse even sounded — barely — plausible in his own head. But barely was enough to get him there, and now that he was pretty much a fixture at the bakeshop, maybe he could stop coming up with excuses.

Watching her as she chatted easily with the customers, smelling the pies as they were baking, the sweet aroma of the sugar mixed with the smooth warmth of the butter, Kellen could admit it brought him a feeling of comfort he didn't know he'd been missing in his place in Atlanta. And sadly, he couldn't quite capture that feeling back at his grandparents' now that his grandfather was gone.

That thought brought on a certain amount of unease and guilt; he knew he had to fix it for both himself and his grandmother. Kellen picked up his coffee cup and took a sip, almost hating how perfect it was once again. Crap, it took him walking past three coffeehouses in his own neighborhood to get to the one that made a cup of coffee this good. How was it that she was able to pull it out on the first try? The thought both bolstered and perplexed him at the same time. He hated that he could find something to grow attached to in this town that he very much needed to detach himself from.

Kellen let out a sigh as his phone beeped three times in rapid succession, indicating that Tracy had sent the files on ahead that he requested. He couldn't believe he was still in Sugar Lake missing meetings, re-arranging them to be video conference meetings, all to try to convince his grand-mother of something — which was now looking to be a fruitless endeavor.

Nevertheless, he still had to figure out a way to salvage the Ronson deal now if it turned out he couldn't get the Redheart back on the table. After talking with his grandmother again last night, he decided to split his time and yes, be more hands on here in Sugar Lake with the reno. Something she'd clearly got on the horn and shared with Miss Joyce between then and this morning. Not that he wanted either the reno or to be in Sugar Lake, but after seeing his grandmother out on the gazebo and the awful fear that brought on, he knew he had to find a way to ensure her safety while still maintaining the relationship they'd come to love and cherish. She was all he had left. All he'd had that he knew he could count on. Kellen couldn't risk losing any part of it. Though he'd still go back and forth to Atlanta, he'd stay and get things settled here at home base, and hopefully when all was said and done, the RPG deal would be signed and he'd have his grandmother settled too, safer and closer to him.

CHAPTER 11
HOPE FLOATS

Drea arrived at the theater later that morning at the same time as Kellen. Though feeling less awkward than at their previous meetings, she still couldn't help the immediate sensations of both tension and excitement when she saw him pull up beside her on his bike after she'd made her way from the bakery once the morning rush had ended.

"Wow, you really are getting in the miles on that thing today, aren't you?" she said, by way of conversation. Clearly, he'd come from his place because he'd changed out of his earlier attire and, though not a Suit on a bike, he was wearing what looked to be a designer T-shirt — she could tell by its fine quality, double stitching, and the silky way it draped across his shoulders and chest — and easy woven shorts of equally fine quality.

"Well, after bringing my grandmother her

breakfast this morning, I found that I was still a little restless. Also, it felt good to get my bike out again. I don't get to ride as much as I'd like when I'm in the city. So, stretching my legs is a nice change of pace. Besides, it's not that long of a ride from our place into town."

A part of Drea inwardly frowned, so she guessed the tentatively scheduled meet up over at Jolie's was now off — well, at least in his mind. Jolie's was quite a hike, heading to the highway. Did he plan to bike it there too? Oh well, what did it matter to her? She'd be better not sharing a meal with him anyway. She inwardly huffed as puzzle pieces started to meld together. He probably biked just for that reason.

So what? She could still head to Jolie's herself. Be the third-wheel little sister. It was a role she was born to play. Enjoy dinner, make her sister crazy, and get a free meal in the process, because Clayton would be too upstanding a fireman do-gooder to let her pay. It was a win-win for her on all fronts. This time she shrugged for real before turning and making her way to the theater entrance.

She and Kellen were stopped short when they found the theater door already unlocked and were greeted by the sound of

Mrs. Betty's voice, full of excitement as she conversed with someone just inside the viewing room's entrance.

Stepping into the space, Drea could practically feel the heat of the annoyance as it radiated off Kellen's body. It was so hot her instinct was to step back to avoid being burned. Mrs. Betty was being all happy and chipper while in animated conversation with Ray Nash, one of the town's biggest contractors. Archer Jove, Mrs. Kilborn's architect, flanked her other side. Drea smiled at the sight of Archer. He'd not been in the bakery for a while, having gone on a low carb diet. The last time he was in, he'd bought two pecan twists and told her it was a last hurrah before saying good-bye.

"Hello, Mrs. Betty, Mr. Nash, Archer. I didn't expect to see you all here today."

Drea nodded toward Ray, and then looked at Mrs. Betty. "Wow, you're here even before we are today. I didn't expect you to beat me," she said with a genuine smile.

"I didn't expect any of you here at all," Kellen said from by her shoulder. "Grandmother, I thought you told me you had an appointment. You could've let me know that the appointment was here. We could have ridden into town together."

"I could have, yes." For some reason Drea

had a feeling that Mrs. Betty was making up excuses on the spot. "But my scheduled plans changed along the way into town and I decided to call up Ray here to discuss our plans for the theater. Let him know what I was thinking after our conversations. We have known him forever and he has an excellent reputation. I think he should work up a bid for us." She turned to Archer then. "And of course, Archer should be here for this. Why, when he called the house returning your call to meet, I thought why not have all of us meet up. That way everyone's on the same page."

Though she didn't know the particulars, judging by Mrs. Betty's tone and the quick frost that came over the air, Drea had a feeling the Suit was in some hot water. She could practically hear his internal groan. He turned Ray Nash's way and gave him a tight smile. "Thanks for coming in on my grandmother's quick call, Mr. Nash." He looked at Archer then. "And thanks for returning my call, Archer. I'm sure freeing your schedule for such a hastily put together meeting must not have been easy."

Archer smiled, showing his perfect white teeth and flashing playful dimples. "It's not a problem. I'd drop anything and everything for Mrs. Betty and I'm happy to help in any way I can, though I know you're in good hands with Mr. Nash here. As I was just explaining, you won't need my consulting all that much. I'm sure Mr. Nash will have it all under control."

"See, darling," Mrs. Betty chimed in then. "Didn't I tell you it would all be just fine? You haven't a thing in the world to worry about."

Kellen smiled. It seemed fluid and easy, but Drea felt that she could pick up on his cues, and everything about the way he smiled and spoke said that he knew this wasn't just a quickly set-up meeting by Mrs. Betty, but something she tactically planned. He was being played and Drea could tell that Kellen hated being played, just like she could also tell that he wasn't about to call his grandmother out in front of this group of people.

Drea watched as Kellen's eyes narrowed further and his brows knit tight when two of Ray's five sons came down from the upper levels — tall, dark, burly, and muscular, that summed up the Nash boys. The eldest, King Nash, gave Drea a quick smile and a nod while his younger brother, Griffin Nash, added a slow up and down and a lazy smile to his drawn-out greeting. "Good to see you again, Drea. Been way too long since I've gotten in some of your sweet honey biscuits."

"Has it now?" Drea kept her voice even. Months ago, she'd gone on a couple of dates with Griffin Nash. Two to be exact, which was one too many. Though the first was nice enough, on the second he got unexpectedly handsy and had to get his behind handed to him in the form of a quick verbal smackdown that let him know who she was and where she was from.

She'd told him that she wasn't quite as impressed as he thought she would be by what he called a fancy dinner at the town's country club. In addition, the fact that lobster bisque came along with the prix fixe dinner didn't entitle him to any more than a kind thank-you when he dropped her off back at home later that evening. Obviously, by the tone of his greeting today, it seemed Griffin might need a bit of a reminder.

Kellen continued to speak then, looking his grandmother directly in the eye with a tight smile. "Grandmother, do you mind if we speak outside for a moment? There is a bit of business we should discuss." He turned to the collective crowd, a gentle hand on his grandmother's forearm to lead her away. "If you all would just excuse us for a moment."

Suddenly Drea had visions of the ultimate western standoff taking place in the movie lobby. A scene from *High Noon* complete with tumbleweeds rolling between Kellen and Mrs. Betty with the old popcorn maker the only witness for the carnage about to take place.

But the standoff wasn't nearly as long as a midday feature and in little to no time Kellen and Mrs. Betty returned, their expressions letting everyone know who'd won the standoff by a landslide.

Kellen cleared his throat and spoke as Mrs. Betty beamed triumphantly from by his side. She may as well have been wearing a WWE championship belt with that smile, and Drea almost wanted to stand up and cheer over the marvel of the sheer force of the little woman.

"Please tell me what you think we need," Kellen said. Somehow Drea knew how much gruffly blurting this out hurt his pride. "And keep in mind, we're on a budget here, Archer, Mr. Nash."

"Says you!" Mrs. Betty added cheerfully, and even Kellen caught on that this bit of extra was just to get under his skin.

He leaned over and put an arm around his grandmother, then bent down to kiss the top of her forehead. "What am I going to do with you, lady?" he said softly, and a small part of Drea melted at the unexpectedly sweet gesture.

Flipping on a dime, he turned to Ray Nash, his tone back to business. "Mr. Nash?"

"You can call me Ray, Kellen. I think you've grown up enough for that."

Kellen reluctantly smiled. Ray Nash, helping break some of the tension in the room. More of his icy demeanor thawed as he shook his head. "Now, Mr. Nash, you know that won't possibly work. How about we do a walk-through and you tell me your thoughts."

They proceeded to start walking through the theater. At this point, Drea was beginning to feel like she could take on yet another job as a Redheart page, giving historical tours, but she was surprised during their walk to once again be pleasantly shocked by some new discoveries in the Redheart. It was the little architectural gift that kept on giving. And when Mrs. Betty was taking them around, the pride and love practically exploded from her.

It was good seeing that spark that had dulled the day her husband had closed his eyes. At least Drea could see that, if only for fleeting moments, Mrs. Betty could get it back. That was something. It was worrisome, the immediate change that had come over the normally jubilant older woman. Sure, it was to be expected, but even to her aunt there was a cause for alarm. She was starting to think her aunt was right; Mrs. Betty needed this project. Mr. Henry went too soon. So quick that she didn't have any time to prepare. Without this project, she may have been forever looking for the goodbye that was stolen from her.

"And you all wouldn't believe the time we had with these curtains." Drea looked at Mrs. Betty as she talked animatedly about the theater's curtains. "The originals were completely destroyed, or nearly so, when we got the place. They were unusable. So these were imported from a theater in Paris. Henry ordered them special. But then they arrived, as is, mind you," she said.

Drea could tell her mind was somewhere back in the year she and her husband had gotten the curtains. "The hems were a mess. Most of it was more down than sewn up. I'll tell you all, it was falling apart. Now we're talking yards and yards and I don't even know how many yards of hemming." She got a conspiratorial gleam in her eye and looked at Drea. "Quiet as it's kept, I wasn't the pillar of the community I am now."

"You don't say," Kellen drawled, and got a light arm whack for his troubles as Ray Nash chuckled.

Mrs. Betty gave Ray a look and a finger wave as she grinned. "Now, don't you start, Ray. You just keep your trap shut."

Ray held up a hand. "I didn't say a word, Betty."

"You're always a pillar to me," Archer chimed in, and Mrs. Betty waved a hand at him as she shook her head, shooing away his compliment.

She went on. "As I was saying, children, I didn't have folks I could call on to help me out, and it wasn't as if I was going to send the curtains out to be hemmed, so I got it in my head that I could fix them myself." She let out a wistful sigh and Drea practically felt the air expelling from her own chest.

"Well, as Henry was working during the day, he'd come and do a bit of painting or something here at night and then we'd head home together. At one point, he got sick of finding me sitting on the stage with these darned curtains. It was the never-ending job. Finally, he looked down and saw me struggling, getting a glimpse of my poor bleeding fingertips; right then and there he got down, grabbed a needle, and started sewing with me."

Drea thought her heart would practically explode over the sweet story.

"So, is that how it is that Grandpa can sew so well? I've seen him do up his own pants and fix buttons. He never sends things out?" Kellen asked.

Mrs. Betty nodded. "It is. It took him a minute to catch on, but he was a quick study all right. In all these years, the hems have never fallen on these curtains. They've practically outlasted the fabric now. And" — a rosy blush came to her soft brown cheeks — "they've seen their fair share of tangles."

Kellen let out an embarrassed groan while Mr. Nash laughed heartily. Drea was about to chime in when Griffin Nash sidled close and whispered in her ear, "I wouldn't mind getting tangled in the curtains with you."

Kellen cleared his throat loudly and was suddenly at her side. "Thanks, Grandma. That's a great story." He looked at Griffin Nash. "Mr. Nash. I think you have all you need to give us a bid." Finally, he turned and smiled at Mr. Nash, his eyes softer, though his tone was still all business. "Like I said, please remember we will be on a budget. And of course, you understand, I'll need to do all necessary business background checks in order to make sure we'll have no unforeseen problems down the road."

Drea tilted her head. His tone and posture had changed. Suddenly he seemed at least three inches taller, if that was even possible on his already tall frame. This had to be his Suit out of a suit negotiating tactic and not have anything to do with Griffin's ridiculous comment. How could he have picked up on that anyway? It was said so low that she'd barely more than felt the unease of it.

Still, it seemed to have the desired effect as Griffin took the smallest step back. He faded slightly into the shadows as his father nodded his agreement to signal the beginning of the ending of the meeting.

CHAPTER 12
WHEN SUIT MET BOOTS

Once again Drea was stuck in a perplexed state standing next to Kellen Kilborn.

This time it was as she was entering Jolie's Bar and Grill, the local "famous" watering hole just on the outskirts of town; you took a left off Main, on the way out to highway 76. Just about everybody knew it, even the tourists, thanks to the newly added signs advertising it out on the highway every three miles leading into town.

WE SET THE BAR WITH BARBECUE.
JOLIE'S 10 MILES OUT EXIT 178.

RIBS THAT WILL STICK TO YOUR RIBS!
JOLIE'S 5 MILES EXIT 178.

And Drea's personal favorite: COME AND GET YOUR JOY ON AT JOLIE'S, NEXT EXIT 178.

She was sure this one referred to the

famous Joy Juice, a sweet rum punch that was just as popular as Jolie's ribs. This sign was new and she didn't know how they got the normally reclusive bartender, Caleb Morris, Clayton's older brother, to pose for it, but there he was, in all his handsome, bearded glory. There were ribs, apps, and a pitcher of Joy Juice featured on the bar and Caleb behind the bar with a semi-welcoming half smile that she was sure had women turning left quick off exit 178 to see what Jolie was serving up. It definitely had her cousin Rena taking that left exit more than a time or two. Though if you questioned either of them about it, they were nothing more than passing friends. But the way Caleb always stepped up for Rena — in a way that her so-called boyfriend Troy always failed to do — made him seem like more than a passing friend.

Tonight though, as Drea stood at the bar's entrance with Kellen Kilborn by her side, she knew what it was serving up. A whole boatload of unnecessary complications and aggravation.

"Come on, you two. Our table is ready," Liv said. Her newfound brightness once again grated on Drea's nerves. She fought the urge to grumble one of her usual retorts with her new, though not quite, boss so near and looming. But really, if this cheery, butterflies, the-world-was-all-sweetness-and-light thing that Olivia had going was what love did to a person, she could have it. Drea couldn't believe she was thinking it but, though she was thrilled for her sister, a part of her missed the old, nitpicky, judgmental Liv.

She reluctantly proceeded, her eyes moving away from the lovely dovely Liv and Clayton walking hand in hand as they followed the hostess to their table. And her eyes definitely avoided Kellen, who was stiffly by her side. She thought then of the crafty Mrs. Betty, and she was sure her Aunt Joyce had her hand in it too, and how they made good and darned well she and Kellen both would be uncomfortable together on this not quite double date tonight with Clayton and Liv. When their meetings were done at the theater, Mrs. Betty made big with an exaggerated, "oh, by the way," as she suggested Kellen take her car and give Drea a ride over to Jolie's since they'd both been invited out for dinner tonight.

The fact that this was done in front of everyone and the Suit didn't hesitate to flat-out refuse was no less than mortifying. "I'm not quite dressed for dinner, Grandmother. Besides, I have my bike and how will you get home?"

Mrs. Betty gave him an annoyed look. "It's Jolie's, darling. Fantastic, though not quite Michelin starred. I'm sure you'll have no trouble getting in." She smiled. "Besides, I'm sure Ray here will drop me at home."

Ray did his duty and nodded in the affirmative.

"Wonderful!" Mrs. Betty said. "Now, off with you two. Better to get your nourishment! As you can see, we have lots of work ahead for us."

In response Kellen's brows tightened and he let out a slow breath of air. Still he nodded, went forward and kissed his grandmother's cheek, and shook hands with the other men before turning toward Drea, placing a hand gently at her elbow, and leading her out.

Talk about the most awkward five-minute ride out to Jolie's ever. Who knew five minutes could last so long. But as Kellen opened the door of his grandmother's car for her, he still protected her head as she tucked herself into the big sedan. "Save me from small towns and women with speed dial," he mumbled as he slammed the door behind Drea and went over to the driver's side and got in. Drea considered conversing with him, but after two false starts and his clear anger over being forced into this dinner radiating off him in waves, she gave up and studied the lines on the road. Just as now she looked around, intent on taking in the bar and not his broad shoulders or how wonderful he smelled even in the midst of all the beer and barbecue.

Instead, she caught Caleb's eye, and despite the bar being moderately busy, he gave her a friendly nod and his usual half smile. He was a nice guy, though hard to crack. A veteran, he'd lost a hand in combat, and she knew there was a certain amount of strain between him and Clayton though, as of late, he and his brother seemed to be getting along all right.

The only time Drea really saw him seem to relax was around his niece, Hope, or when he was with her cousin Rena. Which was why she had her suspicions, but she guessed that was Rena's way — she could bring a smile out of the most stoic soul or, she sometimes thought, in Caleb's case, it could be something more. Despite all Rena's going on about Troy this and Troy that, it was the reserved and reclusive Caleb Morris that made her blush. But then again, Caleb Morris had that effect on just about every woman, hence the big old sign out on the highway. It was then that she noticed

Kellen's nod and Caleb's nodded response.

Drea looked his way. "You know Caleb too?"

He shrugged in that nonchalant way of his. "I know a lot of people."

Ugh. If she had a dollar and a part for each time she'd heard that line, she'd be a star. "Of course you do," Drea said dryly as the four of them went to take their seats.

Seeing the booth in the middle of all the bar's action, Drea suddenly longed for one of the less desirable tables. With a booth and the four of them there was no easy seating set up. Either she would sit across from the Suit and have to look at him and chew ribs in his face throughout the night, or they would sit next to each other, thigh to thigh, which was a whole other intimacy all together. Lovebird Liv struck again, sliding into the booth first and tugging Clayton down beside her.

Great. The thighs were it, Drea thought as she slid in with the Suit next to her. Thankfully, despite the booth size and his thigh size, he kept a measured distance. She'd guess about two and a quarter inches between them. Immediately, Drea shifted a little more left, and paused when she felt Kellen stiffen ever so slightly next to her. She let out a breath. Okay. Maybe she was taking things a little too far. She didn't need to make everyone around her uncomfortable and now she was probably making him quite so. Not that she cared all that much; he did have it out for, if not her, then for Mrs. Betty's plans for the theater, and that affected her. So, there was that. But still, she didn't want to give the man some sort of complex. He was pompous, arrogant, and all those things that went with it, but she supposed his personality was what it was. That couldn't be helped.

Besides, when their server, Shelby, came over — a seasoned Jolie's waitress better known for her ample hips, squeezed into the most incredible, breath-defying stretch jeans, than her winning personality (of which she had none) — Drea was more than ready to get her eat on and get this evening over with. The fact that the four of them were pretty much Jolie's veterans made ordering easy. There was no mulling over the placemat menus or prattling on with questions about the heat levels of the wing sauces.

Everyone ordered either ribs or the chicken specials — in her and Liv's cases combos — with mac and cheese, collards or slaw, a side of baked beans added by Clayton, a pitcher of Joy Juice, and a draft for the table.

Drea was pretty sure they had won the no-nonsense Shelby over with their quick ordering. The fact that she raised her perfectly arched, threaded brows and quirked her dark eggplant lips into what could be considered a smile in coven circles had Drea thinking they might get an extra square of corn bread in their basket when she brought it out.

"Isn't this nice? The four of us getting together like old friends?" Liv said, and Drea leveled her with a look.

"But we're not."

"Jeeze, touchy. We kind of are. There's no need to be like that, Drea. You, me, and Clayton are old friends, and Clayton and Kellen here are old friends, so it's not like we all can't be friends or friendly."

Drea let out a growl and was surprised to have it matched by what she thought was an affirmative sneer from Kellen on her right. "Oh, come on and stop laying it on so thick. I get that you two are all in love and it's cute, it really is, and I'm happy for you. Thrilled even." She turned to Clayton. "Bro, you're a great guy and I've been rooting for you from the beginning. I'm totally in your corner and whatever you're doing, don't stop. You're keeping this one off my back" — she gestured to her sister — "so thanks. But for the record, men and women can't be friends."

"Amen."

She looked over at Kellen, surprised by his cosign, and smiled.

Liv snorted. "Oh great. Suddenly we're out of a scene from *When Harry Met Sally?* On this you two would agree." She let out a frustrated sigh. "Of course they can be friends."

Drea laughed and shook her head. "Of course they can't. None of my so-called male friends didn't end up as something else entirely or have that something else in mind when they set out to start off their 'friendship.' " She thought she may have felt an imperceptible movement from by her side, so she turned Kellen's way. "What about you?"

He looked at her, seemingly shocked at being addressed. "What about me?"

"Do you have any female friends?"

"I, well . . ." he said, seemingly stumped by her words.

Drea turned back to Liv. "That's a no. See there. Men and women can't be friends. Of course, with a guy like this. . . ." She waved a hand in Kellen's direction. "Okay-looking —"

"Don't gush now," he drawled out, and the words rolled over her slow and sweet like Clayton's darned organic honey.

She raised the corner of her lip. "Of course, a guy like him would have women coming at him with ulterior motives."

Liv rolled her eyes. "What about me and Clayton?"

Drea laughed, then coughed. "Do you want me to choke? You two, better than anyone, prove my point."

Clayton nudged Liv. "She's right honey, we do."

Liv shot him a look. Her brown eyes wide, her expression seemingly horrified by the betrayal. "What do you mean 'we do'? We are great friends, have always been."

He laughed, then leaned down to kiss her. "If you say so, buddy."

"Oh gosh. I'd like to keep my appetite up. Some of us plan to eat tonight."

Liv laughed at her sister as Clayton turned toward Kellen. "So, how are things going with the Redheart renovation?"

"Great!"

"It's going to be a lot."

She and Kellen answered Clayton's seemingly innocuous question at the same time, looked at each other, then both looked at Clayton's and Liv's bewildered expressions.

The two of them turned to each other bursting out laughing. Drea held her hand on her thigh to keep from kicking her sister.

"I can see you two are going to be fun," Liv said, and Drea let her foot go, arching out on autopilot as if a doctor had suddenly hit her knee with one of those little knee bangers.

Her sister tilted her head and shot her a glare just when Shelby brought over their corn bread and drinks. Drea gave Shelby a big smile upon seeing they did get extra corn bread, and middle pieces no less! "Thanks, Shelby."

"Nothing to it," the woman responded with a mumble. "No need to go on."

"I see she's still full of charm," Kellen said once she was out of earshot.

"Maybe she just doesn't have time for foolish whims from customers, is all. You know, no time to chitchat or small talk."

"Noted," he said while pulling out a square of bread and starting to butter it.

Liv chimed in after taking a sip of her Joy Juice. "Oh, I'm sure she's not referring to you."

He looked up at her with surprised eyes. "Why would she be?"

"Yeah, why would I be?" Drea added.

Liv shook her head and took another swig

of her drink. "Nice to see you two agree on something."

Clayton laughed. "So, are you going to tell me about the theater? I didn't think it needed all that much work the last time Liv and I went there on a date. Besides, I remember your grandparents doing some updates not more than a couple of years ago with reupholstering the seating and whatnot. They did their best to keep the old gem in good shape." He raised his beer glass, seeming to sober, and looked Kellen in the eye. "I know I told you before but, once more, I'm sorry about your granddad. He was an outstanding man. He'll be missed."

Drea saw Kellen's jaw harden as his full lips thinned. She could see and feel his struggle to hold on to his emotions as he raised his own glass. She found herself struggling against the lump in her throat as she and Liv raised theirs too. Finally, Kellen let out a slow breath. Drea watched as his eyes slowly closed, then opened again. "Thanks. That he was and he will be."

She found herself momentarily stunned, glass still in the air as she watched him drink, the way his lips cupped the rim of the glass and his jaw worked as his Adam's apple bobbed. She jumped, almost spilling her own drink when she received a kick in the shin from under the table. She frowned, coughing as she lowered her glass, realizing that hers was the only one still in the air, and took a quick sip trying to cover up for her ridiculous gawking.

She ventured a look over at Liv, who gave her a glance and an almost imperceptible quirk of her lip, but it was enough to let her know she'd been caught. Crap, she knew she wouldn't hear the end of this one. Either Liv would tease her to no end and continue to push her toward this man who had no real interest in her. Or, and maybe this would be the better scenario, she would see that this guy was not for her and turn into the Olivia of old and admonish her more for being foolish and falling back on her old ways, crushing after a clearly unavailable — at least to her — man that she was in a working relationship with. Been there done that and didn't even end up with a T-shirt for her troubles. Of course, then she'd get on her about focusing and finding her direction in life once and for all. Not that her sister would be in any way wrong for her talk or her thinking at all. It would be last year all over again.

As a matter of fact, as she was thinking earlier, a part of Drea would welcome it.

Just as she understood her parents now starting to put the pressure on her, she could use a bit more. This little Southern sojourn had seen its course played out. Even she could admit it was time for her to make a proverbial move or get the heck off the pot, so to speak.

"So," Clayton continued, "about the Redheart. What's happening with it?"

Kellen looked at her and gave a nod, seeming to defer to her to comment, which Drea didn't know if she should take as him being gracious or as some type of trap on his behalf. She knew she shouldn't be so suspicious, but couldn't help it. Seeming to sense her caution, he spoke up. "Since I'm lagging behind in the initial talks for the theater, I'll let Drea here tell you. It would seem she and my grandmother have come up with quite the plan."

Drea nodded. "Quite, huh? Don't gush now, Suit. I wouldn't want you to pull a muscle."

He shot her a quick side-eye, but instead of speaking stuffed his mouth with a bite of corn bread.

Drea looked to Clayton and smiled. She could've imagined it, but no, she felt Kellen stiffen even more beside her. "I wouldn't describe the renovations as quite," she said, "but more in lines of a grand restoration. Something that is much needed to bring the Redheart up to the standards of today and push it forward into the future. Actually, it's only a tiny bit of me involved. I'm purely there making suggestions, really."

Kellen coughed and Drea immediately leaned over and gave him a hard smack in the middle of his back, not breaking stride in her conversation. "Like I was say-ing, I'm pretty much just there to bring form to Mrs. Betty's vision. We want to update all that is in sore need of updating: the concession and lobby area, carpeting, the screen possibly, and probably the screening equipment."

"All that?" Clayton asked, astonishment in his voice. "Geez, when we were last there the old girl looked good to me."

"That's what I say," Kellen said from Drea's side, and she shot him a look.

"Honey, you're not helping any," Liv interjected out of the corner of her mouth. Her voice was light, but still Drea was thankful for the bit of sisterly solidarity.

She gave Liv a slight nod before continuing. "Plus, we'd like to add in party and craft rooms where there is space, to make the theater not just a stop-by place but more of a community destination. I think an addition of an out-back mini amphitheater may do just that. It will be great for small, outdoor community plays. A different and more artistic venue than, say, the school auditorium."

She watched as Liv's eyes lit up; she could tell her sister was seeing her vision, and even Clayton nodded in agreement. She looked over and the rest of their eyes followed suit to see Kellen looking poker faced, stoic. You couldn't tell if he was holding an ace-high straight or pair of fours. Not that it mattered; Drea knew his intentions.

But it was Clayton who would speak again, making her wonder if he knew what Kellen was brewing. "You're right, that is quite the endeavor, Kellen, and I can tell you're a little hesitant. But it all sounds terrific for the community. It would be a shame to see the Redheart close. It's sad how many of the local businesses already have left and moved out of town just to be closer to the multiplex at the mall. Not that I don't get their reasoning, but if there was a wonderful gathering spot right here in Sugar Lake, just maybe we could keep more of the small town feel we've come to love right here. I for one miss the old businesses that have left, and if we had more top local amenities in town besides just the country club, we'd be able to keep more tax dollars right here in Sugar Lake proper."

She could tell Kellen wanted to say something but was hesitant, but then Liv chimed in teasingly, "Says the honey-harvesting beekeeping firefighter." She reached a hand out and stroked at Clayton's clearly freshly-shaven-for-their-date chin, and goodness help him, Drea might send her next kick in this grown man's direction, as her sister brought a blush to his deep brown cheeks.

She pulled a face, and shifted her gaze. With nowhere to go but the wall or in the Suit's direction, their eyes locked. He swallowed and so did she. Quickly, she turned her attention to Liv and Clayton, and noticed the two of them were like two spectators at a show they didn't order tickets for.

"Seriously, neither of you are lovesick teens anymore. It's not cute."

They both laughed as Shelby came with the food. "Okay, no more of that," Drea said. "This is serious business time. None of that funny stuff that will go and have me losing my appetite."

"As if you would," Liv chimed back.

Eh, she was right. Not even the Suit could get her off course in this moment. They were about to enter barbecue lovers' nirvana and she was ready for the full-on experience. Ribs and chicken, mac and cheese, the type with the perfect ratio of cheese to mac so that you weren't too little or too much in one direction or another. At Jolie's, magically, though condiments were on the table, she'd never reached for salt or pepper; everything was perfectly seasoned. The only thing she'd ever seen patrons do was play around with which hot sauce to add to the perfectly seasoned meat: Trappey's, Red Hot, or Tabasco for the purists.

Even though the Suit was beside her, Drea quickly forgot about his nearness, her awkwardness, and focused all her attention on the plate of ribs and chicken in front of her.

Boots could eat and Kellen found he enjoyed watching her do so. Unlike any of his other dates, though this was clearly not a date, watching her gave him a sense of total relaxation. Like he didn't have to be on. Whenever he was out with other women, be it for business or pleasure — and let's face it both seemed interchangeable — it felt like either he or both of them were on a job interview. You must order the right thing, eat the proper way, drink the precise amount in order to leave the perfect impression.

There was none of that with Drea. It was refreshing to see how she didn't put on some sort of show for him, though why would she want to with the way he'd been acting toward her? Kellen paused at that thought and looked at her, smiling as she tipped her tongue out and licked an errant bit of sauce from the corner of her mouth.

He snorted to himself as he looked back at his own plate and she laughed at something her sister had said. Yeah, why would she put on a show for him? He was definitely not her type and she, with her free spirit, not his. A man like him could never be open enough for a woman like her.

But for now they were stuck together. At least until this project or his deal or both were done, Kellen thought in between delicious bites of rib, slaw, and macaroni. Though he wouldn't want to share with his grandmother and admit defeat, he was surprised at how the evening was evolving. So far Clayton was turning out to be good company. Though they weren't the best of friends growing up, he was an all right guy. Besides, he wasn't the worst back in their school days. Unlike some of the rest, he'd let him be himself and to himself. Which was all he'd wanted out of his years in Sugar Lake after coming here after his parents died. Not a jock, or a nerd, or a drama kid. Just himself without any forced-on extras or pushed upon friends.

So, Kellen guessed he shouldn't be surprised Clayton turned out cool and interesting with his side honey business and a nice woman on his arm. If anyone deserved that he supposed Clayton did. It was nice to see how excited he was when he talked about his business and its possible future growth. Even more exciting than that was the clear faith Drea's sister had in him and his dreams, and the way he supported her and her future at Goode 'N Sweet too.

Kellen spared a quick glance Boots' way. And he was thankful to Clayton for being here and keeping the conversation going. It kept him from having to talk. All he had to do was nod and chew. For the life of him, he didn't understand why his grandma thought this dinner was a good idea. The fact that she and Miss Joyce went to Pentagon-level strategy sessions to make sure this little foursome dinner happened after he'd shown his reluctance at the bakery that morning spoke to how much they must have wanted it.

And he knew what happened when his grandmother wanted something. Mountains. Moved. He was amazed at how much he'd completely underestimated the craftiness of his grandmother.

It wasn't as if he didn't know she was shrewd; growing up with her he knew the woman, but in all his years he'd mostly seen her as sweet, kindly, loving, and mainly a bit of a flibbertigibbet, for lack of a better word, but it was one she used often to describe herself, saying she liked the way it rolled off her tongue in the most unexpected way. At times he thought, as he took his first bite in way too long of Jolie's delicious ribs, maybe his grandmother liked being unexpected. He slid another glance toward Boots — she was laughing and chewing despite him next to her and their awkward start to the evening. He chewed as he thought. She too, like his grandmother, was quite unexpected.

Just then, right as they were so very close to finishing their meal and he was almost in the clear of getting out of there having fulfilled his obligation for the night, there was their server, Shelby, with what he couldn't quite call a smile. She gave them a nod as she held another pitcher of beer and Joy Juice, saying it was compliments of none other than Caleb Morris. Which, judging by the expression on Clayton's face, surprised him just as much as it did Kellen.

"Fantastic! I wasn't quite ready to call it a night anyway," Liv said.

At that, Clayton's mood seemed to shift, and he turned to Liv. "Oh really? Don't you have pies with your name on them in the morning?"

She waved a hand, then shrugged. "There are always pies with my name on them. But we're out now and the night is still young."

Clayton raised a brow. "Does that mean I might get you on the bull again?"

Kellen almost laughed seeing Boots' sister's expression turn to horror. "You wish! No way."

"As if. You know there's no way she's doing that again. Once was enough to get her man. I'd say the bull did its job."

"Hardly!" Liv protested.

"What do you mean hardly? I'm here, aren't I? Saved the damsel from the terrible steed and all that."

Olivia rolled her eyes. "You really are pushing it, Clayton Morris. You act like I was in distress or as if I needed saving. It was just a little mechanical bull and it's not as if, in the nearly year since I've been here, I've heard or seen any such proof of you being some expert rider."

Clayton opened his mouth, then Kellen noticed he smartly closed it again.

Drea started to laugh before taking a rib in hand again as her sister turned her way. "What are you laughing about? It wasn't as if you were so hot on the bull either."

"Well," Drea started, using her waving hands for punctuation, "I made it a good five seconds or more than you tw—" and before the end of the expected *two* the rib slipped from her hand, landing with a splat and sending sauce splattering onto Kellen's cheek, his glasses, and the collar of his shirt.

Seriously?

He looked over at her, pulling off his glasses and wiping them with his napkin, but of course, he only made the sauce smudges worse. *Smooth, Kel. Very smooth.*

"Did you just really?" he said, looking into her surprised eyes.

Boots gave him an embarrassed grimace that had a dangerous hint at a smile on the end of it as she reached a hand out toward his face. As her thumb stroked his cheek and made its way forward, slipping to the corner of his mouth, Kellen jumped back, not from fear of her, no, it was from the immediate zing of electricity that went from his mouth to his chest, taking him unceremoniously over the edge of the small booth's bench and onto the floor. Wham!

And that's where he was, solidly on his

ass when Griffin Nash walked over and looked down at him. As if the likes of Griffin Nash should ever be looking down at him or him looking up at Griffin Nash from this particular angle.

"Gee, I sure hadn't had you pegged as one who couldn't handle your beer, Mr. Kilborn. But then again you have been spending a lot of time in the city," Griffin said.

Kellen's eyes shot back up. Wait just a minute, did he . . . just? Kellen attempted to get up gracefully, but that was darn near impossible from where he was, with one leg on the bench, the other under the table. Drea came scrambling over the top of him, her lithe body wiggling up his leg. *Jeez, Boots, who does these types of things?*

"I'm sorry," she said, reaching out to give him a hand before noticing that her own hands still had a good amount of barbecue sauce on them as she pulled back. Kellen shook his head. It was a smiling Clayton who eventually came to his rescue, though he was sure his reputation was forever sullied having to be rescued at all. He'd just leave it there, on the floor of Jolie's with the discarded peanut hulls to be swept up later that night.

He gave a nod to Clayton and slid a side-eye to Griffin. "Don't worry about what I can handle, Mr. Nash. I've got everything under control." Kellen turned to the table and wiped his hands as best he could, looking over at Olivia, not trusting himself to look at Boots just yet. He still felt the sting where she had touched him on the corner of his mouth. "If you'll excuse me, I'll just go and clean up quick and I'll be back in a moment. Sorry for the" — he looked at Drea, catching the apology in her eyes though he swore it was hidden behind the fact that she was holding back a peal of laughter — "disturbance."

Kellen tried hard to hold on to what little bit of cool he had left as he made his way to the men's room. Everything in him said to make a beeline out the front door, turn right, get in his car, and drive the heck home. He'd had his fill and then some of being cordial. But as he cleared up the trail of red sauce from the side of his cheek and in vain tried to get rid of the stain from the collar of his shirt, the image of Griffin, with his perfect teeth and bulging muscles and leering eyes, came to his mind. Then it hit him. The way she'd instinctively moved away from him in the theater. It was probably nothing, but there was no way he was heading home before making sure that Boots had found her way home first. Kellen let out a breath. What a ridiculous thought. He only just met the woman days ago. It was clear from the interaction at the theater earlier that she and Griffin Nash had a history. If he'd not come into town, and this old theater thing hadn't started, what difference would it make, him bringing her home tonight or not? Kellen's frown went deeper. None. It wouldn't make a bit of difference, just like it shouldn't make any difference now. It wasn't like he had anything going on with her. It wasn't like she needed him interfering with any part of her life. He shrugged and headed back out to say his good-byes to Clayton and Olivia and head home.

On the way out he locked eyes with Caleb Morris. He hadn't seen the older Morris brother in a long time. He'd been kind enough to stop by the viewing and pay his respects to his grandmother, give Kellen a quick handshake, but, as per his usual reclusive way, like a ghost he was gone. Not that Kellen blamed him for not wanting to hang around for the gathering of mourners with tall tales of the Henry Kilborn they knew and loved. Hell, not even Kellen wanted to be there for that, so there was no way he expected the reclusive Morris brother to stay on. No, the only place one saw Caleb Morris, if he was to be seen, was during his shift at Jolie's, where he was known to be a man of few words who knew how to pour a good drink. Beyond that, there was nothing much more to know.

A big difference from the popular, all-star reputation Caleb had had when they were kids looking up to him in high school, Kellen thought, taking a quick glimpse at Caleb's prosthetic limb. But that was high school, when they were children, so they'd best leave those things behind as the saying went.

He reached into his pocket to leave Caleb a tip when the bearded vet held up said hand. "Now, don't go starting, Kilborn. It was just a pitcher of beer. No need flashing your money this way. It's not going to impress me."

Kellen pulled a face, then shook his head. "I was just going to leave a tip. But fine, and who said anything about impressing anybody?"

Caleb shrugged, then laughed. "Okay then. I was just stopping you before you went and made a mistake. A gift is a gift. You rich folks sometimes have a hard time accepting when others are just being nice."

Oh, there you go. "I was accepting it. This is me. Coming by to say hi and thanks for the round."

Caleb gave him what he supposed would pass for a smile up in the woods where he hid out. "Well, you're welcome. I must admit I was surprised to see you come in here. It's not like Jolie's is your type of place. I'd think the country club is more up to your dating standards."

Kellen felt a huff coming on, but held it back. "Who says I'm on a date? I'm just hanging out."

Caleb nodded, distracted by a couple of girls who came in; they were young, early twenties probably, and all full of smiles and waves his way as they took a perch at a round table with a view of the bar. He gave them a quick nod.

"Looks like you have it pretty good here," Kellen said.

"It's a job," Caleb replied in a noncommittal way, then added, "So Drea Goode, huh?"

Kellen frowned. "Huh?"

Caleb smiled. "Oh, those Goode girls. And you're seriously saying you're not on a date?"

"No," Kellen spoke up quickly. "I'm not. She's doing some work for my grandmother at the theater, so we're essentially on a project together."

Caleb nodded as Kellen's frown went deeper. What, did Boots have admirers all over Sugar Lake? Suddenly Caleb put up his hands. "Oh no, I wasn't thinking anything, not that it would matter to you. I was just wondering about old Griff there, saddling over into your spot."

Zeroing in on their booth, Kellen turned so fast that for a moment he thought he'd given himself whiplash. Where were Clayton and Olivia? Why was their side empty and why was wrench-head Griffin Nash wedged into his spot, sitting way too close to Boots and right over his leftover ribs, no less!

"But since you're just working together, I guess it doesn't matter. . . ." he heard Caleb say as he started to walk toward the booth mumbling something about thanks and catching up soon.

"Excuse me, Nash, but I believe I was sitting there?" It was a statement posed as a question that he knew with just one glance at his hardened expression, Griffin Nash should know he didn't need to answer. All he needed to do was get up.

But stupid kid that Nash was — and he really was turning out to be not at all smart — he had the nerve to look at Kellen, his possible future employer, and let his eyes linger on the leftover sauce on his shirt

234

before he said, "There's plenty of room on the other side of the booth. I think Clayton and Liv went to take a spin around the dance floor. Feel free to park it."

Kellen cocked his head to the side, for a moment stunned at the clear dismissal and that he felt every muscle in his body tighten with the overwhelming need to pummel the young jerk. But he took a breath. Why should he want to go and do that? Why should he care? He'd walked away for what, maybe four minutes, and in that time, Boots had let the muscle-headed jerk cozy up next to her in his spot, a spot he really didn't want to be in, no less. He let out a bored sigh. If his grandmother hadn't put him in this awkward situation, he could be in his comfortable apartment right now. Having finished a good workout, shower, and a steam. Things should be well on their way to solidified with RPG and he and Kilborn Properties well on their way up. He should not be marred in rib sauce, dealing with upstart pinheads or annoying waitresses with delusions of grandeur.

He looked around. Trying to make out Clayton and Olivia on the crowded dance floor across the other side of the bar. He'd just settle up with Clayton and be on his way. He'd had enough catching up for one night. Boots had her sister here, more than enough willing participants to the show that was her. He was sure she would find her way home. She'd be fine.

Not quite seeing them, Kellen turned back to the table to leave a few bills and make his way out. "Listen, tell Cla—" he started just as he noticed the clear look of discomfort on Boots' face. And this was not her usual discomfort that came with being around him. No, that discomfort was more like a mild annoyance — okay, it was irritation maybe, the kind that came when a gnat kept whirling around you. With this it was different. Right now, she looked downright mad. And he didn't like it. Not one bit. If anyone was going to make Boots mad tonight it was going to be him.

"Excuse me, Nash. Like I said, you're in my spot. And I don't recall saying I was done there." Kellen leaned over close to Griffin's face. His light eyes meeting Griffin's dark ones. His mouth a flat line as he fought to keep his breathing slow and steady. Griffin stood, trying his best to keep steady eye contact, eventually failing, and only then did Kellen finally tilt his head and smile. It was a smile that he knew conveyed anything but pleasure. "But thanks for keeping it warm for me."

As Griffin walked away, Kellen sat back down and pushed his plate away. Thankfully there'd been only two ribs left before the fiasco. "Guess I won't be having those now."

"I'm sorry about him and the mess on your shirt," Drea said before she waved a hand at his plate. "And ruining the rest of your dinner."

Kellen looked at her. The apology was somehow a surprise. Not for the shirt — she'd already apologized for that — but for Griffin Nash. There was no need to apologize for that jerk. "You already apologized for the shirt. Don't worry about it. I'm sure with a good washing the stain will come out."

"Yeah, but it looks expensive."

He laughed. "It doesn't look expensive. It's just a white shirt."

She gave him a side-eye and he was glad to see her posture change considerably. His Boots was back. Kellen squelched back a reaction. The same old Boots was back. There was no way she was his Boots. But still it was nice to see the side-eye had returned. He was starting to miss it. That weird edgy thing they were doing was getting weird.

"Well, you look expensive." She clapped her hand over her mouth and looked to the left and then the right. "Wait, that didn't come out good at all, but you know what I meant."

"No, it didn't, and I don't," he said. "Was that supposed to be some sort of compliment, because if so, it didn't come out that way."

"Well . . ." She started to pick up her glass, clearly stalling for time as she searched for the words.

She was cute. Cute in that effortless way that had him thinking thoughts that he probably shouldn't be thinking at all. But he couldn't seem to help himself with the way she was sitting there fiddling with her little straw, clearly in that moment trying her best not to make eye contact with him. Fiddle twirl, twirl fiddle, finally she took the straw out, set it on the napkin on the table beside her plate, and she picked up her glass and took a long gulp of the red concoction that had so many flocking to Jolie's Bar and Grill. Her lovely full lips in that moment looked more sensuous and kissable than he felt comfortable with. It made him slightly nervous, her having a chance to think her words over. Because if he knew Boots, her having too much time to think would only make the next words that much more dangerous for him.

Just then, the tempo of the music changed and the bar let out a collective cheer. Boots looked over at him and gave him a bright smile. "Ugh," she moaned, which was so counterintuitive to her smile that it threw him off. "It's a line dance; I hate line dances. But if there's one thing I've come to know being in this town for the past year, if we don't participate, they end up grabbing us one way or another. Come on, let's go."

Suddenly she was pushing at him to get out of the booth, her little hands much stronger than he anticipated, practically sending them over the edge and onto the floor once again.

"Wait a minute," Kellen said, whirling around on her. "I can't stand line dances either. As a matter of fact, I'm not into dancing at all. Come on. We've done our time. Why don't we just pay the bill and I'll take you back to your car. We can go."

Her disappointed look made him instantly regret his blunt words. "I can't leave before I say good-bye to my sister," she said. "And she's somewhere out on the dance floor. It's not like I can very well go out there by myself, right?" She looked around and visions of Griffin and more of his ilk two-stepping all up on her filled his mind.

He shook his head. "Fine," he said, taking her hand, purposely ignoring how perfectly it fit in his. "Let's go, but realize you're not fooling anyone with this I-don't-like-line-dancing act," he said, seeing how quickly and smoothly she slid into line and step with the rest of the crowd. "You may be a New Yorker, Boots, but your feet and hips are two stepping like a true Southern girl."

He watched as her face scrunched up. "Is that supposed to be some sort of compliment?" she yelled at him over the music.

He shrugged as he fell into step with her. "Take it however you want. It wasn't an insult. I'll tell you that much."

The slight smile she gave him left him questioning what thoughts she had going on in that head of hers.

"That's okay, Ray. I'm fine right here."

"What kind of gentleman would I be if I dropped the lady off without walking her to her door?"

Betty looked at Ray Nash, with his perfectly nice smile that she was sure was courtesy of Dr. Levitz over at Eastshore. She took in his fit-for-his-age body, thanks to a no doubt low-cholesterol, low-sodium diet courtesy of Dr. Jones over at EastMed in Augusta, and worst of all his perfectly

240

nice, soft eyes, full of awful condolences, and she couldn't wait to bolt from his pickup truck.

She knew she was making a mistake when she'd agreed to a ride home from him this evening. But Ray was an old friend and a widower himself going on over fifteen years. Ray's wife passed away suddenly way before her prime, leaving Ray alone to raise their four boys. Being widowed fairly young, for better or worse, and poor Ray would probably say it was worse, made him one of the over fifty prime, eligible bachelors of Sugar Lake. She could almost laugh at it now, and in those days, she used to laugh at it quite a bit. Poor Henry and some of the guys used to be quite the buffer for saving Ray from the advances of just about every eligible woman in and out of the church between the ages of twenty-five and fifty-five. Every mama wanted to set up her eligible daughter and every daughter had her sights on him for their mama. Ray Nash and his handy hands were in high demand.

But he'd made it these years without being snapped up. And here he was, still single with only a few scars, dalliances, and broken hearts in his wake. And now though, he had the nerve to be all smiles and talking about walking her to her door. As if they were two young'uns and she was someone who should be door walked?

Goodness, if she hadn't been so determined to get Kellen out with Alexandrea tonight, she wouldn't be in this position. Not that she was in a position — it was Ray Nash — but still, she just didn't like the feeling.

"That's okay, Ray. I'm fine. I'm a big girl now," she said, reaching for the door handle at the same time that Ray came running around to her side of the cab. She shook her head as she took his hand getting down and gave him a double pat on the shoulder. "Thanks a lot, now you get along. I can show myself into my own house just fine."

Ray gave her a nod as his eyes seemed to soften more, the moonlight catching them glistening in the darkness. "You sure you're all right, Bet? I do worry about you. I know that you come off as awfully strong for such a tiny little thing. And you are tough, I'll give you that, but you don't have to be strong all the time. This is me talking to you as a friend. It's been many years since I lost Nita but, truth be told, not a day goes by that it doesn't still feel raw."

In that moment, she saw a little bit of Ray that she'd never seen in all her years of knowing him. Maybe it was something he never showed his friends, or maybe he just never showed her, and it was only something he possibly shared with Henry. A certain vulnerability, a loneliness that looked very much like the reflection she saw in the mirror after she washed her own face at night. Betty swallowed. "Oh Ray, I understand. Maybe for the first time, I really do."

With one last look at him, she climbed the stairs to the front door feeling more tired than she had in a long time, but Betty was careful not to show any of her exhaustion until Ray had turned and she had given him what she hoped passed for a bright smile that gave away none of her true feelings. Closing the door behind herself, Betty was struck once again by the eerie silence of her large home. Coming home used to be such a thrill for her when she was newly with Henry. The two of them would frolic through their great big house, making plans on how they would fill it, and working hard in the early years to see those plans come to fruition. Betty, even at her age, had the nerve to smile to herself and blush just thinking of it. She flipped on the light and let out a sigh. She considered going through to the kitchen and thought against it, instead making a right and heading up the stairs to her bedroom. She was tired; it had been a long day. Her appetite was long gone. Besides, she was full enough, with the hope that Kellen was down at Jolie's with Alex getting to know her and hopefully igniting the sparks of newfound love, as she had planned.

CHAPTER 13
HUSH, HUSH, SWEET BOOTS

That was it; she was done with Jolie's Joy Juice. Drea groaned to herself when four thirty came around way too quickly the next morning and Aunt Joyce was as chipper as a newborn baby bird. Her voice calling her to wake up, get a move on, and the pies don't wait for nobody crackled through the air.

Had it really been her idea to pull the Suit out on the dance floor the night before? How was she supposed to know that the guy was a freaking two-step master? Out there shimmying like he was Luke Bryan, or a K-pop boy group member gone country. Drea saw her reflection in the mirror and shook her head at her sorry state. Eyes red and puffy, skin blotchy from too much to drink, she let out a sigh and patted at her cheeks with a splash of cold water, hoping to revive the tired skin. With her luck, the dancing machine would probably be at

Goode 'N Sweet right at the crack of 6:47 looking pressed to perfection, waiting and ready for his morning coffee.

"Come on, turtle, let's go. I came up with the most fantastic idea for a new pie combo last night. 'Shake-It-Till-You-Make-It Chocolate Caramel Peach Turtle Delight.' "

Drea gave Liv a sneer. The turtle part added to the name of the pie she knew was a direct comment on their little foursome last night. She was so stunned at seeing how the Suit had transformed once he got on the dance floor that for a moment she was struck positively stock-still. She was supposed to be the one with the dance training. But still, he had good moves. Just thinking about it gave her a shiver. Drea was shocked by his quick feet and smooth hips. When he turned to her after a particularly tricky cha-cha and gave her an unexpected roguish wink, Drea's jaw positively dropped to the floor.

Thank goodness the nudge from Liv pulled her out of her stupor. "Okay, turtle, time to come out of your shell and get to dancing. And you're not going to let the Suit show you up, now are you?" It was then that she finally started to have a good time. For the first time in Sugar Lake, Drea had let her hair down and really let go with the person she'd least expected.

But all too quickly, the fun and the easiness of the night had ended. With the change of beats, along with the change of songs, the line dance was over and all of a sudden folks were coupling all two by two on the dance floor. Drea and Kellen were staring at each other in awkward silence. Why did the DJ choose then to head back to a 70s smooth Barry White tune? The song was all bass, from the guitar to the percussions to his deep melodic voice, and that coupled with the Suit's light eyes was nothing but a recipe for disaster.

Drea shrugged and nodded toward the door. "So, about us heading out . . . this seems about as good a time as any," she said.

"Oh no, not yet," Liv chimed in from over Drea's shoulder, and though Drea tried as inconspicuously as she could to kick her, arcing her leg out behind her, her darned sister was too quick, dipping out of the way, swaying into her boyfriend's arms. She laughed. "After this song, we can all head out together. I agree, it's getting late, but let's just get in one more. This has been fun."

Yes, this is as much fun as going to the guillotine, or maybe not, Drea thought as she had awkwardly stepped into the waiting arms of her not-quite boss.

"Knock knock!" The words were accompanied by a loud rapping on the door, bringing Drea out of her thoughts and into the present. "Seriously, turtle, let's go before Aunt Joyce has a conniption fit downstairs. You know her motto."

Drea gave her sister a nod and let out a sigh. "Yeah, yeah."

They looked at each other and laughed, then said in unison, "The pies wait for no one."

Where in the heck was he? Drea thought again at 7:45 when the Suit still hadn't materialized at Goode 'N Sweet that morning. Though she hated to admit it, she'd gotten used to his early morning visits. As tired as she was, she still managed to have the shop open only one minute after she thought he'd be outside lingering at 6:48. But no, he wasn't there. Drea stuck her head out in the predawn light looking up and down the block; seeing no sign of him or his bike, she shrugged and assumed that maybe he'd show a few minutes later doing his punctual 7 o'clock thing. But when he didn't show then and still no sign of him at 7:30, she'd wondered what had gotten into him.

Sure, it was awkward as hell; but at the same time, at least to her, it also felt way too right. So, she'd endured — if enduring it was something like melting into the man's chest like a rocket ice pop on a concrete sidewalk in August. Then yeah, she'd endured it just fine. But still she'd had to. It was their one and only R & B slow jam dance. When would she ever get another chance with the Suit out on the dance floor like that? It was like ticking off an item from her hopeful romantically unobtainable bucket list. Slow Dance with a Stuffy Guy You Have No Chance of a Future With. Check.

As far as bucket list tick-offs went, they'd made it through beautifully. At least she thought they had. His moves were surprisingly smooth, which made her wonder if Mrs. Betty had him take dance lessons when he was a kid. She would so be the type. Possibly for cotillions or some such tradition. And Drea was careful during the dance not to look into his eyes, but only stare at a strong jawline and that tendon in his neck that seemed to throb in such a way that it made her want to lean forward and bite it. Drea swallowed instead, willing her heart to slow down and stop beating at such an erratic pace, willing the song to speed up and get over with so she could let go of his strong hands, step out of his embrace, and get back to herself already.

By the time he dropped her off back at the car, she was a bundle of nerves and wanted to smack him for being as cool as he was.

Kellen was hungry. No, he was cranky. No, he was hungry and he was cranky, he thought as he stood on a ladder in front of the marquee bar changing the sign from THE WAY WE WERE to CLOSED FOR RENOVATIONS. He told himself, as the local town handyman, Errol, tossed him up letters, that his sign changing was in no way an acquiescence to his grandmother's bidding. He also told himself that this in no way had anything to do with Alexandrea Gale or their little dance the night before. But one thing was for sure, his hunger and his crankiness had something to do with both those parties.

He wondered if she wondered where he was that morning since he hadn't shown at Goode 'N Sweet for his usual breakfast. He told himself he had every intention of doing so when he woke up at five thirty a.m. after having finally gone to sleep at three. He told himself it was because he got tied up in his work going over his new proposal for the

Ronson Group and a few other smaller prospectuses that they were working on for other companies. Sure, he said, that was the reason why at seven a.m. he was still in his own kitchen sipping on drip coffee that didn't quite measure up, munching on a toasted bagel that definitely didn't measure up to what was waiting on him at Goode 'N Sweet. But the reality was, while going over his meeting notes and prospectuses his mind kept wandering back to the night before and how ridiculously perfect Alexandrea Gale felt in his arms as they danced.

He had to get over these feelings and quick if he was ever going to accomplish what he wanted to do. Kellen placed the final *S* and let out a sigh. Closed for renovations. But what was he really trying to accomplish? Was he there to actually renovate or excavate? He needed to make up his mind about it and quick. Being a man of a torn mind did not suit him at all, so to speak.

And speaking of torn, as if on cue, there she was. Kellen was just about off the ladder, almost taking his last step, when he saw her. He didn't exactly see her fully, not enough to make out all of her features, since she was silhouetted by the sun at her back, but he'd recognize her at fifty paces with just a glance now. Long and lean every-where, her arms bare and swinging in that effortless graceful, dancer-like way she moved. Like a woman at one with her body, coming toward him, her legs taking long strides in jeans that accentuated every lean curve. He groaned. Get a grip, Kel. This road had a clear dead-end sign on it and he was the one who'd put it up. Why was he even thinking this way? Still, she did make for a pretty view as she made her way from Goode 'N Sweet to the Redheart.

Kellen's foot hit the pavement then, just as her face came fully into view, and for the first time he caught her hard expression. It pulled him up short. Oh boy, she was com-ing at him hard today with dagger eyes and her lips in a firm grimace. His mind did a quick replay of the date/not date last night, and though it had been a tangled ball of awkwardness, it ended congenially enough. But had he gone too far by not showing up at the bakery this morning? What would it matter to her seeing him or not at the crack of dawn? Kellen made a quick dismissal of the idea that she could have actually been expecting him this morning. But before he could even ask, the answer came from her lips after she'd flipped on a dime, bestowing the most radiant smile on ol' Errol before her smile completely disappeared when she turned back to him. "So, where were you this morning? Sleep in and . . . ? Don't tell me a guy like you can't handle a night with a little Joy Juice and dancing. Here I thought you had more of a fighting spirit," she said, tossing long braids over one shoulder and turning away from him to head into the theater. He reached out and grabbed at her wrist, turning her back toward him.

"Don't worry about me, I've got more than enough fight to spare."

She shot him challenging eyes as she pulled her wrist from his grasp. "Did you say fight or bite? Because I've got more than enough in me too, Suit."

Kellen felt a smile tug at his lips. All that fight talk had him surmising he loved the fight in her. It pulled him in while keeping him at the distance he needed.

He found her twenty minutes later up in the wreck of the archives room already waist deep in film reels, dust, and boxes. Actually, she was more than waist deep since she was using precariously stacked boxes to get to something on one of the shelves way up high and her motorcycle boots looked like they were going to slip at any moment.

Kellen went hopping over three boxes and a stack of reels, catching her just in time as she landed in his arms, looking up at him with a shocked expression.

"Are you out of your mind? Do I have to ban you and these boots from this room? It's like every time you're in here it's a disaster."

Her mouth, wide in an *O,* was open, but quickly turned flat as she pushed at him, hard in his chest. "As if!" she yelled, going to stand upright. "You can't ban me from anything or anywhere. Your grandmother said I had free rein around here to get this place in shape and that means you can't stop me."

"Well, la-di-da," he replied, then pulled a face.

"I'll say," she struck back. "And don't you sound mature. La-di-da indeed."

Kellen let out a growl. What was he going to do with her? What had he done to deserve a woman like her coming into his life at a pivotal time like this? It couldn't be more inconvenient. Kellen ran a frustrated hand over his scalp and looked up. "What were you trying to get at up there, anyway?"

She smiled. "Oh, I thought I saw a copy of *Splendor in the Grass* up here on the 1960s shelf and I wanted to get it down."

"What the heck for? It's not like you're

going to watch it now, and besides, who cares?"

She made a face and waved her arms in the air. "Who cares? How can you say who cares? It's Natalie Wood and Warren Beatty's debut. When he was at his hottest."

She coughed and threw her shoulder back, her voice deepening. "I — I was just kidding," she started, then put her hands over her face only to slowly remove them, her eyes taking on a bright sheen of sadness reminiscent of Natalie Wood and days long gone by as she blinked at him with an expression that seemed to reach in and attempt to tear his heart apart. "I can't kid about things, because I'm . . . I'm . . ."

Kellen found it hard to breathe, and the lump in his throat made swallowing an impossibility. She blinked and in an instant, she changed again, her smile going wide as she once again seemed to be back to her true self. ". . . bonkers about you!" she finished.

He let out a breath as she once again flubbed the line. The quick change gave him just the amount of space he needed to come back to himself. Did she know how very necessary it was? However, with the quick flip of Boots' off and on switch, Kellen suddenly wasn't sure who her true self was.

"Don't tell me you haven't seen this one," she said. "It's a total classic."

He frowned. "I don't know. I think I did, but I hardly remember it," he replied, the lie rolling off his tongue for reasons he couldn't fathom. How could he forget the impact of a young Natalie Wood in a tub having a complete meltdown? The scene was so memorable that it was still etched in his cinematic memory and, with Drea's little two-second Natalie homage, he suddenly could way too easily imagine her in some such similar scenario.

"Well then, we should watch it or rewatch it together!"

His eyes widened in shock just as his phone buzzed.

She looked around the room, the sadness in her eyes so great it was like it could be measured. "It would be a shame to have all these treasures just boxed up. They should be viewed."

She let out a sigh. "Viewing all of these will take more time than I'm sure either of us has."

His phone buzzed again, and he pulled it out, checking the screen. Jamina Ronson. Perfect timing. Why was he even having this discussion with Boots right now? If he wanted the RPG deal to happen, he needed to find a way to clear out inventory, not catalog it for viewing.

He looked at Boots. "Listen, I need to take this. Just start making piles. But low shelves only," he said, pointing at her, then clicking over his phone and putting it to his ear. "No climbing!" he warned.

"Oh my, aren't you getting ahead of yourself, Mr. Kilborn," Jamina purred into his ear.

Kellen let out a slow breath, and as if on autopilot he forced a smile as he went out into the hallway to walk as swiftly as he could away from what he thought was Boots humming an 80s disco R & B classic. He shook his head when he heard talk of men pausing coming from her lips. The woman's vintage catalog, when it came to pop culture, was astounding.

"I'm sorry. I wasn't talking to you, Jamina," he said, making his voice as placating as possible.

"I should hope not. I mean, there are those who welcome a good climbing from me. Not to mention I'm in fantastic physical shape. Why, I made Mount Evans my plaything and I'm not talking about that little drive-up route either. The real fourteener."

Kellen laughed as he made it to the end

of the hall, Boots' voice nothing more than a low murmur floating through the air. He was sure, or at least moderately sure, that Jamina couldn't hear her. "I don't doubt it, Jamina." Of course she'd do the fourteener as the expert climbers did. "Now, to what do I owe this call?"

"Well, Kellen, to say I was upset to hear that you won't be making RPG's event the Saturday after next is an understatement. What could be so important that you can't attend? I had you down as one of my special guests and was hoping to introduce you to some of our more influential investors."

Dammit. When he'd told Tracy to cancel all his social events and reschedule his meetings for the next two weeks until he could get a handle on things in Sugar Lake, he'd forgotten about the RPG event. His grandmother was making progress in this deal bad enough. He didn't need to contribute to the quick demise of it. And of course, here was Jamina calling with just the right carrot to dangle his way in the form of investors. Suddenly his grandmother came to mind — her with Ray Nash and her grand plans, which immediately had his mind shifting to Griffin Nash, sitting in his place when he'd returned to his booth the night before.

"I'm sorry, Jamina. I'm here in Sugar Lake right now taking care of personal family business." It's not like he could very well tell her he was currently working on a project for his grandmother that was completely counter to Jamina's own interests. That would essentially take him out of the running with the acreage deal he wanted to do with her on the other Kilborn land.

It was the Kilborns, the Dawsons, the Haneses, the Sharps, the Hepburns, and the Pomeroys who were the largest landowners in the Sugar Lake area. But it was only the Kilborns who had, one, the most land and two, the land that was the closest to buildable on the lake ridge with the best views. Sure, the Sharps came in second, but clearing their land would be hell and he was sure getting clearance, while not impossible, would be difficult since it would change the natural landscape more than he was sure the town council was comfortable with. Virgil Dawson, on the other hand, had a good amount of property, similar to the Haneses, but both farmed on their land and were not likely to budge. Which only left the Hepburns and the Pomeroys. The Hepburns were probably out since they had been leasing a large parcel of their land to the cable company and a local cell company and were not likely to let go of that deal. And the Pomeroys could be moved, but their land wasn't nearly as buildable, and they didn't have the added in-town accessibility that the Kilborn land had. Not to mention he and Jamina had already begun to negotiate.

"It's a shame really. I did hope to see you. Your friend Brent Howell said he would come. I'm finding him quite enterprising. Why, when we spoke he didn't seem surprised to hear about the theater not being sewn up at all. As a matter of fact, he mentioned something about new construction on it?"

Dammit, Brent! What was Boots' cousin doing running his mouth to Jamina Ronson and what would he get out of messing up Kellen's potential business? He thought, well, at least hoped, that Brent had evolved from the slickster he'd been throughout high school and in his early twenties, but perhaps he was wrong. If things worked for Kilborn Properties and RPG, Brent would get his standard commission, so why would he go and try and actively sink his deal? Kellen scrambled. "Brent doesn't know what he's talking about, Jamina. I'm just helping my grandmother clear up some things with the theater." He let out a breath. "Yes, she's still considering things with it being so soon after my grandfather's passing, but rest assured this will all go as it should."

"Oh, I hope so, Kellen. I'd hate to be disappointed in you and so early in what I hope to be our mutual relationship. You know how much I want that property. It's perfect, central to our plan to build a selling hub and offices for the condos we'll be constructing in the area. But no worries, I'm sure you'll clear it up by the time I see Brent at the party. He's bringing an old Sugar Lake neighbor of yours — Rory Pomeroy? Rory also has land that is usable and if, though I'm sure this won't happen, but if your grandmother still is reluctant, we do have our options. Maybe not as central, but workable."

If he was a lesser man Kellen would have kicked the wall. Of course, Brent was now sidling up with a Pomeroy. Why put his eggs all in the Kilborn basket? It was just good business to keep options open and, now that Kellen thought of it, Brent probably had his eyes on an even bigger prize. It could be Jamina herself and a position at RPG. How could he blame him for that? But still. Just then the low hum turned to a louder bellowing as Brent's cousin, Boots herself, switched her tune, now putting the men on full stop to switch eras to the nineties and scream about a girl being poiiisonnn!!!

Kellen turned his head sharply, just in time to see Boots hopping out of the archives room, arms swinging while she held her phone up in selfie mode. Was she singing to herself? Making a video or singing to someone else? When she turned and saw him, Kellen mimed that he was still on the phone. "Do you mind?" he mouthed.

She nodded, shrugged her shoulders expressing an overblown pantomime of an apology, then looked back at the camera and made an exaggerated motion toward his way with an eye roll. "Gotta run, peeps," she said. "Looks like I'm dealing with a case of the Mondays," she pouted, bringing to mind the old line from *Office Space,* one of his favorite comedies, as she hit the end button on her phone and tiptoed in the opposite direction toward what he assumed was her way to the ladies' room. Kellen squelched back a laugh when he remembered Jamina on the line and the problem at hand. Between her, Boots, his grandmother, and now Brent, his well-ordered life was quickly spinning out of control. He needed to nip this in the bud and quick.

But how?

"Don't worry about what Brent says, and,

though I'm sure you'll have an interesting time meeting Rory Pomeroy as he's quite the character, please don't lose focus as to what we'd agreed on. Kilborn land is perfection and I'd love to help you facilitate your Sugar Lake condo building project. Kilborn has been successful with other projects in the immediate area, not to mention Atlanta and Augusta. We know the people and what folks are looking for when it comes to Southern living. Not to mention I know you want connections in New York. We're already there and can accommodate all your needs." Kellen paused. Did he do it again?

Jamina let out a sigh. "Kellen dear. You don't have to sell me. I get that you are a good salesman. Sure, and that's fine, but we're builders. You and your connections to me mean nothing without the land we need to build on. Now, you have what we need, I'll give you that, but I already know I definitely have what you need. Now I really must run. Your place will still be open for you if you can find your way back to Atlanta. If not, I understand . . . priorities."

The pregnant pause in the way Jamina said *priorities* had him suddenly queasy. Was it possible for a man to get immediate morning sickness?

Upon hearing the silence of Jamina hanging up it felt like, if not the final nail in his coffin, at least one along the way toward that direction. Kellen put his head down on the wooden door in front of him. He couldn't believe how much he had changed in just the past two months. He was fine just a short time ago, though he was the VP of Kilborn Properties pretty much handling the day-to-day operations of things, keeping his grandpa updated and pulling him in for advice only on the biggest deals. For the most part Kellen had felt comfortable making decisions on his own. But now with the level of this Ronson deal and the fact that it was putting him in opposition to his grandmother, he was in the rare position of not being sure of his own mind.

He closed his eyes for a moment and searched his mind for his grandfather's voice, wondering what he would say in this moment if he was back in Atlanta at his office calling him under the pretense of just shooting the breeze.

"You know best, son, trust your gut," Kellen imagined he would hear. But why today was silence all he was hearing and his gut giving him nothing but queasiness?

Frustrated, Kellen looked up and pulled his shoulders back, noticing where he had stopped, in front of the other archives/

storage room. He decided after dealing with one disaster, he might as well face another. Opening the door and flipping the switch on the overhead fluorescent light, Kellen was stunned at the scene before his eyes. Piles and piles of video cameras of all makes and models. Years of his grandfather's obsession were piled in this room. He scratched his head and sighed in bewilderment, not knowing where to begin, so instead just choosing to dive in, picking up the closest camera and flipping a switch.

"Hey, Suit? Suit!"

Kellen turned around, video camera in hand, toward Drea's voice, surprised by her tapping him so hard on his shoulder. She ducked, seemingly surprised by the long viewfinder of the camera.

"What is it, Boots? I'm right here. Also, is there a reason you feel the need to make your presence known quite so loudly?"

She frowned, striking what he was coming to know as quite a Boots-like pose. Arms folded across her chest, one hip popped to the side. "And what's wrong with being loud?" she countered. "Making your presence known?" She turned her head, giving him a side-eyed smirk. "What is it? Don't tell me Mr. Suit likes his women meek, sweet, and docile."

He tilted his head and raised a brow. Once again, last night and the feeling of her in his arms while they were on the dance floor flooded back to his mind. "And what would you care how I like my women?"

Her eyes went wide before shifting left, then right. He saw the color rising beautifully on her cheeks. "I — I don't of course." She dropped her arms, looked around, and then folded them again. "Why would I care?"

Kellen laughed. It was the first time he felt like laughing all day and he didn't realize how much he needed it.

She looked at him, confused. "You're so odd, Suit."

He shrugged. "News flash, that's not the first time I've heard that, Boots. And for the record, no, I don't like my women meek, docile, or sweet."

She pulled a face. "Well, good for you. And for the record, I still don't care."

CHAPTER 14
LOVE AND BASKETBALL

Kellen had no real intention of showing up for the cool old guys' nightly basketball game, but when he'd gotten wind from his grandmother over dinner that evening that Brent Howell usually made an appearance, he decided it would be best to keep his defense up even while in Sugar Lake.

"So how did it go with you and Alex this afternoon?"

Kellen paused mid-upswing in bringing his burger from Doreen's Diner to his mouth. "There is no me and Alex, Grandma, and everything was fine."

His grandmother shook her head with a smile and picked up her fry, taking a delicate bite. "You know good and well I didn't mean it like that, dear. Goodness, you go jumping to snappy conclusions like that and you'll have more than me thinking of you two as a couple."

"Oh, come on now," he said. "I wasn't

jumping, and I wasn't snappy."

She looked him up and down. "Kellen, you're practically out of your seat. Now, if it isn't the mention of my sweet Alex that has you on edge, then what is it?"

This time Kellen stuffed his mouth and quick. He'd had a few good days of not arguing with his grandmother and he liked it much better that way. Dinner tonight from Doreen's, though not their norm, was the first moment between them that felt like normalcy in a long while. He couldn't — no, he knew he didn't want to — screw it up by bringing up their clear, dividing opinions on what was happening with the Redheart.

But something had to give.

"Stuffing your mouth with food to avoid talking about what's really happening, Kellen, is not going to make your problems go away. Something's gotta give," his grandmother said, doing that mind-reading thing she did by parroting his thoughts.

Kellen sighed. "Gram, I don't know what you are talking about. I'm fine, we're doing fine, and I got this under control." If control meant being saddled with working on a renovation he didn't want to work on, and turning it around on a dime while being at the beck and call of a New York transplant who happened to also be a bakeshop girl who also fancied herself a designer or sort of designer, then yeah, he had everything under control.

"You're not fine at all," his grandmother said. "You've had all day to look at Ray Nash's bid for the Redheart and you haven't said a word about that."

"Well, I haven't gotten bids back from my guys yet."

His grandmother crossed her arms and looked at him squarely, reminding him eerily of the moment with Boots earlier. "Funny, I didn't hear a thing about you getting any guys up to give you bids."

He gave a huff. "Well, that doesn't mean I'm not getting them. I have sent photos to some of the best contractors in the county and they're getting back to me."

"Oh really? If they were the best, and they actually wanted the job, they would have already gotten back to you."

"These things take time, Grandma."

She rolled her eyes. "Time is a luxury, my darling, that not all of us have. You should've well learned by now, tomorrow isn't promised and Ray and his boys are good. Better than good; they're our people. We can trust them. Plus, their bid is fair."

"Grandma, how would you know if their

bid is fair?"

Her soft eyes turned as hard and as dark as diamonds. "Boy, don't you dare pretend to insult me. You've only had this job a moment while I've been working alongside your grandfather a lifetime. Stop getting ahead of yourself. Besides, don't you think you need to be figuring out what RPG is doing sniffing around the Pomeroys?"

Once again, his grandmother was a step ahead of him.

"How do you know about RPG and the Pomeroys?" The look she gave him let him know how foolish she thought his question was. And it was foolish. Sugar Lake was a small town. If Brent Howell was talking with the Pomeroys, and Brent had connections with RPG, of course it would get around in about the same time as it took Jamina Ronson to hit speed dial on her phone.

His grandmother, instead of answering his question, was just looking at him expectantly. He looked at the remaining half of his burger and realized he didn't have anywhere near the appetite he'd had earlier.

"What do you expect me to do about RPG and the Pomeroys? I'm busy with your renovation."

"Oh, so it's mine and not ours?"

"Come on, Grandma. This is not what I

want. I know closing the Redheart would be hard, but it's still the smarter choice. The fact that RPG is talking to the Pomeroys lets me know they are ready to take us off the table."

"And?" she challenged. "Would that really be so awful?"

He looked at her once again, confused. He'd never understand Betty Kilborn. "Grandma, what are you talking about? Do you want to sell to RPG or not?"

"You know the answer to that, Kellen. I'm not feeling any such sale to RPG. I'm perfectly fine with things as they are. But I also am not stupid, and I know if a company like RPG wants a piece of Sugar Lake, they're more than likely going to get it. I just want to be sure we properly control what piece they do get."

"Exactly!" Kellen said, for the first time feeling like he might be making a bit of headway with his grandmother. "So now you see what I was saying about why we have to sell them the Redheart."

"I don't see any such thing, Kellen."

He blinked again.

"I'm saying you need to find a solution to get what you want and manage all of this."

"I had it managed, Grandmother."

She shook her head. "You had nothing of

the sort. The way I'd read that contract, all you had was empty promises, a bit of cash, and Jamina Ronson managing you. And you managing me in the process."

Kellen sighed. Once again, he was caught. But still he didn't feel wrong. Not completely. "And what's so wrong with that, Grandma? I just want to help you. I want to be sure you secure your future, that the company is secure, and most of all that you're safe. You can come and live in Atlanta near me. It's not like you need to be in this big old rambling house all alone."

His grandmother balked. "So now not only do you want to get rid of our theater, but my and your grandfather's whole life and legacy in one fell swoop. Boy, you are going too far."

The cold way his grandmother put things at times made Kellen shiver. He swallowed. "It's not like that. Of course it's not. I just want to take care of you. Not manage you." He thought of Boots and the reno then and looked his grandmother in the eye. "Though it seems there is plenty of me to be managed lately."

His grandmother surprised him by laughing. "Oh, there you go. Getting all caught up in yourself and thinking too far ahead in everything. Now you're giving your old

grand way more credit than she deserves."
She let out a long breath, then waved a
hand. "You know what? We're going to have
to put a pause on this one. I know you will
think of something that is satisfactory for
both of us. You don't have to worry about
me, Kellen. Life is going to happen whether
here or Atlanta. Your grandfather's sudden
passing should have at least taught you that
much." She smiled at him, then looked at
the clock over the kitchen entryway. "It's
early still. I heard there's a basketball game
on tonight. Clayton, some of his boys, letting off a little steam, and some steam-
letting seems like it could be just what you
need right about now."

Seriously, did the woman implant a *Bourne
Identity*–style tracker on him when he hit
the town limits? Kellen suddenly wondered
where one would go to get scanned for that
type of thing. It wasn't like he could just
call up the CIA.

"Not to mention, I hear Alex will be at
the gym. She's so sweet. Agreeing to help
the girls' dance team with their drills since
their coach had an emergency."

"What would I care about Boots, I mean
Alexandrea, and what she's doing for the
girls' dance team? I see enough of her during the day."

His grandmother grinned. "Of course, dear. What would you care? I only brought it up in case you were going, to let her know I'd see her at the theater tomorrow."

He looked at his grandmother, confused. "Really, Mrs. Smartphone? Since when do you need me to relay messages to Alexandrea for you? From the way I see it, you two have a regular chat room going."

She smiled again. "Like I said. Looks like you could blow off a bit of steam. Besides, I think Brent Howell may drop in too."

Kellen gave her a long look. "Really, Gram, you ought to drop the theater renovation and consider taking up side work as a PI."

His grandmother burst out laughing. "Oh, you flatter me! But this is all such easy information to gather. Though I would like the idea of having an official badge. Or maybe I could make private investigating a side business after the theater is up and going. I always loved Angela Lansbury's work on *Murder, She Wrote,* though nothing beat *Columbo.*"

Kellen shook his head. "I was just kidding. Don't go getting fit for a trench coat that fast, lady." He cleared his area and went around the island to kiss the top of his grandmother's head. He looked down at her dinner to see that she'd gotten through half the burger and most of her fries. No, it wasn't the most nutritional dinner, and he'd make a point to work on getting the fridge and pantry properly stocked and some more nutritional meals on hand, but at least it was something. He couldn't have her missing meals and making herself sick.

She looked up at him and smiled softly.

"Listen, though I won't be late, don't wait up. Maybe you're right. I could use the workout and I don't want my game to get rusty."

A light lit up in his grandmother's eyes as her smile went wider.

"Have fun, dear!"

He sighed. "It's just basketball, Gram. Nothing more than that."

"Of course it is, dear."

Kellen got back into his car fifteen minutes later, frustrated and tired. The last thing he felt like doing tonight was shooting hoops, but knew he had no choice with his grandmother's not-so-subtle hints about Brent Howell being at the gym. With that she was giving him just the opening he needed to face Brent head on and hopefully convince him that shutting his trap to Jamina with weekly Sugar Lake updates was in both of their best interests.

"Okay, and it's one, two, three, four! Twist, twist, dip and up! Perfect!" Drea was surprised at how much fun working with the girls on the junior dance team was turning out to be. She hated it when her aunt was right about something that she was hesitant on, which meant that most of the time she was pretty much salty about something or another. But her aunt was right, dang it.

That morning the dance team's coach, Tia Jenkins, had come into the bakeshop on her way out of town. She was picking up a pie for her aunt over in Cordell who'd fallen ill and had talked about how upset she was about having to cancel practice on her girls for the night. Drea was shocked when Aunt Joyce chimed in with, "But don't worry, I'm sure Drea would be perfect filling in for you tonight with your girls and their practice."

The way it was said by Aunt Joyce and the hopeful look on Tia's face pretty much left Drea not able to use any sort of lame excuse about hair washing. Not to mention the fact that Tia was one of the few people in town who knew how to properly do a boss twist out when her hair needed it, saving her a four-hour drive to Atlanta, meant that Drea really couldn't refuse.

"Thanks so much, Drea," Tia said. "All you'd need to do is sit in on my girls' practice tonight. I'd rather them not take the night off with competitions starting up in three weeks. It's just for tonight. You'd be a lifesaver and I promise to hook your hair up real good next time."

"How old did you say these girls were?" Drea asked while getting Tia's order together and fighting against the building nerves churning in her belly.

Tia's expression turned sheepish. "Thirteen to fifteen."

Drea shook her head and laughed as she handed Tia a pie to take to her aunt and some extra biscuits for her drive. "Oh, you sure will hook my hair up and good," she said. "Now, have a safe drive. Don't forget to let the principal know I'm filling in. I don't want any trouble at the school tonight."

And for the most part she had to admit that both Tia and Aunt Joyce were right. The girls, while at first hesitant and wary of the bohemian Northerner in their midst, quickly loosened up and were eager to show off their moves. They were extra excited when they saw that Drea quickly picked up on their routines and joined in, showing them when they could perhaps sharpen things. She hoped Tia wouldn't mind, but hey, wasn't that what practice was for? All in all, it felt good to move around and let loose in a group, no matter if it was with a group of hyper-hormoned teens.

That was until she looked up at the end of the practice and locked eyes with none other than the Suit himself, definitely out of his suit, in a tank and sweatpants with a gym bag slung over his shoulder, looking like he was heading to the gym down the hall. Drea stilled, her eyes locking with his, for reasons she didn't understand, hardened ones. What the heck was his problem? She was off the clock. They weren't in the shop or the theater. Did the bug up his behind travel with him everywhere?

"Whew! That man is fine with a capital F! Is he a new coach, because if he is, I might actually show up for gym class," one of the girls said over her shoulder as some others burst out laughing.

The Suit had the nerve to quirk a brow at that one and the corner of his lip turned up. Drea's brows drew tight and she tilted her head to the side as she glared at him.

He coughed and continued down the hall, Drea letting out an audible breath before turning back to the girls.

"Okay, ladies. Let's focus and run it once more, then I can dismiss you."

"Sure, miss," the same young commenter from before said. "We'll try. Though focusing may be tough after that."

Drea fought to stay serious, but couldn't help smiling. Remembering being fifteen herself or maybe it was twenty-five and yesterday. "Let's do that, shall we?"

Twenty minutes later as she was sitting on the gym's bleachers next to her sister and watching Kellen post up against her cousin, Brent, she was anything but focused. At least not on the game, per se. Drea thought she'd heard Brent's name when Kellen was on the phone earlier. And now here they both were at the gym squaring off on the court like it was the freaking NBA finals or something.

Darned this small town. She couldn't go two blocks without running into a Goode or a Howell. It seemed that cousins were in no short supply in Sugar Lake. When she first got into town, she enjoyed the novelty of running into family wherever she went and the fact that there was a certain amount of comfort to the routine of seeing the same faces day in and day out. But it was starting to wear on her — the fact that you could never quite escape what, at times, felt like not only prying, but judging eyes of your relatives wherever you went. At least at home, back in New York, even though New York was a lot smaller than folks seemed to realize, there was a certain amount of anonymity to it. She kept her head down there, avoiding eye contact, and walked fast enough to become little more than a figment of the imagination as she was quickly replaced by the next passerby on the street.

But not here in Sugar Lake; it didn't matter if you went out of your house heading to the gym, the diner, the coffee shop, the hardware store, heck, or even the mall — there was always either your family or your family once removed in the form of someone who knew your family who was always right there whenever you looked up. Though tonight Drea thought she shouldn't have been surprised. Not by the sight of Brent, since her cousin had a knack for showing up in the oddest places and at the strangest times.

Known to stay on his hustle, which Drea could respect, Brent was always looking for the next business opportunity or hookup, though she didn't quite get where he would find it here. But it became evident when Kellen sauntered into the gym ready to join the game.

She knew she probably should've gotten over how he affected her, but she still found herself wrestling internal butterflies as she watched him confidently walk across the gym's hardwood. Here he was, looking cool, confident, strong, and casual, shattering her earlier conceived vision of him. Not just going through the motions jogging up and down the court, the man was clearly on a mission, expertly dribbling, taking fast breaks, going on the hard offense as he seemed to be taking out some earlier frustrations on the hardwood tonight. What could they be? The phone call he'd gotten earlier? Though she wasn't trying to listen, it was clear from what she did hear that it had to do with his business in Sugar Lake and, more importantly, with the Redheart.

She knew he was against the remodeling of it, but with the changing of the sign today, she started to think that maybe he'd come on board. Drea didn't even want to consider the fact that he could possibly, in reality, be going against his grandmother's wishes and still have plans to sell the theater out from under her. Kellen playing ball on the same night that Brent happened to be felt like too much of a small-town coincidence even for Sugar Lake.

"What are you sighing about now? You're

finally out and not spending yet another night at home in the den with Aunt Joyce watching *The Wheel* or Internet surfing, but instead you've got a perfect lovely view of gorgeous firemen as they jog up and down a ball court and still you sigh?"

"Maybe I'm sighing because the view is just that lovely," Drea countered.

Liv rolled her eyes. "Come on with that. I know the difference when it comes to you. I'd fall for it if there were any bit of longing or some oomph behind that sigh and if it were perhaps directed at that new boss you say you're not interested in, but this is different, and don't say it's nothing. You've been in a funk for weeks now. What's up?"

Drea shook her head, then looked down. "I don't know." She looked back at the court and her eyes landed on Kellen. Tall, tan skin, muscles. He dribbled, faked left, then flipped right and made a perfect jumper into the hoop, sending Brent scrambling for the rebound in frustration. Kellen turned Drea's way and their eyes locked once again. She let out a breath. Too bad he thought of her as pretty much just what she currently was, a part-time organizer and place filler keeping his grandmother happy and making his life complicated.

"You're doing it again."

"That was a breath, not a sigh," she countered.

Liv looked at the court, then back at Drea, giving her a hard nudge.

"Ouch! All that dough kneading is making you strong as all get out!"

"Good. Just so you know it." Liv laughed, then her voice grew serious as her brown eyes softened. "Look, whatever you're doing to yourself, stop. I can feel you beating yourself up and you need to quit it. You've been doing great at the shop and what you're doing right now with Mrs. Betty is important work."

"Important part-time work," Drea said.

"What does that matter?"

Drea looked at her sister, not hiding the surprise from her eyes or her voice. "Who are you and what have you done with my sister? You're the same one who last year wouldn't stop hounding me about being selfish and getting my life together."

"So?"

"So how is this getting my life together?"

Liv tilted her head. "How is it not? And how is it selfish? Look what you're doing for Mrs. Betty. Plus, you're getting paid, right? And getting paid a good penny for a skill you excel at." Drea opened her mouth to protest, but Liv held up her hand.

"Stop right there. Don't with the down-play. Not to mention you're using skills you were trained in."

When Drea frowned at this Liv went on. "Don't you remember after graduating with your arts degree and your first Broadway disappointments how you were ready to throw in the towel, so you decided to get certified first as a nail tech, then after that, what was it? Your stint as a bounce aerobics trainer."

"Don't remind me. I still get a rebound headache when I think of those back-to-back classes."

"But," Liv continued, "you enjoyed your design and decorating courses. And you excelled at set design. That and acting were the things I saw bring out the most passion in you. And come on, stop beating yourself up. You are a fighter; it may not be in the traditional sense, but you trying so many things in order to realize your one true dream is something I've come to admire."

Drea pulled back and gave Liv a shocked look. "Don't tell me you're complimenting my flightiness now."

Liv shook her head. "I wouldn't go that far. Just take it for what it is in the moment, dear sister. But come on and quit it with the beating yourself up. That's not your role in this relationship. Remember? You're the star of the family. I'm the one who's good in the kitchen."

Drea laughed for the first time in a while, feeling like her sister had truly said something that cut to the core of who they were. "Listen," Liv continued, "I can admit when I'm wrong, especially since it's so rare."

"There she is," Drea said with a nod, and Liv laughed.

"No, seriously, last year you helped me so much by not only calling me on my bull, but also giving me free rein to learn my heart myself, and I'm grateful for it. Now I must call you on yours, though you may not be ready to hear it. Nothing you're doing right now is selfish. You've given freely to Aunt Joyce and now you're helping Mrs. Betty."

"But I'm getting lots more back in return," Drea said.

"And what's wrong with that?" Liv countered. "Is there some sort of life score card that I don't know about that says relationships can't be mutual give and take and in order for us to be worthy of happiness we also have to have more in the giving or suffering column? I truly don't think it works like that." Liv looked out at the court and caught Clayton just as he made a basket and Hope walked into the gym, her girls' club meeting letting out. She smiled. "I maybe used to think that way, but thankfully now I know a little better."

Drea didn't know what to do with her sister. She'd changed so much from the uptight, corporate woman who'd driven with her to Sugar Lake the year before, fighting over food and the radio the whole way. She looked out at the men playing on the court. No, she didn't know, but she sure hoped that Clayton Morris did, because if he messed up this new, wide-eyed Liv, handsome fireman or not, she'd knock his lights out.

CHAPTER 15
I WANT MY OLD SUIT BACK!

"I love how you've already started organizing these. It makes so much more sense, Alex dear. And I think for you and Kellen's watch list you must add *Mahogany*. Diana Ross is simply divine in that," Mrs. Betty said while waving the film canister in Drea's face.

"She and Billy Dee are both perfect," Drea countered. She, the eager budding fashion designer with stars in her eyes, and he, the handsome, way too serious activist who was completely smitten by her but had no time for what he considered the trivialities of the fashion world.

Mrs. Betty beamed. "I know they are the perfect 'opposites attract' couple. When that movie came out with Diana Ross and all those glittering designer costumes and all that glorious color, I just about lost my mind." She flipped the film canister over and over in front of her face. "I wonder if this film even runs well now. I bet it's about darn near worn out. I must have made poor Henry watch this movie no less than fifty times and each time to me was like the first."

Drea loved seeing the exuberance on the older woman's face, and in unison, they looked at each other and mimicked famous lines from the film. Both put on their best Diana cadences. Each cascading into a fit of giggles when it was over, but Drea froze when her eyes hit the doorway and landed on Kellen's once again annoyed, open-mouthed expression as he waved his cell phone.

"What is happening here?" he said to the two of them. "With all the construction you've already got going on with those guys downstairs, I would've expected this room to be completely cleared out, but instead, you two are up here having a fine game of let's make believe."

"And hello to you too, my dear grandson," Mrs. Betty said, her voice soft and unfazed as she straightened her blouse and looked at Kellen stoically.

He rolled his eyes and walked fully into the storeroom, giving his grandmother a smile, though tight, and coming to kiss her on the cheek. "I apologize, Grandmother. Good afternoon. Looks like you two are enjoying yourselves up in here," he said, his voice softer than his looks.

"Funny you say that with a smile, but you don't make it sound like a compliment at all," Drea said.

He looked at her. "And your point is?"

Mrs. Betty let out a huff. "Really, you two, I swear you try the patience of Job. Kellen, you have to admit we have done quite a job in here so far today.

"The storage room is almost cleared, and as you can see, the boxes are already lined up and labeled. They're just about ready to be filled with whatever it is we have to discard, and with this box over here, you can see we'll put in the reels that we need to convert for the new equipment we're looking to get in."

"New equipment? Grandmother, we haven't decided yet on that new equipment and you know how much digital conversion is gonna cost."

Mrs. Betty looked at him as if he had just told her water was wet. "And your point is?" she countered perfectly, using the exact same voice he used with Drea just moments before.

Kellen rubbed his forehead and closed his eyes before looking back at his grandmother and then at Drea. "And this pile, what is this you got going on over here?" he asked.

"Now, this is the start of the pile that's the best of all," Mrs. Betty began, and Drea braced herself for the storm she knew was to come.

Kellen looked at Drea. "What, I feel like I'm being set up for something."

"I wouldn't say you're being set up, per se, but maybe getting more of an opportunity to expand your historical horizon."

"That's an absolutely perfect way to put it, Alex dear," Mrs. Betty said before turning back to Kellen. "This growing pile here contains the kind of movies I think that you and Drea should watch together. It's also part of the digital conversion box. Consider them expanding your knowledge base on movie history."

It was official: His grandmother had lost it. "Have you lost it, Grandmother? In what world do I have time for this and in what realm is this necessary for me to do? Are we opening a Hollywood cultural historic center here in Sugar Lake?"

Mrs. Betty's eyes lit up and Kellen got a knot in his stomach. "Don't challenge me, Kellen. You joke, but now, that's a great idea. We could focus on diversity. There is nothing like that in these parts."

Kellen let out a long breath. "Grandma,

now, I get taking on this fun project and helping you out with it, but there's absolutely no reason for me to watch these movies. You've got *Claudine,* which I've seen already. *Mahogany,* okay I get it, but no reason for me to watch it now."

And to that both Boots and his grandma gasped in unison. Kellen rolled his eyes at the absurdity and somehow cuteness of the combined presence of the both of them. They were truly a dangerous duo. "Then there's *Lady Sings the Blues,* and what's next? *The Wiz?* Must I take in all of Diana Ross's entire film career?"

"Hey, there are plenty of worse ways to spend a day. You act like that's a punishment. Ms. Ross is queen supreme, no pun intended," Boots said.

"You're not helping here," he barked her way.

"I wasn't trying," she countered.

Kellen looked at more of the pile. "What else? *Breakfast at Tiffany's.* So now we're on to the great Ms. Hepburn. Grandmother, is this truly necessary?"

Drea watched as Mrs. Betty's face went from hopeful to desolate in the span of Kellen's short speech. Everything in her told her to stay out of it. Keep her mouth shut. This was their fight to hash out, but unfortunately her wayward tongue started wagging before she could get her brain to stop it from doing so. "Wait a minute! What gives you the right to say what's necessary and what's not necessary when it comes to your grandmother's theater and renovation? Obviously if she thinks this is something that's important to the success of the center that she's trying to build, then there must be a perfectly good reason for it, don't you think? And I would think you being the smart businessman that you are would at least give her the respect that she deserves and the time to hear out what she's proposing."

They both turned toward Drea in unison, with silent, surprised expressions, the five seconds of silence ticking out slowly, like an eternity.

Finally, Kellen spoke up. "You're right, Drea. I was rude, and I was wrong."

Drea looked around the room, not quite knowing what else to do, but not quite ready to meet Kellen's eyes. She didn't know if this was a dream or reality; was the Suit actually admitting to her that she was right and he was wrong? He leaned over and gave her a nudge with his shoulder. "Oh, quit being so dramatic. It's not that big a deal. So I said you were right about something."

He took out his phone and flipped on the camera, holding it up so that the three of them were in frame. "I, Kellen Kilborn, was insufferably rude to my grandmother today, and for that I am terribly sorry."

"And?" Mrs. Betty said as she tilted her head toward Drea.

Kellen sucked in a breath before letting it out. "And I came to this conclusion," he blurted out quickly, "thanks to Miss Alex-andrea aka Boots Gale, who was right when I was wrong." He turned toward the two of them. "There, are you happy now?" he asked, clicking the video button off.

But Mrs. Betty snatched the phone out of his hand and clicked the video button back on. "Just about," she said, and held the camera up so that once again the three of them were in frame. "I will be when you agree to watch the videos on the must watch list."

Kellen sucked in a breath. "Grandmother, I don't have time to do that, plus the renovation, plus take care of Kilborn Prop-erties' business. I really am sorry."

"Fine, Kellen, you don't have to watch all of them on the list. Just my top three or four." She dropped the camera and stared at him. "Please, sweetheart, some of these Grandpa and I haven't watched in years and

I would really like to view them again. Want to join Alex and me?"

Drea found herself watching with bated breath as she waited for Kellen's answer; she knew this was important to Mrs. Betty, but for some reason, she could feel how important it was for her to have Kellen there too. But why was it weighing on her so? She gave herself a mental head shake and told herself it was for Mrs. Betty's sake. Still she wanted to hear his agreement.

Kellen raised the phone back up. "Yes, Grandmother, sure, I will watch the movies with you. Please understand, you still have the company to consider. I know this is important to you, but I also have to protect our interest too."

Mrs. Betty reached up and touched Kellen on the cheek, her eyes and voice soft as she gave him a pat. "Of course, sweetheart, just like I need you to trust me, I have complete faith in you."

Just when Kellen thought he had a handle on things, having gotten Brent, he hoped, at least temporarily in line and in agreement to stay on the hush about the goings-on here in Sugar Lake with Jamina and the Ronson Group, then something else came along. Of course, Brent made no promises about not looking for outside opportunities in case what he had going with RPG fell through. Not that Kellen could blame him for that. At least the slickster had that much sense. But still, here he was on a night he should be home brainstorming, loading the projector for a movie evening with Boots and his grandmother.

Ray and his boys were done for the night and just finishing up packing the trucks. The small town felt like it was closing in on Kellen since he was bumping into his past at every turn. Although, when Griffin cornered him the first chance he got when he came in that afternoon, probably thanks to his father and holding on to the contract, he had the good sense to have an apology on his lips. "Mr. Kilborn," he said. "I'm sorry if I was a little too overzealous over at Jolie's place. It seems when I have a few too many I don't know my own mind."

Kellen immediately thought of Griffin sitting in his spot breathing all over his ribs, not to mention breathing all over Drea, and felt his temper start to rise again. But he knew that he had nothing to really get angry over. There was nothing going on between him and Boots and there never would be. After everything was done with the theater, and he got this problem cleared up, she would be a part of the history of the Red-heart that would linger in the past too. He gave Griffin a long stare before speaking. "Just be sure you keep your wits about you when you're here on this job. I don't go for any fooling around with anyone under my employment. And I mean in any way, under-stood?"

Griffin swallowed as Kellen saw his nostrils flare for a moment as if he wanted to challenge him, but when Griffin's eyes shifted, he knew he thought better of it. He nodded and said, "Mr. Kilborn, I under-stand, and thank you. You know my family's reputation — we always do a good job."

Kellen nodded. "I'm counting on it."

As he made his way back downstairs he could see Griffin, once again, huddled talk-ing to Drea. He leaned in close to her ear and she nodded and stepped back away from him; had the conversation earlier been all for nothing? Griffin looked up at him, his eyes going wide for a moment before he stepped back. Drea turned around and met his gaze, then she smiled wide, walking toward him as Griffin slipped off toward the back door.

"Do you have the movie all set up?" she asked. "You really did such a good thing today by making your grandmother so happy and agreeing to watch the movies with her."

"How about you just focus on your work and let me worry about my grandmother's happiness, okay?" Kellen shot back, the words coming out too quickly and way more harshly than he intended, or she deserved. An apology was on the tip of his tongue, but she spoke first.

"Fine, Suit. Once again, you're right, of course. I should focus on my job. Lack of focus has always been one of my few downfalls." She cleared her throat as she threw her shoulders back, looking at him from under haughty eyes. "Lucky for me, I don't have many though. How about you get the movie started. Your grandmother's been kind enough to provide us with snacks and she's already sitting in the auditorium. You can join us whenever you're ready."

Goodness, one would think she'd been working under the tutelage of his grandmother for way longer than the past couple weeks by the way she had given him such a proper setting down, he thought as he watched her walk away, back strong and full of steel while her long legs carried her away with all the regal elegance of the queen dismissing a peasant outright.

Though Diana Ross as Billie Holiday was

pretty amazing, Kellen was even more mesmerized by the image of watching Drea viewing Ms. Ross on the screen. Though he'd seen the movie back when he was a kid, all his old feelings and more came back as Billy Dee smoothly delivered his line about not letting his arm fall off to a hesitant Diana Ross as Billie Holiday. Kellen fought not to laugh out loud as the memory of his first stunning face to face with Boots and her misquoting of the same words came back to him. She truly was one of a kind and had knocked him completely speechless with her stunning looks and killer attitude. As Billy delivered the line, Kellen looked over past his grandmother to see Drea, her eyes wide and glassy as she murmured the dialogue right along with the actors on screen. In that moment, she looked over and locked gazes with him, giving him the same haughty glare she'd given him earlier.

Oh crap, he really messed up with that smart-ass comment about just doing her job and staying out of their personal business. Why had he let Griffin get him all riled up and why did he take it out on Boots? He gave his grandmother a glance and noticed her eyes growing sleepy. It was probably for the best. It had been a long day for her and, though she was a tough old bird, he was sure all this extra work was taking a lot out of her. Kellen frowned and looked at the screen. Now thinking it over, he was lucky that his grandmother hadn't walked up on him while he was giving that smart-alec, mind-your-business line to Drea. She might've cuffed him on the top of his head for sure if she had.

The movie continued as Ms. Ross still dazzled, her voice strong yet vulnerable as she sang about the man she loved coming along someday. And though he tried to keep his eyes focused on the screen, Kellen couldn't help taking another sidelong glance at Boots, this time catching her wiping tears away as she rocked back and forth in her seat. He looked down at his grandmother again, now snoring lightly, popcorn about to tip over in her hand and career onto the floor. Kellen let out a sigh and took the popcorn, grabbing a few kernels and stuffing them into his mouth.

Great. He had one snoring. And the other one, either in complete misery or having the time of her life — heck, he couldn't tell. She wiped snot from her nose, then had the nerve to look at him like he was bothering her. Kellen shook his head once again, thinking how did he have the time for this?

His grandmother let out a snort just as Miss Ross finished singing "God Bless the Child"; in that same time Drea blew her nose quite loudly.

Kellen fought back a grin. Thank goodness they had the entire theater to themselves.

"Wasn't that just terrific, children?" his grandmother said, looking back and forth between the two of them as if she had been up the entire time and watched the whole movie. She gave a stretch, looking over at Kellen. "What was your favorite part, dear?"

"You can't be serious, Grandma. It's after nine. I'm not sharp enough for a quick pop quiz; can we save that until tomorrow? Besides, honestly my favorite part was a part that you didn't snore through."

She gave him a quick swat on the arm. "Kellen, you know it's not right to point out a lady's bodily functions. And you also know a lady never snores."

Kellen growled at the same time that his stomach rumbled. "What say a lady stops by the drive-through on the way home? Because I'm hungry and I'm sure you are too. Let's get going." He looked over at Drea. "Are you ready, Boots? If you're done being all emotional, we can grab you a burger too at the Rocket drive-through and drop you off on the way."

She shook her head. "Emotional? As if you'd know an emotion if it bit you in the booty. Thanks, but no on the burger, I have my car."

"Are you sure, dear?" Mrs. Betty said. "It is late, and I hate thinking of you driving on those lake roads at this time of night."

Drea smiled down at Kellen's grandmother. "I'm absolutely fine, Mrs. Betty. It's not that late and there's light out there on those old roads now thanks to the cable company having to put them out for the repairmen."

Mrs. Betty pulled a face. "Well, we can thank the cable company for at least that. Okay, you get going now, dear. Kellen and I will lock up here and head home together."

Kellen got up to walk her out, but Drea held up a hand. "There's really no need for you to walk me out — I've got it. Why don't you just go on ahead and get that projector shut off and get your grandmother home. It is late even if she did sleep through most of the movie," Drea said to him with a laugh as she headed toward the back exit.

But Kellen shook his head. "You know I can't do that," he said, following behind her. "I'm already on thin enough ice to see through with my grandmother as it is. Just let me do this. Trust me, it is by no means a reflection on your independence; consider it you doing me a favor."

That seemed to work and she gave a nod and turned away, pushing open the exit door and letting him follow as Kellen put the code into the alarm to make sure that it would be disabled and not send sirens blaring throughout the quiet Main Street. He flipped the lock to leave the door ajar and happily noted that at least the back lot was well lit now that he'd ticked lighting and back-lot clean up off his list. She used her keys to unlock the door of her surprisingly old sedan and opened it. "Well, thanks," she said. "You can go on and I want to let you know, it's been a lovely night." She hesitated and for a moment looked embarrassed. "So, will I see you tomorrow? I mean, will you make it in for breakfast in the morning?" She held up a quick hand and laughed. "Not that you have to be there. I just want to be sure I'm ready and on time with opening if you are."

Kellen blinked. Wait. Was she really saying she wanted to see him in the morning? He nodded before giving a shrug that he hoped came off as cool while inside he felt anything but. "I don't know, I guess. I do have to get in early as my grandmother said; there is a delivery coming in the morning. Why? Did you miss me this morning?"

Did he really just ask that? What was he, all of thirteen? But, he kind of wanted to get a rise out of her while he also desperately wanted to know the answer. He watched intently as Boots' eyebrows drew together. "Of course I didn't. I was just asking as a normal person would." She shook her head and let out a sigh as she slid into the driver's seat and started her car. "Geez, some people and their self-importance. As if I have time to worry about one customer and his morning biscuits."

Kellen didn't let his smile go wide and he didn't go back into the theater until she was well out of the lot and onto the main road headed home, his mind already on the sweet honey biscuits he'd be wrapping his lips around come morning.

CHAPTER 16
AS YOU WISH

Dang it to all get out, she got him again. This time surprising Kellen by opening the shop's door at 6:45, right when he pulled up out front. "Come on in here and hurry up before somebody sees me open the store early for you."

Kellen felt like he was doing some sort of covert ops as he entered Goode 'N Sweet even before Drea had turned on the main overhead lights signaling that the shop was officially open. His heart, for some reason, was beating erratically as the whole clandestine affair made him want to grab her by her wrist and turn her around, see her braids swing wildly and take her in his arms and kiss her. Kellen gave his head a shake. He didn't like this feeling. He didn't like the fear, the sense of loss of control that she brought to his being. The night before he couldn't get images of her out of his mind no matter how hard he'd tried, and boy did he try. Baseball, math, politics. He tried thinking of anything and everything he could, and in the end his mind's eye — and he hated to admit it, but maybe it was his heart — kept bringing back visions of her.

But just as the beautiful visions of her were not totally unwelcome, they also brought on feelings of hope and thoughts of the past that he'd taken careful care to bury, but there they were. Back on the surface as he could clearly see his own father, normally bookish, quiet, and stoic, but light and carefree as he playfully chased his mother around their New York apartment when he was young. Him reaching for her as she slipped from his grasp and slipped on the slick marble floor. As he and a young Kellen rushed over, their eyes full of concern and their hearts racing upon seeing the blood on the floor, his father had the nerve to look up at his mother and smile in that moment. "I swear, you make me crazy, woman. Look at what I have to do to get you in my arms." Then he reached for her and pulled her in for a kiss. Kellen never understood it. And he always knew that sort of irrational, out-of-control feeling about so-called love would lead to catastrophe. Which of course it did.

"Why are you letting me in this early?" he asked Drea, coming back to himself.

"What, you don't want to come in and sit down and drink your coffee like a civilized human being? I know the truck is delivering supplies today between seven thirty and eight and I didn't want you to have to scarf down your breakfast and end up getting heartburn on top of that bad attitude you already have. You coming in and having a leisurely breakfast? How about you consider it doing me a favor this time?"

He appreciated her slick play on words in the way she threw out the fact that he played the favor card to her just the night before. "Fine, since you want to put it that way, but you have to be sure I'm out of here in time."

"Just go on over to your usual table," she said, rolling her eyes skyward, "as if you need me to be a timekeeper for you. They probably call you when it's time to reset Big Ben over in London." She yelled out toward the kitchen, "Aunt Joyce, you still got any extra sausages back there? Your favorite Suit is out here, and he looks hangry." She looked him up and down and darn it all, though it wasn't one of his traditional suits in any sense of the word, today he was wearing a tan summer suit that fit the whole countryman-about-town thing perfectly.

"Sure, tell Kellen to take a seat and you

get his usual order ready."

Kellen was already on his way, and he wouldn't dare tell Drea how good it felt hearing her aunt's voice as he sat down to begin to face his day with her coffee, her sister's biscuit, and her aunt's smuggled-from-home sausages.

The renovation was picking up speed way faster than Kellen had expected over the next week and, though he was grateful for the full days and to be spared any more snot-nosed, snoring/blubbering movie nights, he had to admit that a part of him kind of missed it. Oh well. Plus, Grandmother was correct in her assessment of Ray Nash and his guys. So far, he found them efficient and meticulous in their work on the theater. Not to mention, they were doing everything at a breakneck speed, which spoke to the Nashes' integrity and the fact that they weren't trying to pad their bill with unnecessary time.

But still he was left in a quandary over what to do about Jamina and the Ronson Group. He was sure that nobody would make them an offer for the land at the same price as the Ronson Group, at least not without a high level of marketing on his behalf. Opportunities like this didn't come around so easily. And he also knew that he wouldn't be able to keep Jamina patient for much longer. Kellen was deep in thought, not even noticing the noise as Ray's second and third sons took out a wall off the left of the concession stand that would make space for the new party/meeting room. Suddenly he felt his grandmother tapping him on the shoulder.

"Sweetheart, it's fantastic how quickly everything is moving. The way things are going now, if we stay on track, we'll be able to open by the end of the summer or early September, which I think is perfect timing, don't you?"

He turned and looked at her, his first response, a *no*, ready to fall off his lips, but he stopped when he saw the bright shine in his grandmother's eyes. "Yes, it's perfect timing."

Her smile went wider and she looked up at him again. This time her eyes grew more serious. "You know we need to start seriously considering our fixtures. I don't want to just buy generic things from some catalog. And there are two old chandeliers down at Melbourne's over in Jesup. I asked them to hold them for you and Alex to take a look, and if you like them, you can pick them up today."

Kellen pulled a face. "What? Today, Grandma? I don't have the time today."

"Oh Kellen, you wouldn't have the time any day," she said, opening his hand and placing her car keys inside. At the same time Boots walked in. She was wearing tight black leggings with an impractical tiered, lacy overdress that looked like she'd found it in her grandparents' attic. Of course, she had on her motorcycle boots and the combo made him suddenly want to take a ride with her more than anything else that afternoon.

"It looks like we've been tasked with a scouting assignment this afternoon, Boots," he said, then forced his tone to soften when he saw the hesitation in her eyes.

"We?" She turned to his grandmother. "You aren't coming, Mrs. Betty?"

His grandmother waved a hand. "I've had photos sent over and I trust you two to make a decision on my behalf. Now, get going. I want to keep watch over here a while. Take my car. It's a lovely day and the backseat is big enough to handle anything."

They both looked at her as she giggled. "I mean, it's big enough to hold the two chandeliers." Then she tilted her head and looked at them both. "Why, what did you two think I was talking about?"

Drea quickly waved both her hands in

front of her face. "Oh, nothing! Of course that's what you were talking about. Well, I guess we better get going if we're going to get them back in good time. Are you ready, Suit?"

Kellen looked between Drea and his grandmother, then gave Drea a quick nod as he tightened his grip on the car keys and let out a sigh. "Of course I'm ready. I was born ready. Let's go."

"And don't forget it's a beautiful day, Kellen. You should let the top down, get a little fresh air for a change. You stay way too cooped up. It's not normal," his grandmother yelled to their backs as they headed out the theater through the back door.

At a certain point, you had to know when you were had. And that time for Kellen came twice during their chandelier-gathering expedition. The ride out was uneventful, if uneventful meant constantly arguing over the radio stations until he finally gave up and just went with Boots incessantly flipping between songs and bellowing out wrong lyrics to tracks. It was fine. He was actually getting used to her over-the-top antics and it was nice to have the company and the entertainment on the quiet country road that led to the old thrift shop. Melbourne's was an old institution and off the beaten path, but since being featured on a thrifting reality show, they'd gained quite a bit of popularity and finding deals there was getting scarcer and scarcer. Lucky for them his grandparents were old friends and longtime customers of Mr. Melbourne, so he'd put the good finds aside for his grandmother when she'd let him know about the renovation.

Picking up the chandeliers proved to be an easy task. Though reining in Boots wasn't half as easy. Her eyes lit up upon seeing all of Melbourne's wares. "Wow, this place is fantastic!" she said of the rusty old barn that had been converted into just one of Melbourne's storehouses.

"I'm so glad you approve, young lady," Mr. Melbourne said. His ruddy cheeks got even ruddier as his eyes lit with clear excitement over having someone like Drea traipsing through his piles of dust and junk. When he started in on yet another origin war tale about yet another artifact, Kellen had to take Boots' hand. She looked up at him, her mouth open in shock, and he quickly released her. What was he thinking? "Um, Mr. Melbourne. Thank you, but we really have to get going. I need to get the chandeliers back to the shop and check on progress today. But we will take that *One Night Only* sign that Alexandrea picked out too." He saw her eyes light up.

"Really, I didn't think you liked it, Suit."

"As you wish, Boots."

He turned back to Mr. Melbourne. "I think it will be perfect in one of my grandmother's party rooms. She'll really appreciate it."

Taking the top down to load the chandeliers in the backseat, that's when he saw it, the second time he'd been had. The picnic basket. And not just a basket, but this one was wood and straw and lined with a red-and-white gingham and sitting in the backseat of his grandmother's old convertible like something out of a vintage 1950s movie. He looked over at Boots, then looked over at Mr. Melbourne and noticed the older man's way-too-loaded grin.

"Looks like you'll have time to stop off for a little picnic lunch," Mr. Melbourne said as he placed the chandelier in the backseat.

Kellen set the basket on the floor and put the other chandelier down. He glanced over at Drea, noticed her torn expression, and at the same time remembered how good she felt in his arms as they danced at Jolie's that night. He gently took the sign out of her hand and placed it on the floor behind the picnic basket and looked back up at Mr. Melbourne. "No, we definitely won't," he said, hoping his voice was way stronger than his resolve.

"No, we definitely won't," Drea said, walking around the passenger side of the car. Her voice was deadpan, but then she turned to Mr. Melbourne and, as was so very like her to do, she gave him a bright smile and stuck out her hand. "It was so nice to meet you, Mr. Melbourne. I hope to come back and get a look at some more of what you've got here."

Mr. Melbourne grinned wide showing just about all of his dentures. "Please do, young lady, we only got through two of my barns and I've got two other sheds that we didn't even get to touch; there's still so much more to see."

"Well, I'm looking forward to it, thanks so much for your time," she said as she got into the car, and Mr. Melbourne closed the door behind her. She looked up, her eyes doing that fire aim thing that she did so well. "Well, let's get going, Suit. Like you said, we need to get back to the theater and check on progress. The day waits for nobody — isn't that one of your mottos?"

He gave her a quick nod as he shook Mr. Melbourne's hand when he came around.

On the road back, Boots didn't fiddle with the radio quite as much and she was uncharacteristically quiet — that was, until they hit a bump in the road. Thanks to her quietness, Kellen heard a hissing sound, which caused him to pull over to the side of the road on a lookout point of route 84. That's when he got the feeling they'd been had for yet a second time.

"What is it?!" she asked as Kellen looked down at the back driver's side tire and rubbed at his forehead.

This couldn't be happening, he thought. It wasn't like his grandmother could put a rock in the road. But his grandmother was good with cars; she was meticulous about things like upkeep and staying on his grandfather about tire rotation and things like that. Of course, she could have let something like this slip since his recent death. Kellen knelt down and peered closer at the small nail that looked way too perfect in the back tire. It was small enough to not cause a flat, but just enough to give them a leak that would cause the car to slow down on the way back. That coupled with the picnic basket had Kellen's mind working overtime. He shook his head. His grandmother couldn't be that devious, could she?

"Kellen, what is it? Is there something I

can help with?"

Kellen let out a sigh and looked over at Boots, who had gotten out of the car and was by his side. "Looks like we hit a rock and maybe have a nail in the tire; it's about to go flat. Guess I better change it so we can make it back safely."

Her eyes went wide. "You? You know how to change a tire?"

He gave her a sigh. "Why would you think I would not know how to change a tire, Boots?"

She looked over at him. Silent. Her only answer a slow up and down look, taking him in from his button-down shirt to his khaki shorts to his deck shoes. He held back a grimace, refusing to give her the satisfaction of a reaction, and went for the trunk.

He did afford himself a whoosh of air though when he saw his grandmother did thankfully have the spare and all the necessary tire-changing equipment in the trunk. He was glad she didn't go that far in her stranded scenario and leave him totally high and dry. He pulled the jack, then the tire out of the trunk. "I might as well get this over with."

"You sure?" she said skeptically. "You really seem like more of a roadside assistance guy to me."

He let out a sigh, then shook his head. "You really know how to take an already tired joke to clear past the point of exhaustion, Boots."

"Thanks, boss. I'll take that as a compliment coming from someone as tired as you."

"Really, you shouldn't," he said as he leaned down and started on the tire.

Moments later, without the cool breeze, and the manual labor wearing on him, Kellen was starting to think Boots had something when she'd talked about roadside assistance, but he knew that it could take hours on this road for a service truck to reach them. There'd only been a few cars that had passed since they'd been on this remote scenic overlook and there was no guarantee they'd get help before dark. He might as well just get the job done.

She came over to him, as he was just finishing jacking up the car, her boots and shapely calves making it hard to concentrate on the task at hand. She leaned down and wiped his now sweaty forehead. "I guess it's lucky that Mrs. Betty packed this lunch for us. Who would have thought we'd run into such bum luck?"

Kellen swiped a glance up her way and stuck the new tire on, banging it into place. "Yeah, who woulda?"

She shrugged.

"Do me a favor and hand me that lug wrench?"

She looked at him, then at the tools on the ground, then back at him like he'd grown two heads. He laughed. "It's the L-shaped metal thing right there."

She grinned as she handed him the wrench. "You know that's the first genuine smile you've given me and it's at my expense."

He frowned, pausing mid-wrenching to look up at her. "It is not."

"It is. And there you are. The defiant one is back." She smiled and darn it if his heart didn't stutter. The wrench slipped and hit his other hand with a bang. "Ouch! Crap!"

"Oh no! Are you okay? I'm sorry for teasing you. You can't help your personality." She grabbed his hand and the current that went through him was like no other. He pulled back, then looked at her.

"I'm fine," he said abruptly. Then softened his tone. "Really, I'm okay."

She let out a low breath and got up slowly, leaning over into the backseat. She came out with a small package. "Is it about done?" she asked.

"Yeah, it's all done."

She gently took his hand again and held

out the ice pack she found in the basket, then put it to his fingers. Holding tight and not giving him a chance to pull away. "Good. Now hold this to your fingers for a few moments. Like I said, you can't help your personality. Why don't we sit a moment and eat? If we don't, your grandmother will be all sorts of mad at the both of us. And besides, I'm hungry."

He let out a breath, knowing he should protest, but his finger did hurt, and his stomach was empty. He nodded. "Fine. You're right. But just a few moments. We should get off this road before dark."

She smiled again, letting his hand go. The feeling leaving him more empty than it should have as she went to grab the picnic basket from the backseat.

"This field really is perfect, don't you think?"

"I think this tart is perfect. Who knew peaches, pears, black- and blueberries would all go so well together? Miss Joyce is incredible."

"I'll tell her that," Drea said. "Though I'll be sure my sister is in earshot since this is another of her new concoctions. She's been quite inspired since being back and with Clayton. And I think it's his honey that really makes the magic."

He stared at her. Lunch was delicious all around. His grandmother had packed some delicious sandwiches and even surprised him by making the potato salad that she knew he liked. When she'd done that, he didn't know, but he knew it had taken some definite planning on her part. He was glad that Boots insisted they stop and eat the lunch she'd prepared. It would have been a crime to let that salad go to waste.

And though the pie really was perfect, he was embarrassed that he couldn't come out and tell Boots what he really wanted to tell her. That yes, the field was beautiful with its yellow and purple wildflowers framing her perfection perfectly as the hill sloped down toward the town below. No, he couldn't say that, so instead he copped out and made the conversation all about the pie. He took another bite. *Smooth move, Suit.*

Kellen took out his cell to take a picture of his plate. He'd surprise his grandmother and send her a text to let her know he'd enjoyed the meal. She'd like that. But then Boots stood up and swung her arms wide. "The hills are aliiiiighttttt!!"

Alight? Kellen burst out laughing, raising his phone as he did so. "You really are a piece of work. Is there a musical or a movie you don't know, love, and misquote?"

She shook her head. "What's there not to love? And what are you talking about misquote? Isn't that how it goes?"

Kellen shook his head. She was so darned cute, looking at him with her big brown eyes so earnestly that he didn't have the heart to burst her bubble just then. He shrugged. "What do I know? You're probably right. This is your world, not mine."

She smiled at him then, brightening the already impossibly bright day. "Oh, I don't buy that. The theater is magic for everyone. Where else can you go to lose yourself, even if it's just a few hours, and escape the madness of this world?"

She looked far away and, in that moment, not her normal . . . well, he didn't know . . . resilient self. There was a vulnerability as well as a sweet dreamy quality about her then that made him want to reach out and wrap his arms around her as he breathed in her secret magic. "I mean, you can try by just daydreaming and getting into your own head, but it's hard. Your mind races and wherever you go, there you are."

Kellen suddenly felt like she was speaking to his soul.

She blinked, then looked up at him and smiled. "Besides, musicals and romances are the best! Didn't you love *Lady Sings the*

Blues last week?"

He shrugged. Trying his best to be as nonchalant as he could as the vision of her bright, glassy eyes came to his mind.

"Well, you'll do better when we watch *Mahogany* or when we watch *The Way We Were* or *West Side Story.* Louisaaaa, I just met a girl . . ." Once again, she was singing and doing it wrong.

"Really? So, now I know you're playing with me."

She just grinned at him then. Her cheekiness stirring him with thrills he didn't know he knew how to feel.

"You don't even need batteries, do you?" he asked. "Or are you just self-wind as you sleep at night?"

She frowned to herself and he wondered if she was thinking of an answer. Finally, she shrugged. "Well, I don't know. I guess it just comes natural." Her eyes went slightly cloudy and her voice softened. "Well, sometimes it comes and goes." She brightened almost immediately. "What about you? What gets you going, Suit? Tell me what gets your heart racing? Or better yet, what do you consider a romantic movie? Let me guess. *The Wolf of Wall Street?*"

He laughed, and she shook her head. "Jeez, the things I'm finding that actually get a smile out of you are ridiculous."

"They aren't," he protested, going to put his phone down. He was surprised that he still had it open — he'd been so into their conversation. "And for the record, there are some parts of my grandparents that rubbed off on me. I like plenty of romances."

She made a surprised face and crossed her arms. "Do tell," she snorted as she bent to start cleaning up their lunch from the blanket his grandmother stashed in the trunk. "I'm all ears."

Kellen held back on his retort to that and instead got up to help before they ended up good and truly stuck on this old country road in the dead of night. "Well, I like *Jerry Maguire, Silver Linings Playbook, Say Anything,* and *There's Something About Mary."* He gave her a satisfied look.

Boots froze, then rose up slowly. She stared at him. "Wait a minute. You mean to tell me you're going to look at me now like you just said something cool when you went and rattled off two football movies, pretty much a stalker show, and a comedy filled with bodily fluid jokes and you are acting like you want some applause." Her face got all serious as she looked at him earnestly. It was as if an extra hush came over the already quiet field. She swallowed down hard and blinked, tears filling her eyes. "You. Had. Me. At . . ." She paused long and swallowed again. "Aloha."

Kellen was dumbstruck for a moment, then he burst out laughing at the absurdity of it. She was right. "You're right," he said. "Those really are ridiculous choices." She grinned, a much better expression for her. "How about *High Fidelity* and *Two Can Play That Game*? Also, *The Best Man*?"

She made a face before smiling again. "Quite the list of cheaters' redemption movies, but I can always get behind John Cusack, Morris Chestnut, and Taye Diggs, so I'll give you those."

"You are seriously talented. You know that?"

Her face fell once again.

"Wait, what did I say?"

"Nothing," she responded, and it seemed like all the air was sucked out of the vast field.

"What do you mean nothing? I was just trying to pay you a compliment."

She looked at him, her smile not so bright as she finished reloading the basket and picked up the blanket. He grabbed the other corners and went to folding it with her. "You're right, I should have just said thank you. So, thank you."

He snorted. "Don't say it if you don't mean it."

She shook her head and looked at him as they folded the blanket in half. "No, I do. That was honestly just me taking out frustration on you that wasn't warranted. It wasn't fair." She stepped forward then, as he did too to bring their two parts together. He took the blanket from her hands to finish folding it. Their fingertips touching briefly as she leaned forward and kissed him softly on his cheek. "Thank you," she said, her voice soft. Her breath light as the petal of one of the wildflowers. Kellen was shocked and turned. Surprisingly, quickly, his lips connecting with hers unexpectedly, and more unexpectedly he was shocked when she didn't pull back.

It was soft and sweet and so much more perfect than the field or the pie or even the potato salad. Her kiss made his body tense at the same time it made his heart melt. Kellen was thankful for the blanket between them and the setting sun giving him a much-needed barrier between his body, heart, and mind.

"I'm sorry," she said as she pulled back, licking the memory of their glorious moment from her full lips.

He frowned. "What do you have to be

sorry for?"

She blushed as she picked up the basket and headed for the car. "It seems I got a little crazy. That happens when I get lost in a character and I'm talking about films. I got too familiar. I know we have a working relationship. Please forget that this happened," she said as she eased into the passenger seat. "It won't happen again."

Forget? Did she really think forgetting was something he'd ever be able to do? But then he looked at her and her eyes seemed so earnest, almost pleading with him to just give in and agree with her. He nodded and stepped back, in that moment tripping over a rock and heading feet over head backward down the hill. "Aaaasss youuuu weeesh, Booootsss!!!"

He didn't know if he was right, but he could have sworn he heard laughter in her voice when she yelled down after him, "I get it now, Suit! You really are full of surprises."

CHAPTER 17
SOMETHING HE CAN FEEL

She wasn't okay. As a matter of fact, nothing about this felt okay. Drea thought that she had successfully put her embarrassing slipup and boss kiss behind her, finally had a successful week of renovation, and gotten over some of the awkwardness with Kellen, though the whole down the hill roll almost made her embarrassment worth it all. But now here they were once again with Mrs. Betty throwing boulders into their path.

The three of them were currently in first class on a flight to New York for a quick weekend shopping trip because Mrs. Betty had heard about an old theater down in SoHo that was closing and she wanted to get a jump on whatever supplies were for sale. She also wanted to visit a warehouse in the theater district that specialized in a lot of vintage signage that Drea understood couldn't be sourced anywhere else.

Drea totally understood, and in any other

circumstance would have actually been happy for the paid, not to mention first-class, trip back home. However, in this particular circumstance she was filled with nothing but dread and trepidation. First, it had been months since she'd seen her parents, as they'd only been corresponding by quick text and short phone calls since she'd arrived in Sugar Lake, and she also had only seen them very briefly when they'd gone on their two-month RV retirement trip across the country. Since then they'd been traveling on and off nonstop. But now they were back home in New York, at least temporarily, and she was sure when she got to the apartment they would be quick to pounce on her about making decisions about what to do with the rest of their retirement years. The calls and texts to her had gotten more insistent as of late, and though still in their usual light tone, she could detect a bit of frustration and weariness in their questions about what she planned to do and if she planned to come back to New York. They still wanted to keep the apartment there since her brother was finally finishing up his studies in the fall, but they also wanted to know if she would be returning to New York to continue auditioning and pursuing her dreams of acting and entertainment.

Drea was nibbling on her lips and thinking hard about her upcoming — and probably long — dinner conversation with both her mother and father and she didn't notice the flight attendant trying to get her attention. Not until Mrs. Betty, who was sitting next to her, tapped on her arm. "You okay, dear?" Mrs. Betty asked. "They wanted to know if you'd like another snack."

Drea shook her head and, looking up at the flight attendant, said, "No thank you." Then to Mrs. Betty, "This has been more than enough; you really didn't have to go all out like this."

"Nonsense, sweetheart. My husband and I didn't travel nearly as much as we would've liked before he passed away, but we talked about it very much, and now that he's gone, I realize we wasted way too much time with just talk. Life is way too short and nothing is guaranteed. So, if I am traveling to anywhere I'm going to do it as comfortably as possible with what resources I have." She smiled at Drea, her eyes shining, though the bit of light and happiness that should've been there was dim. "So what that means for you, my darling, is if you're with me, then you're traveling in style too."

Drea grinned, hoping that her smile didn't

reflect the heavy weight she was feeling on her heart. She glanced over at Kellen, who was across the aisle from them, his laptop open, his brows knit tight as he stared at his computer screen. "Lucky me," she said at the same time he turned and looked away. "Well, you at least have to let me repay you in what little way I can. You must come over and stop by my parents' house for dinner. I know once my mom finds out you're in town too, she won't take no for an answer. She's so grateful for the job you've given me."

"Oh, stop it now with all that grateful talk. I'm the one who's grateful that you're working with me. And I'd love to see your mother and your father too — the scoundrel he is taking her from our town. But didn't you let them know you were coming home?"

Drea smiled. "No, I thought I'd surprise them."

Mrs. Betty frowned. "If you say so, dear. Either way, I look forward to seeing your parents."

Drea nodded. "I'm glad, though the idea of my father as a scoundrel is pretty hilarious to me."

To this Mrs. Betty just tilted her head and gave Drea a sly look. "If you say so, dear. He is your shining father after all. Of course, you wouldn't know that's the dashing young man I used to know back in our younger days."

They arrived at JFK and there was a car already waiting to pick them up. It took a bit of finagling to convince Mrs. Betty to not put her up at the hotel/extended stay residence where she and Kellen were staying, which he normally used when in New York on business. But she got through to Mrs. Betty when she explained how much trouble she'd be in with her mother if she took her up on that offer and didn't stay at home. Taking the flight was one thing, but not staying at home, while in the city, even if it was work, was another thing entirely.

Mrs. Betty, being a Southern woman and a mother herself, understood, and they dropped Drea off with a promise to meet up at the SoHo theater in the morning.

"I'm home!" Drea said upon entering the apartment, surprised to find it in total darkness. Where in the world was everyone?

She quickly texted her mother only to get a text back. Sorry. Last minute run up to the Cape. Your father wanted to get in some fishing and there's a fantastic all-you-can-fish weekend frolic for seniors going on. Tonight is the Friday night flash-back party. I've got to go. Will call you in the morning. Good night!

♡ ♡ ♡ ❦ ❧ What the heck was that last one for? How many muscles was she using to flash back and why didn't she call Drea beforehand to let her know she wouldn't be home? Darn it, she really had a taste for her mother's ham and greens and yams! Now all the foods she was dreaming of were up on the Cape Friday night frolicking with a bunch of wild seniors. And of course, her brother was not in town either. Out and about doing his own sort of frolicking. Making himself quite the social media stunter as she'd seen him doing of late. It seems he'd picked up where she'd left off.

Drea shook her head and headed to her room. Gee, it was nice to not be missed. Flipping on the light, she half expected to find it converted to her mother's dream craft room, but thankfully her bed was still there, and she couldn't wait to flop into it and worry about tomorrow — tomorrow.

The ArtMart turned out to be a treasure trove of finds the next day, even more so than the closing theater down in SoHo, though that was fun and interesting to walk through also. Drea was already waiting in front of the theater at nine thirty the next morning when Mrs. Betty and Kellen pulled up in front of it and got out of their town car. She was immediately struck by how sharp Kellen looked in his dark denim jeans, a black T-shirt, and dark sunglasses, finishing off his very New York–looking outfit with a pair of black and white Adidas, which were the perfect finishing touch to the whole look. This was definitely not the Suit she'd first met. If this man had shown up at the bakeshop's door early that morning, instead of walking forward to open the door, she might have run over and put the double lock on before pulling down the shades in order to guard her fast-beating heart.

In contrast, Mrs. Betty looked her usual stylish and eclectic self in a pair of dark, baggy, linen overalls with a graceful cardigan, clunky sandals, and cute striped knit socks completing her ensemble, and of course, she wore her signature red heart pin on her chest.

"You look so lovely today, dear."

She leaned down and kissed Mrs. Betty on the cheek. "Thank you. This is old, but it was fun to go through my closet again. I'll admit that." This morning she'd found an old favorite dress of hers. An easy fit and flair black and white print V-neck sundress that had black piping to accentuate the waist and a flirty high-low handkerchief hem. She was also thrilled to find her summer moto boots with the back and toe cut out. They were so impractical and fun, and she knew that, though he didn't comment on them, Kellen so very much wanted to. She gave him a raised brow and tapped her toe before following Mrs. Betty into the theater to meet the owner, Mr. Lee.

As they toured the historic theater, Kellen was found seemingly intent at times on taking in the fixtures and the ambience, but then at other times he seemed completely distracted by the happenings of his cell phone, excusing himself from time to time to step out and take a call or two.

"I'm so sorry about my grandson, Mr. Lee, and all his distractions, but we do appreciate you taking the time to show us around. The theater is beautiful; it's a shame that you're closing it down," Mrs. Betty said.

Mr. Lee nodded. "It really is a shame; both my wife and I are heartbroken about it, but with New York rents being what they are and ticket prices being what they are, there's just no way we can keep this old theater running. Not with the number of screens that we support, and we just don't have money to do a full renovation to get in the seats that would cover what the rent would cost." He looked around at the beautiful old lobby with its intricate marble carvings, lovely scrolled Oriental carpet, and golden chandeliers. "Even with us doing a random concert here and there, there are still not enough funds to bring in the amount of rent as a full-scale multiplex or even a complete tear-down and condo unit building. The property is just too valuable to the owners as something else, so we have to let it go."

Mrs. Betty reached out and touched the old man's hand. He looked up at her and smiled. "Oh, don't feel too bad for us. My wife and I are making grand plans right now. At least we're young enough to do a little bit of traveling and thus able to spend time with our grandchildren. Now that we've got our minds set on that, we're actually both looking forward to it."

Mrs. Betty smiled. "Well, I envy you, especially on the grandchildren part." She looked over at Kellen, who had just hung up his phone and reentered the space where they were.

"What did I miss?" he asked.

Mr. Lee chuckled and walked over and gave Kellen a pat on the shoulder. "Nothing much, young man. Though I suggest you get a move on any plans for children if you expect to keep your grandmother happy and not be hounded in the near future."

Kellen's stare turned dark as he looked at his grandmother and shook his head. "Really?" he said. "We're here to look at pictures for the theater and still you've got great-grandbaby fever?"

Mrs. Betty shrugged. "What can I say, Kellen, I'm a multitasker."

In the end, they negotiated a good price for Mr. Lee's digital conversion equipment as well as his popcorn machine, which they may not have needed but he threw in for a bargain. Both Drea and, she knew, Mrs. Betty could tell that Kellen was not happy with the purchases, especially the digital equipment. They knew that Kellen was still torn about the renovation and the fact that he was so intense on his cell phone during this trip had her a little bit nervous.

Although Mrs. Betty seemed to be shrugging it all off admirably, Drea knew that she was taking note. Lunch at the Midtown Investor was delicious, but quick and slightly tense due to the fact that Kellen was so distracted.

The only time he seemed to perk up was when they went to ArtMart and happened upon a showroom with a bunch of old Panavision cameras. Both he and Mrs. Betty's eyes lit up at the same time. Their smiles looking so very similar, bright and wide as their faces shone with the thrill of the new old find. "Grandpa would've loved seeing these," Kellen said, seemingly in awe of all the old cameras.

"Yes, he sure would've, sweetheart," Mrs. Betty agreed. "Not that he needed any of them," she said, looking around. "Honestly, I think some of these he actually has. I guess we'll know when we get them all labeled and organized."

"They're mostly organized," Kellen said, already making his way through the shelves of cameras.

Mrs. Betty looked over at Drea, the surprise evident on her face. She then looked back at Kellen. "They are?"

Kellen turned back to his grandmother and gave a nod. "They are. I organized most of them about a week ago. Grandpa loved his old cameras and I thought the least I could do was get those together like he'd like them." He shrugged, seeing the look of pride on his grandmother's face. "Besides, I want to go through some of the boxes anyway and see some of the films he took, but I know that's gonna take quite a bit more time than I have right now."

He stopped suddenly, and his expression turned excited. "Wow, look at this one," he said, pointing to a Panavision camera that looked decades older than all of them. "It's a true classic. I wonder if it's still in working order."

Mrs. Betty shrugged. "Well, all we can do is ask," she said.

Kellen shook his head. "What for, Grandma? It's not like I'm going to buy it. It's nothing but a collectible. Something to have because it makes you feel good but has no function." He reached into his pocket and pulled out his cell phone. "I can take a video in an instant with my cell phone."

Mrs. Betty looked at him and sighed. "What am I going to do with you, dear boy? Since when is making a person feel good not a function? That is what art, love, heck, all the best things in life are truly about. Sure, you can record a video, make a call, answer e-mails, post on social media, even do a deal with that gadget in your pocket, but your eyes don't shine with half the light as they did a moment ago when you were holding that old camera."

Kellen swallowed and put his cell back in his pocket. He hated that his grandmother was always so annoyingly right.

Stopping in front of the condo where Kellen and Mrs. Betty were staying, Drea fully expected to part ways when Mrs. Betty squashed those plans. "I'm so sorry your parents are away this weekend, sweetheart, and I won't get to see them, but you have to understand we seniors can't and won't go letting grass grow under our feet."

"I am starting to get that," Drea said.

"Why don't you come up for a while? It's still early," Mrs. Betty said upon the three of them exiting their car with their wares from their final excursion of the day.

Drea thought about it, but noticed the bit of fatigue in the other woman's eyes. "No thank you, ma'am. I think I'll be going. You go on up. This has been quite a full day. I do think we got a lot accomplished though. I'm just going to hop on the train and head uptown."

Kellen looked at her and frowned. "The train? But it's late. How about you come up with me to take these packages and my grandmother upstairs and then let me put you in a cab."

She looked at him as her brows drew together. "It's barely six p.m. It's pretty much rush hour. The train will be fine and faster for me to get uptown." She looked at Mrs. Betty and noticed the lines of fatigue around her mouth and the glaze upon her eyes. She was worn out, not that Drea blamed her. She had to be after their flight yesterday and their full day of shopping. She didn't have time to listen to the two of them arguing. Seeing her glance at Mrs. Betty, Kellen seemed to notice her condition too. "Please, Boots," he said, and she nodded.

"Sure," she said, taking the small shopping bag full of souvenirs and trinkets that Mrs. Betty had collected from her hand as she also took the older woman's arm and led her into the modern doorman building's lobby, Kellen following, his new old Panavision camera in hand.

"Thank you for giving in without too much of a fuss, Boots," Kellen said once Mrs. Betty had retired to her bedroom to put her feet up.

Drea turned away from the magnificent East River view from their twenty-sixth-floor condo to look at him. He really seemed to be in his element in this cool, sleek apartment's stainless-steel kitchen, dressed in minimalist black with Manhattan as his backdrop, but it was deceiving now that she thought it over, because this Kellen wasn't the country suit she'd come to know. Now that she thought more about it, the country suit she thought she knew also somehow seemed in his element pacing on Main Street in Sugar Lake and at that back table in Goode 'N Sweet, and in that darned field of wildflowers where they'd accidently kissed. "I didn't do it for your thanks," she suddenly blurted out.

He sighed and handed her a bottle of water. "Well, you have it all the same."

Drea took the water and, not careful enough, let her pinky finger graze over his index as she did. The sensation was just about as thrilling as their kiss. "I think I should get going. You know the train."

"Why don't you stay?"

She looked at him, wanting to leave, but not able to move.

"I mean, sure, of course. It's been a long day, but let me call you a car. I can't let you take the train."

"Really, I'm fine."

He shook his head. "What you are is stubborn. Why don't you at least let me, as your boss, send you home in a car? Does it help when I put it that way, Ms. Gale?"

Drea smiled. "A little."

Kellen snorted, but his lips quirked up in a little smile too. "Good. Let's go! I'll walk you down."

She went down the hall to say good night to Mrs. Betty, expecting to knock on the older woman's door and not get an answer. Along the way, she stole a glance at what she was sure was Kellen's room. It was so like him, sleek and gray and minimalist and still somehow disarmingly sexy. Drea turned away quickly and knocked on Mrs. Betty's ajar door. "Good night, Mrs. Betty, I'll be going. Kellen's going to walk me down and put me in a cab."

"That's great, dear. But why don't you come on in first."

Boy, she sounded pretty awake for a woman who seemed so tired a moment before. Drea entered and found Mrs. Betty already changed into a flowing housedress and ballet slippers; she was propped up on the bed, her television set to the classic movie network.

"Thanks for a fun day, Mrs. Betty. I'll see you tomorrow and we'll get in a little more shopping before our Sunday flight back?"

Mrs. Betty smiled. "I look forward to it. Though I do feel bad you're not going to be able to get together with your parents while you're here and your brother being out of town too. Are there any friends you wanted to see? We don't have to meet too early. I understand if there are those you wanted to catch up with while you are in town."

Drea thought it over a moment and came up flat. Honestly, there really weren't any old friends she wanted to catch up with. She hadn't formed many close connections during her high school days, and being a theater girl these past few years, it seemed like everything was all about the competition. She never quite felt comfortable forming any real friendships, since each person she met was always about the next come up or hookup anyhow and would just as soon literally break your leg for the next big shot at fame and fortune. She did hope to see some of her old connections at the workout studio, just to see if some of the old spark was there and she could get her mojo back, but her hopes sadly weren't that high. That feeling caused her no small amount of fear.

She shook her head. "No, ma'am. I'm free pretty early. I did want to get in a quick dance workout class since I'm feeling a little rusty, but that's early. Can we meet right after?"

"That sounds perfect. Take your time. How about we meet at noon by your class and then take it from there. I won't keep you out too long so there is time to change before the show. Is that good?"

She nodded, then stopped and looked at Mrs. Betty, confused. "The show?"

"Oh, I'm sorry, dear," Mrs. Betty said with an apologetic smile. "I was feeling terrible about not being able to get together with your parents tomorrow and you not being able to see them, but luckily enough I was able to score a couple of tickets to the off-Broadway revival of *Sweet Charity*. Would you like to go? I do hope I'm not overstepping my bounds."

Drea sucked in a breath. Would she? Of course she would. The Shirley MacLaine classic had long been a favorite of hers and she'd never dreamed she'd get a chance to see it live. Although as a kid, watching the original movie over and over, she'd learned all the dances and dreamed of performing it.

"I'd love to see it with you, Mrs. Betty," she said. "Thank you so much."

"No thanks needed at all." Mrs. Betty smiled and suddenly started to belt out lines from the musical. "The minute you," she started.

And Drea picked up the line with, "walked in the joint . . ." They both began to laugh through their tears and tune.

"Now, you go and get some rest." Mrs. Betty said after they finished their song. "Make sure Kellen gives you enough money for the cab."

"Of course I will, Grandma. I'm the original big spender."

Drea turned, surprised to hear Kellen's voice from over by the doorway.

Mrs. Betty laughed harder. "Well then, I've taught you well, my dear."

CHAPTER 18
BIG SPENDER INDEED

Finding Kellen waiting for her outside the gym alone when her class was over pulled Drea up short. She had just looked up from saying her good-byes to Stephen, Maia, and Angelo. And Angelo, taking her in his big arms and lifting her effortlessly, twirled her in the air. "Oh girl, what have they been feeding you down in the South?" he said as he put her down. Then he gave her one of his sexy grins that had men and women from Brooklyn to Battery Park swooning over him.

Today's class was just the spark that Drea needed. There were a few friends still in New York. She'd somehow let her past disappointments overwhelm her and had forgotten them. Angelo raised a brow. "Not that I'm complaining, mind you; it's hitting on you in all the right places. You need to hurry up and get back here auditioning.

With that body, you'll be booking jobs like crazy."

Maia chimed in. "He's right, girl. You're looking fantastic," she said, "and we miss having you around. When are you coming back?"

Drea briefly weighed the question over in her mind as her eyes glanced to the family of tourists walking along the street. "I don't know yet," she started, "but maybe soon. I'm just finishing up a job right now and weighing my options."

"Well, don't think too long. I hear there are a couple hot new shows that are going to be in casting come this fall. And since you've been gone, your name's been on the lips of quite a few of your exes."

Drea's eyes seemed to roll on their own. "Don't tell me. I don't need to know. It's not like they were any help in the past anyway. An ex is an ex for a reason."

"Amen to that," Stephen said.

"Finally, somebody gets me." Drea laughed, doubling over and, when she came up, locked eyes with Kellen, who was leaning nonchalantly on a nearby car. How long had he been standing there? Why hadn't she noticed? Goodness, was she getting rusty in her observation skills since her time in Sugar Lake? *Girl, get on your game,* Drea told herself.

She gave Kellen a nod at the same time he gave her an almost imperceptible one, but their interaction was enough for the trio she was with to notice. "Look, I gotta get going; my boss is here."

"All right now," Maia said. "Boss, huh? I see now why you got things to think over. If he was my boss, I'd be thinking things over nice, hard, and slow."

Drea frowned and looked Kellen's way. Though he pretended to be engrossed in his cell phone, she could've sworn she saw the corner of his lip quirk up. Darn him. He probably heard the compliment. Which meant, depending on how long he was there, he probably heard the whole conversation. She quickly hugged her friends, saying her good-byes and promising to keep in touch more than she had been. Walking over to Kellen, she covered his cell phone with her hand by way of greeting, and he looked up at her.

"What's happening, Suit?" she asked. "And where is your grandmother? Is she already at the restaurant meeting us for lunch?"

"She's not," he said stoically.

"Not?" she questioned, looking at him surprised. "Why ever not?"

He shrugged, then shook his head. "I don't know, she claimed to be tired. I guess she truly is. But you know her." He let out a sigh, then clicked some buttons on his phone. "Either way she gave us this list of supplies and companies she'd like us to check out today. It's extensive, so I think we'd better get going if we're planning to have lunch first."

She leaned over and looked at the list. There were poster cases and some lighting that they didn't find from the day before, plus ticket receptacles and roping equipment.

She looked up at Kellen. "Wow. That's a lot."

His eyes were wide through the lenses of his glasses and he looked ridiculously cute. "You're telling me."

"Well, we'd better get going," she said. "Poster supplies first stop?" She was already starting off toward the West Side and the first company on the list when he grabbed her wrist.

"Wait, you don't want lunch first?"

Confused, she looked at him. "Well, if your grandmother isn't joining us and there is so much on this list, why waste the time?" Drea paused. "Did we have a reservation? Was it fancy? Can you cancel, because I really think it's more important that we get this done first. If you're hungry we can pick up something quick. I know of a great noodle place that's right near the poster supply store. We can stop there after we check on those. If that's okay with you. I know your grandmother was eager to archive the vintage posters and display others properly."

He continued to look at her strangely for a moment, then finally nodded. "You're right. We have a lot to do before the show tonight. Lead the way, Boots."

Drea fought against smiling, but she liked hearing him defer to her and she also liked this more amiable out-of-suit Suit that she was meeting while in New York. Still, she couldn't help the feeling that was niggling at the base of her spine, causing her hairs to stand on end.

As it turned out, they didn't make the noodle shop at all, instead ending their day of shopping, their arms loaded down with bags and their stomachs growling late in the afternoon, at a nondescript warehouse at the tip of Manhattan. Drea was excited after having scored a vintage original poster of the classic *Stormy Weather,* with Bill Robinson, Cab Calloway, and featuring Lena

Horne prominently on the poster. She was also thrilled to get ones from the films *Black Orpheus* and *Murder in Harlem.*

Kellen let out a groan and she turned to him. "If I don't eat soon, there may truly be a murder in Harlem."

Drea shook her head. "Your grandmother is so right. You really are a dramatic one. I think your talents are wasted by you not taking the stage as a vocation."

He rolled his eyes and she looked around. "Come on, let's eat," she said, remembering a Spanish restaurant not far on Broadway that was fast, and all their dishes were great. "Let's get you fed."

Drea stared at Kellen as he polished off his stewed pork chops, rice, and beans. To be so fit, the man could sure put it away. He looked up at her and swallowed, reaching for his Coke and taking a long sip. "Why are you staring at me like that?" he asked.

She frowned, then took her own sip of Coke, trying to make time to gather her thoughts before saying the wrong thing. It was true he was all sorts of confusing and this afternoon did nothing but muddle her brain just that much more. As they ate, they were surrounded by shopping bags, and not just her purchases for Mrs. Betty, but things he'd picked out as well: lighting updates, ticket holders, and reel adaptors. "I really don't get you," she finally blurted out.

He looked at her, confused. "What is there you don't get?" Then he turned away as a text came through on his phone. He checked it, then frowned before looking back at her with a sigh. "Better yet, what is it you need to get, Boots? Trust me, I'm not someone you need to be trying to figure out."

"That's just it," she said, frustration setting in. "You go hot and cold at the drop of a hat. You claim to be fully against this reno for important business reasons."

"You're right, I am."

Her eyes went wide. "Then why is it half these purchases are items you picked out and not me?"

"They were on my grandmother's list. I had to pick them out," he replied smoothly.

I seem to also be on your grandmother's list too, but you got over that kiss fast enough. Drea's eyes went wide with the thought, although she'd buried it weeks ago, and she quickly stuffed her mouth with a big forkful of chicken and rice, willing herself not to say the wrong thing. Shaking her head and getting herself together, she cleared her throat. "Still though. You're going a little overboard." She remembered hearing his earlier call and the talk about the Ronson Group. "What are you going to do when it all comes crashing down?"

His eyes went wide. "What do you mean 'crashing down'?"

Drea looked at him seriously. "I hope I'm not overstepping, but do the Ronsons want the Redheart as a theater or do they want it for other reasons? My understanding is they wanted it for their in-town corporate headquarters sales generator. What is outfitting it as a theater going to do for them? All you're doing now, if the sale to them goes through, is putting money into a teardown."

She could tell by the tightening of his jaw that she was hitting some nerves and smiled because of her accomplishment. "Or have you decided to see things Mrs. Betty's way and not sell? She really does have great plans for the theater. At least I think so. It may not be the biggest revenue builder, like the Ronson Group, but it sure will add a lot, in my opinion, to the Kilborn legacy."

He looked at her, hard. "Legacy, huh?" he asked with a laugh. "You sure weave a pretty story, lady. Though you have a good eye, I'm sure on the stage you are fantastic."

Drea shook her head. "Yeah, you and nobody else, but thanks."

"Now who's being dramatic?" His tone

grew soft. "So, is that what brought you to Sugar Lake? The lack of jobs? Because, if you haven't seen, Sugar Lake is definitely not any sort of creative arts, entertainment metropolis."

She snorted. "Oh, I've seen. And well, yes. Partly it is, but I really came for my aunt and stayed to get away for a bit. But now I'm thinking it's time I made some tough decisions."

"Like what?"

She shrugged. "Like anything, frankly. For so long my only focus has been on auditioning and getting a part, any part, in a movie, TV, or Broadway show. Taking classes, studying theater, hitting up each and every opportunity I could, only to get nothing further than maybes and empty promises." She sighed and pushed her plate away, suddenly not hungry. "I don't know. . . . I thought for a while it looked like I was close to getting some work, but maybe not. Maybe I'm just not as good as I thought I was."

Kellen shook his head and finally he laughed.

Drea looked up at him, her temper rising. "What the hell, Suit? You laugh at me now? You really are the pompous ass I tagged you for when I first saw you. When am I going to finally trust my gut and stop giving handsome jerks the time of day?"

He grinned wider. "So, you really do think I'm handsome, huh?"

She snorted. "You're missing the point. I also think you're a jerk."

He leaned forward, his lips connecting with hers and darn it if without even thinking she didn't tip her tongue out and taste the spicy peppercorns from his pork chops and want to dive in for more. She pulled back and covered her mouth.

He laughed again. "You're adorable with all your outrage, you know. This whole pity party, while moving and glorious to watch, was just that. A show, and something to watch. Why are you so worried about what others are doing for you when you need to be out there making your own destiny?"

Drea dropped her hands and stared at him hard, her lips tingling and her mind working overtime. "Well, I can say the same thing about you now, can't I, Mr. Double-Talk. Why are you out here getting pulled in every direction but the obvious one? The one where your heart is telling you to go, toward the Redheart and your legacy."

His eyes dimmed and Drea knew she'd hit on a nerve. He turned away from her and glanced down at his watch. "Listen, we'd better get a move on if we're going to get to the show on time."

She checked the time. Crap, he was right. "Is your grandmother meeting us there? We need to drop off these bags."

He signaled for the check. "That was her with a text. She's not. It will just be you and me tonight."

What? Bait, hook, and catch. Dang, Mrs. Betty was good.

CHAPTER 19
SWEET, SWEET CHARITY

Once again, Kellen was in a theater and should have been paying attention to what was in front of him, but instead his eyes kept wandering to the woman in the seat beside him.

He was a damned fool, and he knew it, for kissing Boots in the restaurant like he did, and he knew this time there was no covering up and no excusing himself for it. And crap if she didn't know it too. What were they starting here?

They hurriedly made their way out of the restaurant and, though he knew she was a bit apprehensive, Drea made the executive decision to stash their bags at her place, which was closer to where they were.

As they awkwardly got into the elevator, jostling for position with a mother trying to wriggle a stroller, he finally felt safe enough to breathe as Drea picked up the baby's dropped pacifier and handed it to the mother.

The mom got off one floor before them, causing another stir as she jostled the carriage into a suitable position to get off the elevator, and Kellen had to forcibly hold the door open with his body, so it wouldn't shut and leave him and Boots with at least one of her children.

But when they were off, and even though it was only one floor to go, Kellen was surprisingly, awkwardly embarrassed by the isolation between the two of them. Maybe dropping the things at her place was a bad idea. He rubbed his hand along his tightening neck. Hell, who was he fooling about this whole damned day? Honestly, this whole trip was a bad idea. She was right about that part. He was playing way too fast and loose between two worlds.

Drea fumbled awkwardly with her keys. Kellen felt his brows draw together when she dropped them and he noticed the slight sheen of sweat on the back of her neck as she went to open her apartment door.

He bent to pick them up, handing them to her and clearing his throat. "Here," he said. "Please don't be nervous. I can wait out here if you'd like while you put the bags in. You don't have to be nervous around me,

Alexandrea."

She looked up at him then her eyes cool and calm as she gave him that smile that seemed to come to her so easy. "The only thing that makes me nervous is you suddenly calling me Alexandrea."

She turned away from him and flipped the key, unlocking the door before smoothly slipping inside.

Well fine, she might not be nervous, but he sure as squat was.

Drea cleared her throat but her words were still soft and shaky. Definitely not her norm. "You gonna let my arm break off, Suit?"

Surprised, Kellen's head shot up from where he'd been studying his shoes like an anxious schoolboy. Finally, he smiled, getting past his surprise and feeling more than a bit of relief over seeing his own feelings reflected back in her big brown eyes. "So, is that becoming our line now?" he said, walking into the apartment, more at ease after being reminded of their first meeting. She really had a way with him. Like she knew how to get right to where he needed getting to.

She quirked her lips and shrugged. "If you say so, handsome. Now, get in here so we can hurry this up and get to the show."

The suggestiveness in her tone had him practically choking on his own saliva, but thankfully he was able to swallow it back down and take in her family's apartment. Though small, it was sweet and homey, and he could both see and feel the Goode family touches all over. From the BLESS THIS MESS sign over the entrance to the kitchen and the LOVE IS WHERE WE ARE saying over the family portraits that crowded the wall over the living room couch. They put the bags in a corner of the living room and she offered him water as he looked around.

"I can't believe that was you. Seriously, you're really wearing your hair like that?" he said, looking closely at the photo of her and her sister, their backs to each other, arms folded, smiles wide, with a younger boy standing in the center of them, his attention clearly more on the melting ice cream cone in his hand than the photographer's instructions to pose. He knew that background, those trees, and that lake. It was Sugar Lake. Suddenly the thought of her summering on the lake so close to where he was and them not meeting until now filled his heart with a sense of longing and missed opportunities.

"Hey, those little afro puffs were the jam back then. Don't knock them!" she said.

He turned her way, pulling back from the photos, and for some reason was almost breathless by the image of her presently right in front of him. Like a gift, a second chance that he didn't deserve. "No, it's you that's the jam," he said. "The total jam."

He reached his arm out and pulled her to him, gratefully tasting her sweet lips once again. He was even more grateful when he felt her body grow soft and meld with his. He knew he was fighting a losing game when it came to her. Everything in him tensing up as his nerve endings went thin and tight, all at once impossibly sharp and on edge, while blood coursed through his body like it was to the boiling point. Kellen suddenly released her and was surprised when she still stayed glued to him. He turned his head and took long gulps from the glass of water in his other hand. Only then did Drea step back, giving him a shy smile while looking up at him from beneath her eyelashes. He almost laughed at the unexpected coyness of it, especially coming from her.

He raised a brow and cleared his throat. "Yeah, I think we need to get a move on. Remember the time, right?" he said, proud of himself for being able to bring up the fact, which was the opposite of what he really wanted to say and do.

Drea suddenly blinked and stepped away. Her hands quickly running down her chest and to her hips. "Goodness, you're right, no time for this," she said, giving him a quick slap on his chest as if they were just playing a game of cards moments ago, and not totally lip locked. "I'll just be a few. I'd like to freshen up and get out of these workout clothes."

As his mouth began to protest, she held up a finger and stopped him. "Don't worry, we won't be late. All my years of training, if not bringing me my big break, have definitely made me a fantastic quick-change artist."

True to her word, near moments later she was calling out to him. "Suit, just about ready. Are you available to help here?"

Help? In there? If he wasn't enjoying the way things were working out so much he'd have expected his grandmother to pop out from behind the plant with a big "tada." Kellen swallowed and headed down the hall. At her doorway was where he lost all other motor functions.

She looked beautiful; by now he should be used to her stunning him with her beauty, but this time it was different. This time, she had a whole sleek, almost untouchable quality to her that made touching her the only thing he wanted to do. It wasn't just what she was wearing: a simple black dress that was dipped low in the back to show off her amazingly curved spine, and rather high in the front, just showing off her beautiful collarbones, which he'd never known up until this moment could be so attractive on a woman. The dress went to just past her knees, accentuating her shapely calves and ankles he'd gotten used to rarely seeing. And on her feet, she didn't have on boots, but black stilettos that were secured by straps so thin, they must have been made by NASA engineers.

She turned and looked at him seriously, then bent down. "I'm sorry I'm taking so long. It's just the other strap on this shoe is giving me trouble. Do you mind buckling it for me?"

His eyes went wide as he looked at her, then down at her shoe for the first time, noticing that indeed one of the cute thin ankle straps was yes, undone. Then he looked at her feet as she turned her cute little foot. He noticed then that her toes were painted a pretty candy apple red. Jeez, how many tests were men to endure?

She snapped a finger in front of his face. "Well, can you?"

"Oh yeah, sure," he said, bending and just about tipping over from the weight of how light her body felt as she leaned on his shoulder and how heavy it felt on his heart for reasons he didn't understand and didn't want to mull over. Kellen went to buckle the strap and couldn't quite get an angle, causing her to tip over onto the bed, her legs flying up, everything about the situation too tempting, too perfect, and too dangerous for him to even contemplate. He knew they needed to get out of there.

Kellen quickly grabbed her ankle.

"Hey there, do you mind? I'd like to be able to use that when you're done."

He looked up at her and loosened his hold. "Oh, sorry." He quickly fastened the strap. Careful to keep his eyes on the shoe, he stood and took her hand, pulling her up.

"Come on, let's go. Though your room is adorable." He looked around. "And you can explain to me about those K-pop boy band posters you've got on the side wall later, we should go."

She looked at the posters and grinned. "I will not. A woman never has to explain or make excuses for her wants or desires."

He raised a brow and pulled her out of the bedroom. "Let's go. You saying words like *desire* in your bedroom is way more than I can take right now."

And now here they were, in the beautiful Broadway theater where he could be taking in the show, the music, heck, the historic theater around them, and he couldn't keep his eyes off her. He was watching as she pretty much acted out every action as it happened on the stage from right there in her seat. She was a show within a show and a delight to watch.

He told her so an hour and a half later as they dined at a small French bistro that stayed open late for the theater crowd. "So did you enjoy the show?" Drea asked between a mouthful of her fries. "My favorite part was 'If My Friends Could See Me Now.' " Then instantly, as if someone had put a sudden spotlight on her, she started rocking her shoulders and broke into an exaggerated short rendition of, "If they could peep me now, that old crew of mine!"

He leaned forward then, not caring about the smudge of ketchup on her upper lip or her messed up lyrics. All his focus now was on her bright eyes and gorgeous lips. Throwing caution to the wind, he leaned in and stole a sweet and tangy kiss before quickly pulling back.

"That was my favorite part too," he said.

"Well, watching you acting it out."

She froze briefly then grinned, her cheeks coloring with the most delicious berry hue. "Was my acting that over the top? Now I'm embarrassed. I must have made a fool of myself. I always go too far when I get excited about something. Breaking out into song and scene at the drop of a hat." She looked around, then waved a hand at him before shoving a big bite of steak in her mouth. "Let's hurry up and eat. You can throw me in a cab and we can get this night over with. You must have been so embarrassed. Here we are having a nice night out and I'm about as classy as Charity Valentine."

He laughed. "Slow down, sister. Have a glass of wine. I think after all the work we've been doing, we both deserve a bit of an escape. But seriously, you really do have a passion for the theater. I don't understand you giving it up."

He watched as a bit of the light dimmed from her eyes. "Oh, this? It's nothing. I have a passion, sure. But passion and talent are two different things."

"Not for you they're not," he said. "It's obvious they go hand in hand. If doors are being closed on you, why don't you find a window you can break open?"

She snorted. "That sounds like a felony to me. Trust me, I don't need a record, mister."

He laughed. It was nice to get out of his own head for a while and think of someone else's problems for a change. He thought of the little clips he had of her from when she was at the theater and the one from when she was in the field, right before their first kiss. It was almost embarrassing how many times he reviewed it on his phone. He looked at her. "You know, I bet there are those who would love to watch you on video."

She shot him a sharp look. "Where have I heard that before?"

Kellen put up his hands and shook his head. "I'm not going to ask, but hear me out. I'm asking you to think out of the box here. If auditioning is not working out for you, why not create your own space. People do it on the Internet all the time. And, hey, you never know where it might lead."

She opened her mouth to protest, then shut it quickly, her brows coming together as she seemed to think over his words. Then she shook her head. "I don't know, it all sounds great, but those success stories are one in a million."

He sighed. "Aren't those the stats for every success story? But still it didn't stop you from going out and pounding the pavement time and time again on auditions, did it?"

She frowned, and he could see the images of the rejections as they washed over her, and in that moment he regretted bringing them to her mind.

Finally, she spoke up again. "I can see your point, but you don't understand. You see where I'm from. My parents are just starting to live their lives and barely able to do just that. It's time I started thinking a lot more seriously about them and all they've sacrificed for me. A person can't go through life just playacting at fulfilling her dreams."

Something in her words stopped him cold as at the same time he heard his name come from over his shoulder.

"Kellen Kilborn, I thought that was you."

Kellen turned, not wanting to put face to the voice that was attached to the words. But he did. Jamina Ronson. "Yes, it is you. I thought surely that can't be Kellen Kilborn here having a late night in New York." She paused and let her eyes slowly and coldly assess Alexandrea. "Since you couldn't make it to my RPG new acquisition meet and greet last week."

Kellen bit back a groan and plastered on a smile as he removed a hand that he didn't even realize was covering Alexandrea's and gave Jamina a wave and stood. "Jamina, it's great to see you. What are you doing in New York this weekend?"

Her eyes narrowed despite her deep crimson smile. "Me? I should be asking you the same thing."

Kellen fought not to sputter. But still, he found himself making excuses. "I'm here on business with my grandmother."

Jamina's eyes went to Drea. "I can see that."

Kellen looked Drea's way and everything in him willed her not to blurt out anything about the Redheart. Thankfully she didn't, but as they were all in the same place and time, he had no other choice but to introduce the two women.

"Alexandrea Gale, this is Jamina Ronson of The Ronson Group."

Kellen noticed Boots' almost imperceptible tightening of her lips as her nostrils flared slightly. Boots stood, and he couldn't help but notice her uniquely slim but lush figure was almost polar opposite to the sleek, somehow too put together Jamina.

She gave Jamina Ronson a cool up and down that rivaled the one she just got. Kellen would have laughed if the situation wasn't fraught with so many pitfalls. But as if a switch was flipped, she suddenly smiled brightly and reached out to shake Jamina's hand. "Nice to meet you. I've heard a lot about you. Your reputation precedes you," she said.

Jamina gave Drea a cool smile in return. "I'm glad to hear it. If they are not talking about you, then you might as well be dead. Or so they say."

Drea pulled a face. "I don't know about that. Dead is pretty final. But I'm not going to argue with you. You're the one with the reputation preceding and all."

Kellen wouldn't mind being dead in this moment or at least out of this situation.

The young man next to Jamina looked to be in his early twenties, and about ten years or so younger than Jamina. He seemed to be about to introduce himself when Drea intercepted and started speaking. She held out her hand to the younger guy. "Hi, I'm Drea. I feel like I've seen you before. Don't you train over at Core Circuits and More? No, wait, didn't I see you dance in XPat's latest video?" The young man, who was trying to look stoic up until that moment, perked up and gave Drea a beaming grin.

"Yes, that was me. I'm Rick and I do train there. Part time. I do personal training too, for special clients."

Jamina gave him a quick nudge in his side and he gave her a sheepish side-eye and looked back at Drea with a grin. "I have many part-time jobs," he said low, under his breath.

Drea nodded then and Kellen couldn't help but notice Jamina's bored expression as her eyes moved away from her and Rick with the fine core and all her focus went back to him. Jamina sidled up to him then and snaked her arm through his. His body suddenly stiffened, giving away his emotions.

"It's a shame you two are just finishing up right when we're coming in. We would have joined you." She looked Kellen in the eye. "As you know, there are things to discuss."

He gave her a long stare. "And we will. But now is not the time." He looked to her friend, Rick. "It was good to meet you, man. I'm sure your table is ready."

Jamina continued to give Kellen a hard stare, then her gaze went over to Drea. Then back to him. "That's fine, Kellen. You're right. Now is not the time, since both our hands are full. You just be sure when the time is right, you have my theater in hand."

Though she did no more than blink, Kellen felt Boots' reaction in that moment as if it was a hard right to his left jaw. Wham!

He glanced at Drea, their eyes connecting for a moment, hers giving him that blazing fire thing that she did so well, but amped up to blowtorch status. She turned to Jamina and flashed her brightest smile. "It was so nice meeting you. Next time, maybe we can get in on one of Rick's classes together. He really is incredible when it comes to core workouts." Then her gaze strode over to Rick, slow, languid, and incredibly sexy, before she landed on Jamina again and chuckled. "But then again, I don't have to tell you that, now do I?"

CHAPTER 20
SPEED

Renovation work over the next few weeks went at a much faster clip than anticipated. But everything else in Kellen's life felt like it was going impossibly slow, stuttered and uneven. Even his breathing felt ragged.

After Jamina, in all her perfect timing, had interrupted the almost perfect day and night Kellen and Drea were enjoying, there seemed to be no coming back from it. Kellen had tried to explain once they left the restaurant and in the cab home, but Drea seemed to have shut down, shaking her head.

"You know what, no; you don't have to do that, Suit. You don't owe me any answers or excuses. I don't need them and frankly I don't want them. This whole Redheart deal is your business. Your grandmother hired me to do a job and I'm getting paid to do that job. Beyond that, I have no control."

He knew it was awful, but part of him had

been relieved by her response. Even though he knew the implications of it. Still, fool that he was, it didn't stop him from reaching across the car seat and attempting to place his hand on hers.

Idiot. Why should she have expected any less when she pulled away? She folded her hands on her lap. Way too quickly they were pulling up to her place and she was facing him. "Thanks so much for the show." She had put on what he'd now come to know as one of her well-trained acting voices, sounding like a cultured British woman straight out of a period piece. "Miss Alexandrea Gale gives her most heartfelt regards," she said, and she reached for the door handle.

He felt his cheeks burn with embarrassment then. Not only was she mad over the whole Jamina thing, but he'd blundered it further by using her full name. He let out a long breath. "What was I supposed to do, Drea, introduce you as Boots?"

She shot him a glare. "I don't know, but maybe you could have dropped the pretense at least a bit. And if you chose not to be honest with Jamina Ronson, you could have been honest with your grandmother, with me, or at least yourself." She had let out a frustrated huff and rubbed a hand across her forehead as she blinked back what he feared were unshed tears. "You know what? I've said too much and gone too far. You were right all along. I should mind my own business. It was silly of me to have forgotten that."

Once again Kellen reached for her, and she pulled away; still he didn't want her to go. He didn't want her to leave his side. Not tonight, not tomorrow night, not any night that he could imagine. He wanted to be with her and it had nothing to do with her dress or her lips or her shapely exposed ankles. . . . Well, maybe something to do with her ankles, but still he wanted to be with her to talk to her and explain the churning feeling he had going on inside him.

"Alexandrea, please," he started as she went for the door handle.

She turned to him, her smile bright once again and a total kick to the gut. Damn, she really wasn't a bad actress at all. "I told you I get nervous when you call me that, Suit. Thanks again. I'll see you in the morning for our flight. Please thank your grandmother again for the tickets. Ta-ta!"

Kellen could do nothing else but laugh against the pain as he watched her leave. *Ta-ta indeed, Miss Gale.*

And he did thank his grandmother, though

she wasn't too happy with his thanks or his attitude when he had nothing fantastic to report after seeing the show. Way too perceptive, even with Drea's stellar acting skills, she picked up on the tension between the two of them, and that was saying a lot given their history. Still Kellen was grateful for the fact that with them bickering less, and the reno in full swing, his grandmother was so wrapped up in it that she'd barely had time to focus on any more elaborate match-making scenes. She was like a woman on a mission. He tried to make her slow down, fearing she was pushing herself too hard, but she would not be deterred.

His grandmother even went as far as to send him back home late one morning for her plan book, which she had forgotten on her shelf. Kellen was rushing back when he was slowed down by a late model sedan on the service road in front of him. Pumping his brakes, he bit back a curse when he noticed who it was. Boots. What was she doing here? Usually she was at the theater by this time. Trying her best to be in whatever part of the building he was not.

Seeing her in front of him made him immediately think of his own growing hunger and how much he'd missed his morning breakfasts at Goode 'N Sweet. He showed up at the bakery the Monday after their return and was shocked when Miss Joyce opened the door for him at 7:00 on the dot instead of Boots, who'd stayed firmly behind the counter making herself busy with other customers the whole time he was there. She did the same for two days following, so he'd decided to give her space.

The whole idea of it made his blood boil. The coffee just wasn't the same if she didn't make it!

Frustrated, Kellen revved his engine and whirled around her, sparing her a quick glance as he shot past her on his way up the road.

Of all the freaking jerks! First he thinks he can humiliate me in New York, then stop coming in for my breakfast, act all two-faced in the theater, and then he had the nerve to pass me in that souped-up roadster of his!

Drea was mad. No, she was more than mad; she was furious, and the object of her ferocity was currently speeding away in front of her like he owned the road as well as her heart. Well, she'd show him. Drea hit the gas and willed her dad's old sedan to go like never before as she fought to gain on Kellen and his sleek sports car. When she reached him and was neck and neck, she suddenly didn't know what to do so she looked him in the eye, then stuck out her tongue. His reaction, instead of being one of outrage, came back at her as only confusion.

Crap. Who was she? Who stuck out their tongue? It wasn't like she'd passed him. She tried to floor it, but the old car wouldn't do it. It couldn't push past him and it started to sputter and cough, making her afraid it was going to peter out.

Not now, old girl, don't embarrass me like this.

Sputter, cough, cough, sputter. She was pushing it too hard. With a sigh Drea let off the gas and pulled to the side of the road. Letting Kellen go and herself and the car both catch their breath. He wasn't worth it anyway. The project was going well. It would be done in a matter of weeks and she could get on with her life. A life where she would not have to see Kellen Kilborn ever again. New York or maybe even LA — she hadn't decided yet, but both were starting to look more and more appealing.

Drea looked up as she saw another car approaching from the front. *What the — ? Did he turn around?* Kellen had turned around and was now pulling up behind her. She briefly thought about slinking down in her seat and hiding, but nope, that wouldn't work. Bracing herself, she turned to him as he rushed over to her window.

"Yes," she said as if this was the most normal greeting.

"What was that all about back there?" he asked, his eyes slightly wide. "Are you and the car okay?"

She looked around at first, guilt grabbing her, but then it quickly turned to anger. "The car is fine and I'm fine too. And I should be asking you what you're about. Who do you think you are speeding around me like that? You don't own the road, you know. You can't just do whatever you want, contrary to what you may think."

He let out a breath. "You're right. I was an idiot for doing that. I don't know what came over me. I was completely stupid."

"Well, you're right about at least that, Slick."

He rolled his eyes. "So, I've gone from Suit to Slick?"

She shrugged. "If the slick suit fits."

Kellen let out a breath. "Come on, that's not fair."

She got out of the car and slammed the door, meeting him face to face, then instantly realized that might not have been the best idea. It had been a while since they were in such close proximity. "What do you know about fair? Is it fair that you're essentially lying to your grandmother with this whole reno ruse? Why are you even doing it if you plan on selling the space to that Jamina woman? How can you do that when you know how much it means to Mrs. Betty?"

She saw his jaw harden as he said, "You're talking about something you don't even know about. I have the company's future to think about — there are employees, a history to consider, and a legacy to build."

Drea folded her arms across her chest. "You say all that and then tell me I don't understand. Man, you really are dense. Seriously, it doesn't take a rocket scientist to figure things out, but you act like you have to take the world apart and put it back together again. And here you were talking to me in New York about out-of-the-box thinking and all that. Why aren't you doing the same? There are builders here that you could utilize to do exactly what the Ronsons want to do and keep it all in the community. What I don't get is why you're continuing the ruse. Why don't you just tell your grandmother straight out that you're a sham? That you're still going forward with that Ronson woman."

He looked at her hard and the look seemed to cut her right to her core. "How about for the same reason that you haven't told her? I don't want to break her heart."

Drea was just about to say something when the words got held up in her throat. He was right. She could have said something to Mrs. Betty and, if not Mrs. Betty, then at least to her aunt, which would have been practically the same as telling Mrs. Betty. Why didn't she?

Just then Kellen's phone buzzed and he reached in his pocket. Drea watched as he clicked it over, answered, and then his face seemed to pale.

"Yes, I'll be right there," he said, clicking off but not moving.

Drea looked at him as fear suddenly grabbed her by the throat. "What is it, Kellen? Why are you not moving?" He blinked and then looked at her. "It's . . . it's my grandmother. She was feeling short of breath at the theater and they took her over to county hospital. I — I have to go."

Oh God. Not Mrs. Betty. Drea blinked back tears that seemed to spring out of nowhere, but then she looked at Kellen, who seemed in no shape to drive. She reached into her car, grabbed her purse, and locked the doors. Turning to Kellen, she took him by the hand and led him to his car, opening the passenger side door. "Get in."

"It's okay," he said. "I've got it. Don't worry about me."

She looked at him sternly. "Be quiet, Suit. I've got you."

CHAPTER 21
BLUSH MEET BASHFUL

"My sweethearts, I'm so sorry. I didn't mean to worry you two so."

"Grandma, stop. Really you shouldn't talk. Remember, the doctors were saying you need to get your rest."

Mrs. Betty rolled her eyes, softening the look by patting Kellen on the cheek. "I was afraid of this. Sweetheart, it's nothing for you to worry about."

Although she said it was nothing, Drea could see the clear strain behind her eyes. She was trying to put on a brave face for Kellen, who was only getting his color back after seeing his grandmother's weak smile once they'd made it to the hospital. By the time they'd gotten there, she was already in an ER bed, having been hooked up to an EKG. She'd gone through a battery of tests and was diagnosed so far with fatigue and slightly elevated blood pressure, but the doctors wanted to keep her overnight and would no doubt prescribe a reduced work schedule.

She knew but she hated to admit it, and Drea did too, that taking on so much so soon after the death of her husband had to have taken a toll on her. And judging by Kellen's reaction to seeing his grandmother even just sitting in a hospital bed, it all took a toll on him too.

Drea's heart practically broke seeing the large, capable man emotionally shattered over the fear of losing a person he loved.

Mrs. Betty coughed and Kellen choked back a sob.

"Aww, come on with the tears now, sweetheart. I can't have you falling apart," she said. "You've got my theater to finish. I've already got my eye on a couple of dresses that will be stunning for the big opening night."

Kellen looked up at his grandmother, his eyes wide, and shook his head. "Lady, you've got a one-track mind."

She shrugged and gave Drea a wink. "You ever see a train make it to its destination riding on two tracks?"

Two tracks — as if? His grandmother's words were still running through his mind the next week as he left her at home early and made his way to Goode 'N Sweet. He'd placed the package he had for Drea in his car and as he watched the video of her in the field one more time before heading out, he hoped she'd accept it and his heartfelt apology.

His mind went once again to the video he'd found in his grandfather's archives of his grandmother on that same field. She looked so young, happy, and carefree as she did a little dance for him, then swung her arms wide, spinning, then coming forward and out of frame as if to give him a kiss. The video ended and then picked up in front of the Redheart with his grandmother again. She was opening a box in front of the theater. It was the lovely heart pin she always wore. She pinned it to the lapel of the little cardigan she was wearing and once again she came forward as if to kiss the holder of the camera. This time the videographer turned the camera around and Kellen saw them both. His grandmother and grandfather, younger and happier and more full of hope and promise than he'd ever thought possible in a time when hope was something that seemed impossible.

He started the ignition and headed to Goode 'N Sweet, hoping that this time Boots would be the one to answer the door.

"What's this?"

"It's for you."

"Why?" she asked, staring at the outstretched bag in Kellen's hand as he stood outside the shop's door at 6:47 a.m.

"So are *you* gonna let my arm break off? Or will you take a chance on this Suit and finally take my hand, Boots?" he said.

She smiled then and his heart lit up with just enough of a glimmer of hope to propel his feet forward as he walked inside Goode 'N Sweet.

Drea was stunned as she looked inside the bag Kellen had given her. A camera, tripod, bell light? She looked at Kellen then with confusion.

"It's just a little starter kit for you to get going on your Web show," he explained.

She frowned. "What Web show?"

He looked back and forth. "Um, whatever Web show your fantastic, creative mind comes up with. I don't know, the one that you write and direct, or the one where you put your own special spin on the classics, remixing the lines and all. It can be whatever you want just so long as it's you and your unique voice is out there."

Drea couldn't believe what he was saying. *Wait, what was he saying?*

"Who cares about doors? Make yourself a window, Boots. It's not like you don't have more than enough talent to set the world on fire from wherever you are."

She couldn't help but smile, but then it all hit her. Though this was a nice gesture, nothing had changed; things were still the same with the Redheart progressing quickly and answers unclear. "Thanks, Suit, but I don't know. This is all very expensive. It's not like you can buy me and then just move on."

"You're right, it is. And for the record, a woman like you I don't know a man in the world who could ever afford. But you sure as heck are worth going into emotional debt for."

He clicked play on the camera and Drea watched as clips of herself and the times she'd spent with him took over the screen. Had she really made a fool of herself in front of him that many times? She guessed it didn't matter though, because at the end of the video there he was on the screen. Those eyes, that smile, declaring his love for her. "You are an incredible woman, Boots, and I believe in you," he said earnestly and oh so cutely, wearing the same suit jacket he'd worn when she first saw him. "I just wanted to thank you for pushing and believing in me too. And to tell you that I only want to be a small part of a world that is made better with you in it."

Drea fought back tears at the same time she tried to wrangle the flock of butterflies once again stirring in her belly, but they were so strong they were about to fly right out of her mouth. Wow, this man was dangerous with a capital *D*. "Watch it, you're veering off into slick territory and you still haven't had your coffee or any biscuits yet, Suit." She moved to go and get his order when he stilled her with his hand.

"You think you can add a sausage or two to that order? I'm gonna need my strength being that the Pomeroys and I have a meeting with the town council this afternoon about permits on building new townhomes on our lands."

Drea looked at him, shock and excitement flooding her body.

"Yep," he said, leaning back. "It's the oddest thing. Some headstrong Yankee was preaching to me about legacies, and it got me thinking, why can't I start a legacy of building right here in Sugar Lake? What do I need with a conglomerate like RPG anyway? If it's something done local for locals and by locals, we'll have that much more support and honor the town history and the legacy. Also, if I work in conjunction with the Pomeroys instead of against them, it will be a lot better down the road. And my grandmother is thrilled now that the RPG deal is officially off the table as it was and the Redheart will stay in Kilborn hands. My hope is that you'll be by my side for the official re-grand opening."

Drea shook her head and started to walk away.

He stood up and ran in front of her. "Wait. What's that for? Why the head shake? I thought you'd be happy?"

She smiled at him. "I am happy. I'm just completely at a loss. It's going to be hard to keep calling you Suit when you go around acting like anything but a Suit."

She reached her arms around his neck and kissed him. His lips were strong, then soft, then strong again as they made her weak in the knees. Just then the bell over the door chimed and there was a cough behind her.

"I'm sorry," he whispered close to her ear. "And if I haven't made it clear enough, I love you like crazy, Boots."

"Don't mind the two of them. What will you have?" Drea heard her Aunt Joyce's voice call out. "They seem to think this here is some sort of kissing booth and not a bakery. Just give me a minute and I'll grab the hose and cool those two off."

Drea laughed as she turned to her aunt. "Don't you dare, Auntie," she said as she pushed Kellen toward his favorite seat at the back table. "Now, do we have any of those sausages left? My Suit here seems to have worked up quite the appetite this morning."

Epilogue: Sweet Home, Sugar Lake

Mrs. Betty was happy. Wait, happy wasn't the right word, she was excited, no thrilled, no maybe she was content or at least as close to it as she ever could be on this night with the memory of her Henry as her guide.

"It's time, my love," she said, taking one last stroll around the Redheart before the big premier. "It's opening night. The theater is finally all we dreamed it would be. We've got a new screen, the curtains are in perfect condition, the seats are not only all updated and recushioned, but we've got a new sound system and have gone digital. I think you'd be so proud." She let out a long breath as she looked up at the shiny, restored ceiling, then made her way to the concession area.

The snacks were all in place, both hot and cold. She'd made extra of her own special pigs in blankets and had a lovely baked goods display from Goode 'N Sweet for the night. The local teens she'd hired looked fantastic in their new uniforms of black pants, white shirts, and red vests with gold trimming. Sure, it was old-fashioned, but it fit the ambience of the old Hollywood style of the theater. Everything was ready for the night's double feature premier of *Mahogany* and then Alexandrea's first installments of her new Web series, *Being Boots.*

"Yep, it's time," Mrs. Betty said again to the memory of the love in her heart. "We did it."

"No, *you* did it."

She turned, almost expecting to see her Henry there at the sound of that voice. Instead it was her Kellen: tall, handsome, and smiling as he came toward her looking so dapper in his tuxedo with Alexandrea holding his hand. Tonight, she was wearing a gorgeous strapless silk minidress with a taffeta overskirt that flared out to a long train. And true to form, she pared it with a pair of cool sparkly stiletto ankle boots.

"Are you ready, my loves?" Mrs. Betty asked as they each took one of Kellen's arms and a ticket agent opened the brass doors to flashes of light.

Mrs. Betty beamed. "Let's break a leg. We've got a red carpet to walk."

RECIPES

Now, our dear Drea is no great whiz in the kitchen, pretty much like your dear narrator here. But she does have spirit, and like your narrator, she likes to give things a good ole college try. So here goes. The following are a couple of recipes of my own concoction, but let's just say they are made up by Liv with Drea and Kellen as inspiration. I hope you'll give them a try, and please let me know what you think. Feel free to change to suit your own personal taste and health needs. Enjoy!

OH HONEY YES YOU MAY PIE

Prep time: 30 minutes
Baking time: 35–45 minutes
Nonstick cooking spray

1/2 cup diced plums
1/2 cup chopped granny smith apples
1 stick butter
1 cup diced canned peaches
1/2 cup granulated sugar
3/4 cup brown sugar
1/4 cup honey
1/4 tsp cornstarch
1/4 tsp baking powder
Dash of nutmeg
Dash of cinnamon
2 rolls ready-made phyllo dough
3/4 cup chopped pecans

Preheat oven to 350 degrees

Dice apples and plums and melt 1/2 stick of butter. Sauté until softened.

In a large mixing bowl mix diced peaches in liquid, softened plums and apples together. To that add in: 1/2 cup granulated sugar, 3/4 cup brown sugar, and 1 tablespoon honey.

In a separate bowl mix 1/4 teaspoon cornstarch, 1/2 teaspoon baking powder, and add to mixture slowly and stir.

Add dash of nutmeg and cinnamon to taste.

Separate out phyllo and stretch to fit pie tin. Add half the mixture for one layer and top with pecans. Add another phyllo layer and the rest of the mixture on top, plus rest of pecans. Add on another layer of phyllo, pecans, and butter. Drizzle with honey and bake 35–40 minutes or until golden brown. Let cool about 10 minutes. Enjoy!

Honeyed Peach, Pear, Black- and Blueberry Pie

Prep Time: 30 minutes
Bake time: 45 minutes
Nonstick cooking spray

1 29 oz large can of peaches
1 14 1/2 oz can of pears
1 stick of butter
1 cup brown sugar
2 tbsp of honey
1 tsp cinnamon
1 tsp cornstarch
1 tbsp white sugar
2 oz fresh blackberries
2 oz fresh blueberries
2 premade roll-out pie crusts

Preheat oven to 375 or 400 degrees depending on your oven.

In a large mixing bowl add peaches and pears cut into medium bite-size pieces with about 1/2 of the peach liquid.

Then add in 1/2 stick butter diced into small cubes and brown sugar. Add in honey and cinnamon. In a small bowl mix cornstarch and white sugar and add to mixture. Lightly fold in blackberries and blueberries, careful not to break them. Set aside.

Spray or grease your pie pan as usual and roll out your premade pie crust. Lift and cover the bottom of your pie pan. Fold in your filling.

Roll out other pie crust and use to cover the top, decorating as you wish. Have fun here. Weave pie crusts, make shapes, or just do what you will, just be sure to cut a few holes to vent. Brush the top with a bit of melted butter and bake at 375–400 degrees (depending on your oven) for 45 minutes to 1 hour or until golden brown. Take out and let cool.

Enjoy!

Serve pie warm or cold, and topping with ice cream is always a good idea!

ABOUT THE AUTHOR

A native New Yorker, **K.M. Jackson** spent her formative years on the 'A' train where she had two dreams: 1) to be a fashion designer, and 2) to be a writer. After spending over ten years designing women's sportswear for various fashion houses this self-proclaimed former fashionista took the leap of faith and decided to pursue her other dream of being a writer. K.M's self-published novel *Bounce* won the Golden Leaf Award for best novel with strong romance elements from the New Jersey chapter of Romance Writers of America. She was also named Author of the Year by the New York Chapter of Romance Writers of America. A mother of twins, K.M. currently lives in a suburb of New York with her husband, family, and a precocious terrier named Jack that keeps them all on their toes. When not writing she can be found on Twitter @kwanawrites, on Facebook at KMJacksonAuthor, and on her website at KMJackson.com.